Cross Checking

by

Laura Strickland

A Buffalo Steampunk Adventure, Book 7

This is a work of fiction. Names, characters, places, and incidents are either the product of the author's imagination or are used fictitiously, and any resemblance to actual persons living or dead, business establishments, events, or locales, is entirely coincidental.

Cross Checking

Contact Information: info@thewildrosepress.com

Cover Art by *Diana Carlile*

The Wild Rose Press, Inc.
PO Box 708
Adams Basin, NY 14410-0708
Visit us at www.thewildrosepress.com

Publishing History
First Fantasy Rose Edition, 2020
Print ISBN 978-1-5092-3047-1
Digital ISBN 978-1-5092-3048-8

A Buffalo Steampunk Adventure, Book 7
Published in the United States of America

Maddie shivered. “I’d better get Roddy home. It’s getting colder.”

“Going to snow some more, too,” Gilbert offered, not taking his eyes from Maddie’s. “I can always tell.”

“Oh, yes?”

He wagged his dark head. Maddie had a sudden and completely inappropriate impulse to plunge her fingers through that black hair. But he still held her fingers captive.

He told her, “I get an instinct for certain things—sometimes I just know.”

“I see. And are you never wrong?”

He shrugged those wide shoulders. “Seldom enough.”

“Come on, Maddie,” Roddy demanded, completely immune to any undertones. “I’m hungry.”

“Yes, all right.”

She tugged at her fingers again; this time Gilbert let them go. Together, they climbed up over the bank and trudged to the foot of Ferry Street.

“Do you live far?” Gilbert asked. “Can I see you home?”

“Peach Street,” Maddie told him, wishing this somehow enchanting encounter had happened on any other day than the one during which she’d destroyed her life. “I think we’ll be all right.” She hoped so.

Gilbert nodded. “Maybe I’ll see you again on the ice.”

Later she wondered if he, with all his bright instincts, had uttered a prophecy.

Praise for Laura Strickland

Laura Strickland's novella *FORGED BY LOVE* won first place in the short historical category of the International Digital Awards.

~*~

"The world building is phenomenal."

~Daysie W. at My Book Addiction and More

~*~

"Laura Strickland creates a world that not only draws you in, but she incorporates it…seamlessly….the kind of book that keeps you awake well into the wee hours, and sighing with satisfaction when you've finished the very last page."

~Nicole McCaffrey, author

~*~

"As I read I became so involved with the story, I found it difficult to put down the book. …Definitely …an author to watch."

~Dandelion at Long & Short Reviews

***

Previous Buffalo Steampunk Adventures

Dead Handsome
Off Kilter
Sheer Madness
Steel Kisses
Last Orders
Tough Prospect

Dedication

Dedicated to the hockey fans of Buffalo who never,
and I mean *never*,
say die.

A word about early hockey…

While doing research for this book, I discovered the game we love was a bit different in the world of the 1880s. Games were still sixty minutes long, but they were played in two halves of thirty minutes each. Teams consisted of seven players: three forwards, two defensemen, a goalie and a rover, who appears to have been something like the star defensemen of today, and who ranged up and down the ice making plays rather than just protecting his goal. What we would call the starters, today, were the main players of the game—players didn't change every few seconds, and the only substitutions came when someone received an injury and could no longer play. Equipment was rudimentary, at best. There were no blue lines yet, and players received warnings before a penalty was imposed. Most teams would have followed the Montreal Rules, and even the puck was a relatively new invention.

I've tried to retain enough similarities to today's game so we can all relate. Think pond hockey, and you'll be close to what fans would have watched in Steampunk Buffalo. I think you'll agree it's every bit as exciting as our games.

Here's to winning the next series played in Buffalo!

Chapter One

Buffalo, the Niagara Frontier, February 1885

"Is he dead?"

Madeline MacGillicuddy posed the question while peering doubtfully at the man who lay sprawled across the stone floor of the laundry. Six feet tall and at least two hundred fifty pounds—mostly flab—he'd gone down like a pole-axed steer when she hit him, and now lay motionless as a pile of bricks.

He certainly looked dead.

Not a good thing, Maddie thought, struggling to draw a breath in the stifling, hot air of the place. Especially since the man in question was her boss, Ralph Trinedore. Killing one's boss in front of at least ten witnesses could scarcely be considered a likely recommendation for retaining one's job.

And she needed this job, darn it. She needed it just as much as she hated it.

She glanced at the witnesses—also her fellow employees at this hellhole officially known as the Trine Laundry—and tried to discern what they thought. This was made more difficult by the fact that only a small fraction of her fellow employees were human. The rest stared down at the prone Mr. Trinedore from a variety of molded metal faces, some dented, some scratched and corroded, all covered with a faint mist of moisture from the hot, damp air. The extreme heat and humidity of the place proved detrimental to machinery. Well, it didn't do humans much good, either. Mr. Trinedore hadn't cared.

For a moment, as they all gazed down at the man—and he stared at the rusty tin ceiling—it became quiet in the laundry, or as quiet as it ever got.

Then Timmy, the boy who ran their errands and helped lift the steaming vats of water, spoke out. "Dead? I hope so, the old bastard."

Timmy had a thick, Irish brogue, which lent a certain eloquence to his final word. He also had an old, yellowing bruise around one eye, acquired when Mr. Trinedore had swatted him some days ago.

For the last time?

Maddie dragged another breath into her lungs. She'd snapped and lost control this one time, out of an endless number of instances, that was what. Her temper, all too often on a short hook, had got away from her. It was something her ma—God rest her soul—had always warned Maddie about.

It's that red hair of yours, girl. You've got your father's hasty temper. It will cost you, one day.

Would this be that day?

The steamie standing to Maddie's left—the one she'd privately dubbed Rita—stirred. Officially, the unit's designation was Number Twelve. Old Trinedore didn't give his steam units human names, but they had personalities all the same, even the ones who worked here nearly twenty-four hours a day and never left the premises.

Maddie had named them all in her head, and assigned them gender. Rita was female because she just seemed like a female. Maddie couldn't quite say why.

Now Rita rolled forward a few inches and jostled Mr. Trinedore's foot with one rusted wheel. Her voice came out in a cracked, metallic whine.

"Mr. Trinedore, are you dead?"

More silence.

A couple of the other mechanicals shifted uneasily. Maddie strained her eyes, trying to see if Mr. Trinedore was breathing.

He didn't appear to be.

Edie scrambled to her feet from the floor, where Mr. Trinedore had put her just before Maddie knocked him down. Because Maddie hadn't delivered her blow in self-defense—oh, no. She probably never would. She hadn't even acted in defense of Timmy, who could likely take care of himself.

Instead, she'd acted at the prodding of her indignation, and in defense of poor little Edie, who always seemed to get the worst of Trinedore's abuse, though they all took a share.

Only eight years of age, weedy and underweight, Edie had lost both her parents, one after the other. Her ma had worked here at the laundry, and after her death Edie had begged Mr. Trinedore for a job. He'd granted that to her, but only as the lowest of the low, mopping up endlessly and scrubbing the vats with skin-destroying lye.

Now she tiptoed forward, blood still trickling from the torn corner of her mouth. She peered at Mr. Trinedore judiciously and spat on the floor, a shocking gesture in one so young.

The gob of bloody spittle landed beside Mr. Trinedore's head. At first, Maddie took it as disdain for their employer. Then Edie lifted enraged blue eyes to Maddie's face.

"That was a stupid thing to do. If he's dead, what will happen to us? I'll be blowed if I go into the orphanage."

No, Maddie thought, no one in her right mind would want to enter one of Buffalo's orphanages, grim and cheerless places of sickness and, oftentimes, starvation. People in the city were working to change conditions there, including that hybrid automaton, Lily Michaels, and her husband, Reynold. Still, Maddie couldn't blame Edie for her anger, or her fear.

Everyone standing around Mr. Trinedore, human and mechanical alike, now stared at Maddie. She swallowed.

"Edie," she said earnestly, "I was trying to stick up for you."

"Well, sure, but did you have to hit him so hard?"

Sometimes, Madeline MacGillicuddy, you don't know your own strength. She heard her mother's voice again, rife with the brogue of Scotland. Now several years silenced, the sound provided both criticism and a strange kind of comfort. To be sure, Maddie—a big, strapping girl—had gained considerable muscle working here, doing the heavy work of the laundry.

One of the mechanicals, the one Maddie called Ben, chuckled. It might not sound like a chuckle to anybody who didn't know him. It might be mistaken for a stutter in his ancient, broken voice box. Half of Ben's head was staved in where Mr. Trinedore had once, in a fit of pique, hit him with a copper kettle. And he was probably the oldest unit on the premises, a real survivor.

Maddie looked at him. He had no eyes, just faint depressions where eyes should be, yet to her his countenance displayed plenty of emotion.

"Our Miss Maddie could take down a prize fighter in one round," he said almost proudly.

"Oh, yeah?" Edie returned. "And what good's that goin' to do us now?"

"Maybe he's not dead." Maddie fell to her knees at Mr. Trinedore's side. She didn't want to touch him. Add it to the long list of other things she never wanted to do. She prodded his shoulder with one finger, hard enough to make him wiggle back and forth a little on his flabby back. "Mr. Trinedore, sir?"

Another of the units, Otis, observed, "His head is leaking."

So it was. A horrifying puddle of red now spread out, rapidly increasing in size.

"He must have cracked his head open on the floor when he fell down," Rita said.

See, Maddie thought, that was the thing about steamies. People considered them stupid, especially basic, rundown models like these. Having worked with them so long, Maddie knew better. They had a lot of good qualities including being patient, endlessly loyal, and unexpectedly perceptive. Rita, for instance, had just drawn a conclusion.

A distressing one.

The floor here was made of big flagstones, impervious to water. A terrible, hard surface on which to land.

Mr. Trinedore's head had probably crumpled like an egg.

Dinty, who stood on Maddie's other side,

contributed, "He is leaking from the other end, too."

So he was. Mr. Tridedore must have evacuated his bowels upon death.

"Pee-yew!" Timmy pinched his nose. "I thought he smelt bad before."

"What are we to do?" Edie bleated.

A good question. What were they to do? More precisely, what was she, Maddie, to do? If the police came, she'd be on the hook for murder, and no mistake. And her responsible for the care of her younger brother, Roddy. Not that Roddy was much younger than Maddie, only two years. But it couldn't be denied that, although big and strong like her, poor Roddy was a bit weak between the ears. And ever since Ma's death, she'd looked after him.

What would he do if she got thrown out of here or, worse, tossed in jail? He'd lose their room, for one. And starve soon after, that was what.

Darn it.

She got back to her feet, even though her knees felt strangely wobbly, and looked around at her co-workers. Her mind whirled.

"Edie's right," she said. "We can't let anybody find out he's dead."

"Why?" Timmy asked.

"Because if people find out he's dead, they'll close the laundry. And we'll all be out of jobs."

"But," Ben pointed out with faultless logic, "he is dead."

Maddie wetted her lips. "Yes. But nobody knows that, except us."

Everyone, human and metal alike, continued to stare at her, now with increased interest.

Ever since the riot in Niagara Square last fall, mechanicals had been speaking up for themselves, seizing a measure of autonomy. Some had started their own businesses, and most were required to be paid a wage, though at Trine's Laundry these poor mechanicals received very meager pay indeed, and didn't even get basic maintenance.

Yet they had a place to stay, to *be*. If Trine's Laundry closed, they'd be out on the streets and, in their conditions, in danger of being scrapped.

Everybody here had a stake.

"People are gonna find out he's dead," Timmy pointed out.

"How? It's not like he has any family. Or friends."

"Customers come in, to drop off and pick up."

"And merchants," Otis put in, "sometimes."

"Timmy and I can run interference with them. We do all the work here anyway, us lot." Maddie barely restrained herself from aiming a sharp kick at Mr. Trinedore's head. "He never did anything but yell at us."

"What about paying bills? Or keeping the books? Ordering soap and other supplies?" Timmy wanted to know.

Otis said, "Ben and I can do that. Someone would have to forge Mr. Trinedore's name on the payment checks."

"It might work for a while," Edie conceded.

They all continued to stare at Mr. Trinedore for several minutes while the great steam plant at the other end of the room thudded and moisture dripped from the ceiling.

"And," she added decidedly, "keeping out of the

damned orphanage even for a little while is better than nothing."

"So," Maddie demanded, "are we agreed? We say nothing about him being—er—dead? And it's business as usual?"

The human workers nodded. One by one the steamies squeaked their assent.

"Well then, just one question remains," said Timmy. "What to do with the body?"

Chapter Two

"I still say he should go in the river." Timmy had expressed that opinion several times already. In fact, the argument over what to do with Mr. Trinedore's body had gone on so long, and the smell coming off him was so bad, Maddie's head had started to ache.

"Someone would see us dumping him," Curtis objected in his somewhat spectral voice, as he had each time Timmy made the suggestion. "It is too far to the river."

"Not if we cut him up, see, and take him in pieces," Edie chimed in enthusiastically. "We could transport them separately, all covered up in dirty laundry."

Maddie heard herself say, "And wouldn't people wonder why we were taking loads of laundry to the river?"

"Miss Maddie is right," Otis agreed staunchly.

"Not if one of the steamies went," Edie said. "Nobody ever takes an interest in what they do."

"Except these days," said Rita, "people watch us with suspicion."

"So we get rid of him over a number of days." Edie shrugged.

"He's going to start to smell bad."

"Already does," Timmy reiterated.

"Look." Edie crouched over the body and illustrated, using one finger. "We cut him here and here.

Head, arms, legs—"

Mr. Trinedore groaned.

"What the hell was that?" Timmy asked.

The supine man groaned again—a sound loud enough to compete successfully with the pounding of the steam plant—and moved his head.

Edie shied like a frightened horse and leaped away. Everyone else, including the rusty mechanicals, expanded their tight circle, staring still harder at their employer.

Somebody swore.

Maddie's heart kicked double time in her chest. "My God, he's alive."

"Can't be."

But even as the words fell from Timmy's lips, Mr. Trinedore defied them. He moved an arm, a leg—both so recently candidates for amputation—and then his head. His eyelids fluttered, though they didn't open.

One of the steamies set up a wail that sounded like a distant fire siren. They couldn't weep as such, but Maddie had heard them make this sound once or twice before, when Mr. Trinedore hit or otherwise abused them.

It seemed his return to life, despite all their debate, gave no cause for joy.

Except, possibly, to her. She whispered again, "He's not dead," and added, "I didn't kill him." Raising her voice, she went on, "He's bad hurt, though." She had a sudden vision of the coppers coming, arresting her and dragging her away to be charged with assault.

Better than murder.

She turned to Timmy. "He needs an ambulance. You run along to the new emergency hospital." It was on Michigan Street, just down the block. “Ask them to send someone.”

“Right.” Apparently happy to get out of the miasmic atmosphere, Timmy scampered. The rest of them watched Mr. Trinedore flail his arms and legs feebly, like a beetle on its back.

Edie edged around to Maddie’s side. “You’d better get out of here, too.”

Maddie, whose brain didn’t seem to be functioning properly, asked, “Why?”

“’Cause if he comes to, he’s gonna tell the ambulance men who knocked him down, ain’t he?”

Damn it. Had she just done herself out of a job?

Rita also trundled closer. In her squeaky voice, she said, “Maybe he will not remember. A lot of fluid has leaked from his head.”

“Yeah,” Edie objected, “but he just might.”

Staunchly, Rita said, “If not, when the authorities come, I will tell them it was I who knocked Mr. Trinedore down.”

Maddie stared into Rita’s face. “Why would you do that? Take the blame for me, I mean.”

Rita gazed back solemnly from her chipped and damaged face. A corroded spot on the indent that represented her left eye made her look particularly plaintive. “You knocked him down in our defense, did you not? Thus, I will return the favor.”

All the breath whooshed from Maddie’s lungs. In this city, at this time of her life, few people did anything for her sake. She found this—well, stunning.

And folks said steamies weren’t human. Darned right—in many ways, they were better than humans.

She placed her hand on Rita’s rusted arm. “But if

they find you at fault, they could…decommission you, or something." She didn't want to say *kill*. But being shut down and sent to the scrap yard was a death sentence for steamies, just like hanging would be for her.

"I will say it was an accident. We will all say so." Rita faced the others present. "And that is the truth. Miss Maddie did not mean to push him so hard."

Maddie didn't demure, though she hadn't actually pushed Mr. Trinedore. She'd treated him to one of her best roundhouse punches, with all her muscle behind it.

Everyone else—including the other steamies—either nodded or grunted assent.

"Still," said Edie, "you'd better get out of here for the time being. If he wakes up and sees you, he's more likely to remember what really happened."

As if to reinforce the advice, Mr. Trinedore moaned and stirred again.

Maddie fled.

She didn't like the idea of running. Her parents—both staunch Presbyterians—had taught her to face up to her obligations and responsibilities, especially any misdeeds. But as Maddie had learned since their untimely deaths, there were degrees of responsibility. Her brother Roddy's welfare had to come first.

If she got taken for assault—still better than a murder charge—and lost her job, Roddy wouldn't survive long. True, he picked up a few pennies here and there running simple errands for some of the stable owners down on Sixth Street. Simple being the operative word. Neither she nor her parents had ever wanted to admit it, but in truth Roddy was simple.

If he couldn't pay the rent, he'd definitely lose

their room. It wasn't much of a room, being cramped and located at the top of a house on Peach Street, hot in summer and unheated now, in February. But he'd wind up on the streets and then heaven alone knew what would become of him.

She ducked out the rear door of the laundry, only to discover it was snowing. The interior of Trine's always felt like a world apart—the time of day and even the weather disappeared in the drone of the steam plant and the general sameness of it all.

Now though, she shivered in the wind off the river and wondered where to go. Back to their room, to hide? But if Mr. Trinedore remembered she'd attacked him, that might be the first place the coppers would look.

She snuck down the back alley and through another narrow cut to Michigan. She could see the ambulance coming from the direction of the emergency hospital, several blocks down.

She walked very quickly the other way. Streets passed by, and houses and businesses, all in a blur while she thought about what had just happened. She strained her ears for sounds of pursuit and didn't realize till many blocks later where her feet had taken her.

Most of the city's stables—at least those that served the commercial cab industry—were tucked away along Sixth Street. The horse-drawn cab business, so Maddie had heard, was a dying prospect. Steam cabs appropriated more and more of the shared custom. Plus, people in the city were becoming conscious of the welfare of the horses, due to efforts of folks like those in the Anti-Cruelty League.

Still, Maddie smelled the stables before she entered the area: the scents of horse, manure, and moldy hay assaulted her, though not unpleasantly.

She wanted to see her brother, just to reassure herself he was all right, or maybe to assure herself *she* was all right. But she had no way to tell where, in this labyrinth, he might be.

Vehicles and people came and went. She ducked out of the way of a shabby black cab, drawn by an even shabbier black horse, emerging onto the main thoroughfare, and squeezed her not-so-slender body to one side.

Often, Roddy picked up a bit of money working for Mr. Crabbe at Crabbe's Cabs, located about half way down the long rows of stables.

She decided to try there first. But she kept her eyes peeled for a tall, lanky figure topped by a mop of hair as red as her own. He could be sweeping out almost anywhere. And she needed to tell him—

It hit her then, in full, what had happened. What she'd done. Knocked down her boss. Hurt him very badly indeed. Not that the bugger didn't deserve it, but Roddy, who depended on her, didn't deserve the consequences.

God help her, she couldn't go back to Trine's, at least not yet. And how was she going to earn her brother's bread?

Chapter Three

"Say that again," Huritt Gilbert growled. He could feel blood trickling down from one corner of his mouth, and bruises rising on cheekbone and jaw. He'd be a mess come morning. Right now, though, he didn't care.

The young man opposite him—big as sin and twice as ugly—grinned and spat out some blood of his own.

"Injun," he taunted, and grinned a grin that showed off his big, gapped teeth.

The men who'd gathered around hooted. Most of them, men and boys alike, worked here in this dim world of stables and alleys, often for wages barely enough to keep them alive. Some slept here at night. Many drank their meager pay and had nowhere else to lay their heads. When it came to netherworlds, Gilbert often thought, the stables were prime.

Still, for Gilbert there was the compensation of the horses, and the self-respect of the labor. At least until some damn fool started calling him names.

This time it was Carl Mueller, who worked at the next stable down from Stanley's, where Gilbert was employed. Gilbert had caught Mueller beating on one of his employer's horses—again. Gilbert might take a certain amount of abuse on his own part, but the horses deserved a better life than what they had.

"Injun horse-lover," Mueller added. "I'll bet you poke 'em at night, when nobody's watching."

Gilbert saw red. He used to think that was just an expression. It wasn't. A fiery mist arose and blocked the satisfying spectacle of his fist crashing into Mueller's face.

Mueller went down like a tree at the final blow of the axe. Chaff and stray bits of straw billowed up in an opposite reaction. A couple of the horses turned their heads interestedly.

Gilbert wiped his chin on the shoulder of his shirt and eyed the crowd. "Anybody else?"

They shook their heads and backed off, most of their enjoyment flown. It usually ended this way, though not always. He'd been caught and pummeled on a few memorable occasions, always by a gang, never one-on-one.

Two of Mueller's cronies picked him up and dragged him away. Carl Mueller was the kind of man who had cronies. Gilbert wasn't, although he liked to think he had the respect of his boss and a reputation as a hard worker.

Mueller seemed to feel that, as the nephew to one of the stable owners, he had some clout. He expected to be part owner someday. That didn't give him call to beat the animals or go around slinging epithets.

Not that *injun* was an epithet, exactly. And not but what Gilbert was indeed half red-blooded, as he liked to call it. Half red and half French, by way of Canada.

It was just the way Mueller said it. Insultingly.

Gilbert was going to have to do something about Mueller. Not the name calling. He could take care of himself. But his nastiness with the animals.

With the others gone, Gilbert slid into the nearest of the cab stalls, where the old horse stood, blowing.

The horse had been brought in exhausted from a hard day's labor, and had proved uncooperative going into his stall. Mueller's answer had been a crop.

Now Gilbert crooned reassurance to the animal and soothed his hand over the flanks, which had taken most of the abuse. He could feel livid welts.

"Damn fool."

Only an idiot abused the stock, or *slaves* as Gilbert privately considered the horses. No stock, no job. No job and a man found himself out on the street. He'd been there before and didn't fancy doing it again.

His father, a good man, had been an adventurer. He'd brought Gilbert down out of the wilds of Ontario as no more than a babe. Gilbert's mother wasn't in the picture, and Pa barely spoke her name. She'd been Algonquin, and she hadn't stuck around. That was all Gilbert knew.

He and Pa had done all right for the first dozen years or so. Paul Gilbert had worked training horses, up until his death by misadventure during a boat race on the Niagara River. That's why Gilbert had gravitated here afterward, starting out as an errand boy and working his way up.

He thought about all this as he comforted the big horse and forked him some hay from the haymow of the stable owner, Mr. Philips. Didn't look like Mueller would come back and do it, and he didn't think Philips would mind.

At least, Gilbert hoped he wouldn't mind.

He caught a flash of red from the corner of his eye and turned. Somebody stood at the end of the block, poised in the full light of the winter's afternoon. A woman, it was.

She had red hair—bright red hair—which was what had caught his eye. Gilbert, uncommonly partial to red hair in a female, felt his interest quicken. She seemed very tall for a woman and blocked a considerable amount of daylight.

Who was she? He stepped out of the stall to get a better look. By God, she must be nearly as tall as he was, and he topped six feet.

She turned her head to peer into the dark cavern of the stable, and he caught a glimpse of her face, a pale oval with unnaturally bright eyes.

Crying? Was she crying?

He started forward, but before he could take more than a couple steps she hurried off, leaving behind only another tantalizing gleam of red.

Gilbert stood where he was, struck far harder than by Mueller's fist.

****

Maddie located Roddy at last, sitting and taking a late supper with Mr. Crabbe, who ran Crabbe's Cabs. Mr. Crabbe frequently let Roddy sweep up for him and often gave him a bite to eat. Maddie always packed her brother a meal, but Roddy tended to eat it early and then got hungry all over again.

She *had* always packed him a meal. Heaven knew what they'd live on if she couldn't go back to work.

Her throat went dry as she paused a minute, watching her brother talking away to Mr. Crabbe, confiding as a child. Mr. Crabbe sat and listened, puffing on his pipe.

Roddy was like a child in many ways. He loved to talk and give away secrets. He loved games and playacting. In other ways, though, he was very much a young man. Maddie remembered that incident last year when he'd been caught in the back of a stable with Mr. O'Dell's daughter. She'd thought O'Dell would thrash him within an inch of his life.

She'd had to do some fancy talking, that was for sure. No harm done, Mr. O'Dell. They'd barely got their clothes off.

Now she sighed. How was she going to tell Roddy she might have lost her job? Maybe she hadn't, though. Mr. Trinedore might not remember what hit him, namely Maddie's fist. She'd have to check back with the others in a day or two and find out what was what.

Meanwhile she might be able to pick up a few pennies as a scrubber over at the sausage factory, or some work at the canning plant.

Her nose wrinkled involuntarily. Women's work—she hated it. Why did it always pay less? Women who worked at the exact same job as a man got a fraction of the wage. Anyway, she'd worked at the cannery a while back when the manageress—a horrible woman—had got put through the canning process. She'd sworn after that never to go back again.

Still, she needed to put food in her brother's gullet, didn't she?

Mr. Crabbe looked up when she stepped into his tiny office. He nodded at her pleasantly.

Roddy kept chattering away, something about a pair of ice skates he wanted. He and Maddie already had blades and sometimes skated on the river, one of the few times Maddie truly felt free.

"The fellas say they're a whole lot better than the old blades. Stay on better, too. See this scar on my chin, Mr. Crabbe?"

"I do, son," said Mr. Crabbe, who'd no doubt heard the story before. Roddy tended to forget to whom he told what.

"That's where I fell when my blade came off. You never saw so much blood."

Wasn't that the truth? Maddie had been terrified, newly responsible for him as she was following her ma's demise.

Roddy glanced up and caught sight of her then; his expression transformed to pure surprise.

"Maddie? Why are you here? Is it that late?"

"No." A twelve-hour day at the laundry was normal, fourteen or even sixteen not unheard of, when they were busy. "There was a—er—breakdown at Trine's. We got sent home."

"That's good. Let's do something fun. Let's go skate on the river."

"Oh, I don't think so, Roddy."

"Aw, come on, Maddie. It's still light out, and it's plenty cold enough."

That was for certain. It had been a cold winter, with wave after wave of icy air swept down from the Canadian territories, blown across the vast expanse of Lake Erie.

Maddie, about to refuse her brother, hesitated. Maybe it would do her some good to go out on the ice, distract her from that awful scene back at Trine's—the terrifying sight of Mr. Trinedore laid out like a corpse. It would definitely serve to amuse Roddy.

"All right, but just for a while, mind, till the sun goes down."

Roddy's face lit, before he sobered a bit. "But I promised Mr. Crabbe I'd do some more sweeping up after I ate."

Mr. Crabbe spoke around the stem of his pipe. "You can come back and do that in the morning if you want to, lad."

"That's very kind of you, Mr. Crabbe. You run away home, Roddy, and get our blades. I want a word with Mr. Crabbe."

Roddy went.

Mr. Crabbe pulled the pipe from his mouth. "What is it, Madeline?"

"Thank you for looking after Roddy, Mr. Crabbe. It's nice of you."

"I don't mind. These stables can be a rough place."

"I suppose so."

"He comes here if he feels he needs to duck away for a while."

"I do appreciate that. Mr. Crabbe, you wouldn't know of any work going here, would you?"

"For Roddy? He already picks up a few pennies here and there."

"No, I meant for…for me."

For the first time, Mr. Crabbe's expression altered to one of surprise. "Job for a woman, here?"

"Why not?"

Mr. Crabbe sounded scandalized when he replied, "It just isn't done. The place is too rough, and the work's too hard."

Maddie sighed. Did he think she didn't work hard at the laundry? Hauling wet, heavy garments out of the vats, backbreaking load after backbreaking load.

"Look at me, Mr. Crabbe. Do I look like a delicate flower? Don't you think I'm strong enough?"

"Strapping, for a lass," he admitted. "Still, there are

fist fights. And," he added as if it closed the discussion, "there is foul language."

As if she hadn't heard that before.

"Anyway," Mr. Crabbe went on, "I understood you had a good job at the laundry. Roddy never leaves off bragging about you."

Maddie experienced a pang. "There might be a few changes at the laundry, that's all I'm thinking. If you don't mind me asking, how much could a fella expect to make working here full time?"

He named a sum that made her eyelashes flutter. "That much?"

"Not so much, is it? Not for mucking out, grooming the 'orses and keeping 'em fit."

"It's more than I make at Trine's. Considerably more."

"Don't matter," Mr. Crabbe declared categorically. "No one will take you on, not so long as you're wearing them skirts. And no decent woman would take 'em off, would she?"

Probably not. But when push came to shove, nothing said Madeline MacGillicuddy had to remain a decent woman—whatever that meant.

Chapter Four

"Watch me, Maddie—watch!"

Obediently, Maddie paused and eyed her brother as he glided over the ice.

They weren't the only Buffalonians on the river this afternoon. Indeed, even though the port authority chased folks off the ice time after time, boys—and some girls—flocked here after school let out. And grown men came too, like the crowd of fellows farther down who batted with sticks at a little black ball, making an uncommon amount of noise.

But Roddy held his own. Indeed, even as she watched him, a big smile creased his face, and for an instant Maddie forgot what lay behind her at Trine's.

With the old blades strapped to his shabby shoes, Roddy became a creature transformed. The surface of the ice couldn't be called smooth—anything but. It contained pocks and ridges, yet Roddy sailed over it like a swan, arms outstretched, all his awkwardness flown.

Both of Maddie's parents had been tall, her Da, Murdoch MacGillicuddy, a strapping fellow up for any labor. Roddy had inherited his build along with his red hair, as had Maddie, for that matter. A tomboy all her life, she rarely showed anyone her feminine side.

Rarely could she afford to, though sometimes she yearned for it. Now her heart mourned over the fact that her strong brother couldn't always be as confident as he looked on the ice.

Then maybe she could quit taking care of him.

She finished strapping on her own skates and pushed off over the ice. The city had been cold today, but the chill here struck right to the bone. She'd feel warm once she started moving.

She stuck away, not toward Roddy but out for what open ice remained, between him and the noisy crew with the ball and sticks. The frigid wind streamed past her face and loosened her hair almost immediately. She should have tucked it all up under her cap.

She shed all thought as bliss enfolded her. She shed everything else too—the poor, distressed steamies back at the laundry and Mr. Trine, lying stiff as a plank. She forgot the scarcity of pennies in the teapot at home, that served as a piggy bank, and even all the meals to be provided, stretching away ahead of her.

Freedom. That was what she felt when she got out on the ice. She loved the way her muscles stretched and bunched in fine fashion, and the rush of air. She rose to the challenge of keeping balanced over the ridges in the river's surface.

Working up speed, she whirled and spun, turned on an edge and headed back the other way, careful not to let her skirts trip her up as she dug in for traction, reversed and skated backward.

She never saw other skaters do this. Few people who took the ice here got fancy. But Maddie MacGillicuddy could skate. She considered she did few things well. Sure, she could bake a decent oat scone and lift heavy barrels of lye. She hadn't been bad at math, back in school, and she was a patch at mending socks.

But out here, she felt graceful. She flew with the cold wind stretching her hair out like a banner, owning the ice.

Still stroking strongly backward, she made a wide arc and stopped in a spray of frost, looking for Roddy. That was when she became aware folks were staring. All the fellows with the sticks had paused to watch her.

Embarrassing. She struck out for Roddy, identified by his wild red mop, and away from the gawkers.

Roddy had met up with some other skaters, a mismatch of street ruffians by the look of them, who'd started a game of their own.

Instead of proper sticks like the fellows farther down, they had lengths of broken plank. Their ball looked like a wad of rags tied up with string.

These were the sort of lads who would normally pick on Roddy mercilessly. Now, though, his skill on blades looked to win him a place in their game.

Maddie skated up, feeling protective. "What's all this?" she called.

One of the bigger boys gave her a glare. "Hockey. Haven't you ever heard of hockey?"

"Sure." She'd heard of it. She suspected that was what the team at the far end was playing, but she'd never been part of a game.

With an eye to ensuring Roddy's fair treatment, she asked, "Can I join in?"

"Do you know the rules?" asked one of the other fellows.

She didn't, but wouldn't admit it. How hard could it be? She shrugged.

"You can't play," objected the first.

"Why not?"

He sneered. “You’re a girl.”

“Woman. And what difference does that make?” She thrust her chin in the air. “I can skate, can’t I?”

“Sure, we saw you can skate. But women don’t play hockey.”

He turned his back on her, just as if that ended the discussion, and started giving the others orders. Was he in charge, then? Tall, lanky and sandy-haired, she thought she’d seen him around the stables.

Her temper simmered. When he began calling out positions and added, at the end, “And the halfwit can play goalie,” she skated back up to him.

“What did you say?”

He turned back to face her. He had pale gray eyes and a crescent-shaped scar on one cheek. His gaze moved from her wild mop of hair—disarranged by the wind—to Roddy and he seemed to tumble to the truth. “Your brother?”

“Yes. And you’ll no’ be calling him that vile name, hear?” Her Scottish brogue, usually barely noticeable, tended to thicken when she got angry.

The young man said, “I calls ’em as I sees ’em.”

“And what’s this you want him to be doing—goalie?”

“Somebody has to stop the ball, and nobody else wants to do it.” He smiled. “If it hits your brother in the head, it won’t do much damage.”

Maddie blinked. She was having a bad day, she truly was, and that made it very difficult to hang on to her temper. She didn’t suppose it would be smart to lay out two men on the same day. But she had the impulse, she surely did, and she just didn’t know if she could hold herself back.

****

Gilbert spotted the woman as soon as he pushed off onto the ice. He thought she must be the same woman he'd glimpsed at the stables—at least, her hair looked the same, and it caught his eye just as it had back there in the gloom.

But what was she doing, facing off with Stewie Grant, who just happened to be a crony of Carl Mueller's and an even bigger ass than his friend?

By Abe's beard, she looked like she might be fixing to thump him.

Gilbert snatched up a length of broken two-by-four from among the others left along the shore, and struck off in the direction of the argument, for such it appeared to be. He could hear raised voices even before he reached the site, Grant's an ugly growl, the girl's sharp like a fishwife's and carrying a strange cadence.

She wore blades and stood on the tips of them—no mean feat. She also wore a shabby gray coat much too small for her and skirts that looked too short and showed a bit of ragged stocking. A deep green scarf streamed away in the wind, but it was her hair that captured Gilbert's attention.

Rarely did he miss a redheaded woman. There were all kinds: pale, strawberry blonde, auburn brown with a coppery gleam, eyeball-assaulting orange.

This woman's hair fell somewhere between the last two—a true, lustrous red with lots of curl.

A man could lose himself in hair like that. Not him, of course. He was certainly no charmer, and none of the encounters he'd had with women—a modest number—had ended particularly well.

Besides, she looked big enough to knock him

down—or to knock Stewie down, for that matter.

Would she? Did she need help?

He paused at the edge of the crowd where she and Stewie faced off, to listen, and rested his two-by-four lightly on the ice.

"My brother's not a punching bag," the woman declared, "or here for your amusement. Why can't you be decent about it?"

She fairly spat the word "decent" and Gilbert could see she held on to her temper by a thread. Ha, and if she expected anything close to decency, Stewie Grant was the wrong man. He had a right reputation around the stables for cruelty; Gilbert despised him to his toes.

Still, Stewie was one of those fellows—and there were enough of them—who always seemed to feel they were in charge. Gilbert didn't know how they got away with it, but they fair populated the world.

Now Stewie drew himself up and yelled in the redhead's face, "I'm captain here, and if the halfwit wants to play hockey, he'll take the position I give him, understand?"

A second redheaded figure sidled up. This one Gilbert also recognized from around the stables. Roddy MacGillicuddy, it was. He and the woman had to be related. The resemblance allowed for no other possibility.

"It's all right, Maddie," Roddy said. "I'll play goalie. I don't mind." Just so he could play. He didn't speak those words, but Gilbert, on a flash of sympathy, heard them.

Smelling imminent trouble, he edged up closer. The potential for disaster lay in the redheaded woman's balled-up fists.

She cried to Roddy, "And let them whack that ball at you? Does that sound like a fun time? Anyway, all your skill's in skating. What good's standing in one place?" She turned to Stewie. "Let him skate."

Stewie waved an arm in an expansive gesture. "He can go skate all he wants. This is my game."

Gilbert pushed himself into place at the woman's side. He didn't know what made him do it—a bad impulse, no doubt. But thinking he might defuse the situation, he gave Stewie an easy grin. "Hey, Grant. It's gonna be dark before you play at all, if you stand there arguing."

Stewie turned outraged eyes on him. "Yeah? And what's it have to do with you, half breed?"

Gilbert felt his own anger spike, but his smile never wavered.

"Let the kid play. What's the harm?"

The redhead shot him a grateful look from tawny hazel eyes. Gilbert decided he'd do a lot—probably almost anything—to be on the receiving end of another look like that.

"What am I supposed to do for a goalie?" Stewie whined.

Gilbert shrugged. "I'll go in goal, if you let the boy play."

Stewie eyed him up and down, apparently decided he was big enough to stop shots, and gave a hard nod. Muttering something about the team being called the Misfits, he moved off.

"Thanks." The redhead gave Gilbert another look. What had Roddy called her? *Maddie*. "I hope you don't get hurt."

Gilbert shrugged. "I can take my knocks."

She too eyed him up and down, but it felt nothing like the way Stewie had glared at him. This glance seemed to measure him in a purely feminine way, and not find him wanting.

Softly she said, “I’ll just bet.”

Gilbert’s grin widened and became genuine. For several heartbeats they stood gazing into one another’s eyes, until Stewie shouted, “Get in goal, Gilbert, if you’re going.”

Chapter Five

"Gilbert." Maddie spoke his name under her breath and turned her eyes on the man who crouched in place, in front of the makeshift goal formed of a wooden beam balanced on two metal barrels. She'd figured out the rules of the game as she watched, at least most of them. In truth, it was only half a game. There were two sets of players, but they shot at the same goal, since they had only the one.

Practice, the repugnant Stewie called it.

So far, Gilbert had let in only one goal from either side. He'd been hit countless times in the chest, and in the head twice. Not that Maddie kept track or anything.

As for the blows to his head, she hoped they hadn't hurt. He had a lot of hair—thick, black, and glossy in the dying light. She'd like to think that cushioned his poor skull.

The epithet Stewie had uttered floated through her head again. Half breed. Was he? Hard to tell. He was tall—taller than her, which was saying something—and had wide shoulders, but not a lot of weight. His eyes matched his hair—black—the kind of eyes in which a woman could get lost.

It didn't matter what Stewie called him. He had a kindness about him that, in Maddie's book, counted for more than anything else.

Now, though, the daylight rapidly faded. It grew

dark early in Buffalo at this time of year. And it rapidly got colder. Of course, it didn't help that she, Maddie, stood still. How stupid that they wouldn't let her play.

At least it looked like Roddy was having fun. He'd been all over the ice and had made some good moves—some blunders too—which made the fellows holler at him.

He didn't seem to mind. Poor Roddy just wanted to be part of things.

It struck her again, the grave responsibility of looking after him, and just how terribly she'd erred this day. When she lay dying of fever, Ma had made Maddie promise to look after her brother. But if she couldn't go back to Trine's, she'd buggered up the chance to do just that.

Stewie bellowed something, and everybody left his position—calling the game on account of darkness. The other team, farther down the river, had already departed; most of the children and casual skaters had also gone.

Maddie sat down, on a plank set in place at the shore, and unbuckled her blades. Roddy skated over to her. After a minute, Gilbert followed. Roddy looked flushed and happy. Maddie hated the prospect of ruining his high spirits with her ill news.

Both men sat and removed their blades. Roddy popped up first.

"I'm hungry, Maddie. What's for supper?"

Knowing the cupboard back home lay nearly bare, Maddie mentally counted her pennies. The day after tomorrow was pay day. Would she be able to collect her wage for the days she'd already labored this week? It would be pretty unfair if she couldn't.

Her stomach clenched with dread. “Not sure,” she told Roddy. She looked at Gilbert and held out her hand. “Gilbert, right? Nice meeting you. And thanks for going in goal so Roddy could skate.”

He reached out with alacrity and enfolded her fingers in his. She half expected to feel something—some momentous jolt of attraction, perhaps—but it didn’t happen, maybe because she wore her mittens.

“Nice meeting you,” he returned. She liked his voice, both deep and soft, with the faintest of accents. She wondered where he came from. Since moving to this city, she’d learned most everybody came from somewhere else—Eastern Europe, Britain, the Deep South. Mostly places she’d never see and could barely pronounce.

It always puzzled her how people who came from some far-off country could pick on somebody else who came from another far-off country, but there you had it. Seemed folks just had to pick on someone.

Including the steam units.

She became aware that Gilbert had failed to relinquish her hand. Now, she did feel something, a kind of warmth that crept up her arm.

Roddy said, “Maddie, maybe next time they’ll let you play, too. It’s no fun just watching, I know.”

“Uh—” Maddie said, giving her fingers a tentative tug.

“Gilbert, you should see how good Maddie skates.”

“I’d like to,” Gilbert said in his dusky voice. The dark—which somehow matched that voice—seemed to close around them. It made the encounter feel more intimate than it should.

Maddie shivered. “I’d better get Roddy home. It’s

getting colder."

"Going to snow some more, too," Gilbert offered, not taking his eyes from Maddie's. "I can always tell."

"Oh, yes?"

He wagged his dark head. Maddie had a sudden and completely inappropriate impulse to plunge her fingers through that black hair. But he still held her fingers captive.

He told her, "I get an instinct for certain things—sometimes I just know."

"I see. And are you never wrong?"

He shrugged those wide shoulders. "Seldom enough."

"Come on, Maddie," Roddy demanded, completely immune to any undertones. "I'm hungry."

"Yes, all right."

She tugged at her fingers again; this time Gilbert let them go. Together, they climbed up over the bank and trudged to the foot of Ferry Street.

"Do you live far?" Gilbert asked. "Can I see you home?"

"Peach Street," Maddie told him, wishing this somehow enchanting encounter had happened on any other day than the one during which she'd destroyed her life. "I think we'll be all right." She hoped so.

Gilbert nodded. "Maybe I'll see you again on the ice."

Later she wondered if he, with all his bright instincts, had uttered a prophecy.

****

All that night, lying sleepless in her little cot, Maddie told herself everything would turn out all right. She would report to Trine's in the morning and discover she'd exaggerated yesterday's situation. Mr. Trinedore would prove to be only slightly injured and would not remember what had happened. She would escape the consequences of the wallop she'd given him on Edie's behalf.

She shifted on her cot again, listening to Roddy snore. Despite her mental state, her stomach rumbled. She'd given Roddy most of their shared supper, and her belly protested its emptiness.

What would they eat tomorrow? And what if she couldn't pay the rent when it came due?

This place certainly wasn't much, a single room that stayed too hot in summer and too cold in winter and, no matter how she scrubbed, seemed always somehow malodorous. But she couldn't have Roddy out on the street.

Maybe he could sleep at the stables. It would just be her, then, without a bed.

She shuddered where she lay. If she'd finished things at Trine's, she'd just have to get another job doing anything. Well, almost anything. In her younger days, she'd had a few ill-advised encounters with men and didn't fancy it all that much. She certainly wouldn't want to do *that* for a living.

Before dawn, she got up, washed her face with cold water, and tamed her hair mercilessly. She always started her shift early. When Roddy woke, he'd know where she'd gone.

Snow had swept through the streets during the night, as if driven by a giant broom. Gilbert had been right.

Gilbert.

Snow still fell in little, icy shards that stung where

they hit her skin. On mornings like this, she always told herself that at least the laundry would feel warm. It didn't help this time. Her stomach sick from dread, she stuck outside the door.

No cops—a good sign. It also had to be a good sign that they hadn't come looking for her.

Not yet. They could be waiting inside, a row of coppers in blue uniforms ready to pounce.

She heard her mother's spectral voice, as so often. *Such an imagination you have on you, lass! In this life, you need your feet on the ground.*

So she did.

She pushed open the heavy door and went in. The moist, steamy air of the place reached out and greeted her, along with the pounding of the steam plant. Business as usual, then.

Some of her panic subsided. Maybe, just maybe, she would get away with this blunder.

A number of heads turned toward her—humans and mechanicals alike. For an instant everything seemed to pause. Then Rita trundled toward her, waving stubby mechanical arms.

"Maddie, Maddie," she squeaked. "You came back."

Maddie waited for the steamie to reach her before she asked, "Is Mr. Trinedore here, then?"

"No. Nooo," Rita wailed. "He is in the hospital. His condition is unknown. We are doing as you suggested and continuing to run the laundry."

Maddie puffed out a long breath and eyed Rita, trying to gauge her mood. She'd worked beside this unit a long time—slaved and suffered beside her—and knew that Rita did have what for lack of a better term could be called feelings. She believed most steamies did, a fact that had nearly caused a riot in this city last fall.

Now steamies demanded their rights. Many of them received a wage, though markedly lower than their human counterparts. They owned property, married one another and, some folks said, even applied to adopt children. There was a couple, one a hybrid mechanical and one a human, who had succeeded in adopting right before Christmas.

The hybrids—now, they were a proposition all their own, with little relation to poor Rita here. You couldn't tell them from humans, being steel and coal underneath but with flesh overlaying it all. And smart. People whispered they were building others just like themselves.

That being said, Maddie could feel Rita's distress. The steamie stared at her out of those chipped, molded eyes and waved her hands again.

"You must go, you must gooo."

Maddie's dread re-blossomed in her gut. "Why? If Mr. Trinedore's not here—"

Edie hurried up, closely followed by Timmy. Both looked grim.

"You'd better do as Rita says and scamper," Edie said. This morning, the bruise on her face where Mr. Trinedore had thumped her looked rich and dark, a plummy purple. The eye, around which it spread, looked red.

"But—" Maddie began.

Timmy interrupted. "The coppers came here yesterday after you left. Questioned all of us. We told them Trinedore slipped in a puddle of water and fell. We also told him you weren't here yesterday—sick."

"Well, then—"

"Look." Timmy narrowed his eyes. "We stuck up for you like you asked, 'cause you flattened old Trinedore for Edie's sake, right? But if he wakes up and tells them the truth, you're for it."

Maddie's thoughts raced. "He hasn't come to yet?"

"Not as we've heard."

"I can keep working, then." Maddie unbuttoned her coat.

Edie grabbed her arm. "Only if you want to do your work unpaid."

"What do you mean? I'm supposed to be here. I'm on the payroll. I'll get paid on Friday."

"Not if Trinedore remembers you swatting him, you won't."

"We'll keep mum," Timmy vowed, "out of loyalty, like I say. If he remembers, though, it won't be good for any of us."

"Oh, Christ." Maddie breathed the words in a prayer. "What am I going to do? He owes me for the beginning of this week, and tomorrow's Friday. Maybe he'll send an agent or somebody, to pay us."

Edie shrugged, a glint of sympathy in her eyes. "Nobody's telling you what to do. If it was me, I'd find another job. Look." She dug in the pocket of her soggy pinafore and produced a single penny. "Take this to tide you over, like."

"I couldn't. That's all you have till tomorrow, isn't it?"

Edie shrugged.

"I can let you have a penny too," Timmy contributed. "I was gonna spend it on smokes, but the air's so bad in here I probably shouldn't bother."

Two battered pennies now lay in Maddie's palm. They would buy Roddy something to eat but wouldn't pay for their rent.

Anyway, look at Maddie MacGillicuddy taking charity from children. Oh, how proud her parents would be!

She stuttered, "I can't."

Edie closed Maddie's fingers around the coins. "We'll try and keep you posted. Timmy will run to your place with news, or else the coppers will show up there. Then you'll know."

"Yes." Maddie stared at her own fingers.

"And thanks," Edie said more softly. "Been a long time since anybody—boneheaded or not—stood up for me."

They both went back to work. Maddie felt a touch on her arm; Rita's rubber-coated fingers lay there, white with lye.

"I wish you could come back to work," Rita squeaked the incredible statement. "I have labored beside you a long time. I miss you."

"Oh, Rita." Suddenly Maddie wanted to weep. "I miss you, too." Could a steamie be a woman's best friend? She certainly had few others. Useless to suggest they see each other outside the confines of the laundry. Rita rarely left here.

"Perhaps I can stop by sometimes."

"I would like that. But the others are right. It is not safe for you to come here, if Mr. Trinedore is alive."

"I suppose not." What the hell was she going to do?

"You are worried about your brother."

"How did you know?"

"You often talk about your concern for his welfare. Here, allow me." The unit opened a door in her side and fumbled with her worn and stained rubber digits. "I too have money. Since the new ordinance passed, Mr. Trinedore has paid each of us mechanicals two pennies a week."

Two pennies for upward of a hundred hours of work—it was something, but still smacked of slavery.

Rita began extricating pennies from her side. "Please take these."

"I can't. You worked too hard for those."

"I have nothing to spend them on. And this will keep you, yes? Until you find another job or go to jail."

"Yes." Wonderful choices—jail or even worse slavery than she'd endured here.

She looked into Rita's chipped face and felt a very real pain at her heart. "It's terribly generous of you. And I will pay you back every penny, I promise."

Rita seemed to fumble for words. She struggled, and a squeak came out ahead of the statement. "No debt. You—you are the one who made working here bearable."

Maddie embraced the damp, sticky unit and, with tears in her eyes, once more fled.

Chapter Six

"He killed that horse. I have no doubt of it."

The words rang loudly through the dusty air of the stables and turned heads. Gilbert, busy mucking out the stalls since his charges were all out pulling cabs, set aside his shovel and went to see what might be going on.

Except for an occasional fracas with Carl Mueller, and the general rooster-pecking that went on in such arenas, life here remained pretty quiet, a seemingly unchanging round of mucking-out, feeding, and grooming.

In the past few days, he'd been to the river twice with his blades, but he hadn't seen Maddie there. He hadn't seen her brother round the stables, either, and hoped nothing had happened to them.

Things tended to happen in this city, he knew—oft times bad things.

Now he, like half the other grooms in the vicinity, drifted up to the next stable down, where the cab owner, Mr. Philips, stood bellowing at a couple of his boys.

"He hasn't come back here? You sure?"

His employees, who looked both sullen and intimidated, shook their heads.

Old Mr. Crabbe, from down the way, stepped up. "Philips, what's going on?" Crabbe was a decent sort, like Gilbert's own boss, Mr. Stanley. Few and far between, in this trade.

Philips' face looked purple with rage. "That ass Mueller has killed one o' my horses."

"You say so?" Crabbe looked around pointedly, as for a corpse. "Where?"

"Not here," Philips struggled visibly to get a hold on his temper. "We had a report of one of our horses down. I sent Mueller to get it up again."

A bad idea that, Gilbert thought. Mueller had not a drop of mercy in him. Philips' horses feared and detested him.

"What happened?" Crabbe prompted.

"Damn fool went over there and whipped the beast, screamed at it to get up—only it didn't. It died right there on the spot."

Gilbert's stomach turned. He could picture the terrible scene all too well. Mueller was a brute with the horses.

"My good horse," Philips lamented, "good for nothing now but the boneyard."

A release for the poor animal, Gilbert reasoned, when it came down to it.

Mr. Crabbe pulled his pipe from his mouth. "You going to fire Mueller?"

"Of course I'm going to fire him, as soon as he sets foot in here."

Well, and that made a good outcome. The onlookers murmured.

One of Mueller's cronies stepped up. "I'm sure it was an accident, Mr. Philips. Carl's always careful with your stock."

Gilbert snorted. Unfortunately he did it aloud, and heads turned toward him.

"You there—you have an opinion?" Philips asked.

"Don't listen to him," Mueller's crony, whose name was Bertram, said quickly. "He's got it in for Carl—socked him, the other day."

Gilbert shouldered his way through the onlookers. "If I have ill feelings toward Carl Mueller, Mr. Philips, it's because he abuses your stock. Just as soon as the rest of them get back here, you give a feel to their backs. You'll feel the ridges where he straps them."

Philips shrugged. "Nothing wrong with strapping a horse, if it won't obey."

"But, Mr. Philips, they do obey—they're good horses. He beats them to take out his temper or 'cause they don't move fast enough to please him when they're tired."

Another of Mueller's cronies, named Strace, stepped up. "What d'you know about it, Injun?"

"I know. I've felt those welts."

"Yeah, and what you doing feeling up Mr. Philips' stock?"

Ignoring him, Gilbert gazed at Philips. "You can bet that's exactly what happened today, Mr. Philips. Carl Mueller couldn't persuade that horse up, when it went down from exhaustion, so he lost his temper and beat on it until it died."

"Maybe so. Either way, he's out of here. Spread the word, all of you—there's a position open at Philips'."

Philips stalked away. Mr. Crabbe gave Gilbert a salute with the stem of his pipe and made off also. Strace, at the head of Mueller's other cronies, stood on, as did a number of the onlookers.

"Carl ain't going to be happy you spoke out against

him," Strace said.

"I don't give a rat's ass if he's happy or not. He doesn't deserve to work here."

"And you do? Dirty injun! Get him, lads!"

The brawl that followed was short and sharp. Most of Mueller's friends were cowards, which was probably why they let him bully them, and why they preferred to attack in a pack. They got in one or two jabs and, when they saw Gilbert wasn't going down, cleared off.

Gilbert was left with scraped knuckles, a throbbing ear, and blood trickling down his chin.

And worth it, he grinned to himself as he went back to work.

****

"What the hell happened to you?"

Gilbert turned around when his boss, Benjamin Stanley, came bustling in. "One of the horses kick you in the face?"

"None of your horses would do that, Mr. Stanley," Gilbert replied. "They're good animals. Not that there hasn't been an uproar here today."

He filled Stanley in on what had been going on. Benjamin Stanley, a fair man in Gilbert's estimation, stood and listened.

Stanley treated his employees—Gilbert and a man named Robinson, with whom he traded shifts—with considerable respect. He didn't condone mistreatment of his horses, either. Not but what their lives were still hard.

"I heard something about it," he said once Gilbert finished. "What's that got to do with those bruises of yours?"

"I spoke up and told Mr. Philips how Mueller's

been beating on his horses. Didn't go over too sweet with Mueller's friends."

"I don't approve of brawling, especially here in the stables. But I'll overlook it this time. I like your work ethic, Gilbert, and I like the way you treat my animals. But if Mueller gets fired, I imagine you'll have to watch your back."

"He brought it on himself, sir."

"I agree. But he won't thank you for speaking out against him. Good riddance, for all that. Here—look at this."

"What is it, sir?"

"Come over by the light."

Stanley spread a sheet of paper across the rough table where Gilbert cleaned tack. On the paper, Gilbert saw a drawing. Of a horse.

No ordinary horse, though. All the parts of this animal were numbered and, well, pulled apart a little, like the beast had exploded from within.

He shot Mr. Stanley a look and quirked an eyebrow. "That from a butcher?"

"No." Stanley waved a hand. "Something much more extraordinary. I've just come from paying a call on the hybrid automatons. Did you know they've set up shop?"

"No, sir." Hybrid automatons?

"They've been building mechanical dogs. Very popular they are, especially with ladies of means. They come in all varieties. You don't need to walk them unless you want to, and you never have to brush or pick up after them. Just a little coal and water, and—*voilà*!"

"*Voilà*," Gilbert repeated, his gaze on the paper. "But that's no dog."

"Indeed, Gilbert, it is not. This is the very latest innovation to come from the hybrids' shop. A mechanical horse."

"Eh?"

"You might well look surprised. So was I. But the hybrid mechanicals are building them. And I've just ordered one."

"Sir?" Gilbert's world rocked.

"I wanted you to be the first to know. Think of it, Gilbert—no more mucking out. No more currying. No more feed—just coal."

No more job?

"But—but, Mr. Stanley, the city is already full of steamcabs. What need for this?"

"Of course there are steamcabs. They're fast and they're noisy. A lot of people detest them. This way, customers are still riding in a cab—the experience remains the same. Just, there's a mechanical up front."

Gilbert said nothing.

Stanley rushed on. "No more worrying about them being mistreated, son. No more needing to rest them. Just an occasional spit and polish."

"But, Mr. Stanley," Gilbert objected again, "the mechanicals have been asking for their rights. Folks say they do have feelings." He gestured at the paper. "Won't these?"

"Well, I don't know about that. I can't imagine they'll mind the work as much as a regular nag."

"It looks very expensive."

"It is, almost prohibitively. But you know me, Gilbert. I like to be on the cutting edge of things. You don't look very pleased."

Gilbert shook his head.

"Ah," Stanley said, "you'll be worried about your job."

"Yes, sir."

"Don't worry. We'll still have all the others, and as I say, you'll need to keep the new one cleaned and full of coal. But we may be able to retire old Jessop, eh?"

"That would be good. His fetlock's still bothering him, and he shouldn't be working all day."

"Precisely." Mr. Stanley folded up his paper and slipped it into his vest pocket.

"How long, sir?"

"How long?"

"Before the—er—steamie horse gets here?"

"Oh, it will be a while. Premium construction takes time, you understand. I do believe only the hybrid automatons are capable of this kind of manufacture. But rest assured, we will have one of the first units in operation."

"How very…innovative."

With a wide smile, Stanley clapped Gilbert on the back. "Isn't it, though?"

Chapter Seven

"What the heck happened to you?" The tall redheaded kid called Roddy echoed Mr. Stanley's words of yesterday. Gilbert, newly arrived at the river side, gave him one glance before focusing on his sister, who stood beside him.

She was here. Gilbert had to admit, the hope of seeing her again had been the only thing to bring him to the river today. And beholding her, he felt a wave of…well, he guessed it was satisfaction.

He could see her much better today, in the bright afternoon sun. Freckles, she had lots of freckles on her face—tiny, light brown ones. He wondered if they stretched everywhere under her clothes and what it would be like to play connect the dots with them, using his fingers. Lord, what an idea.

She had incredible eyes, wide and filled with light, hazel, and fringed by dark-brown lashes. Her nose was bony with, frankly, a bump in it, a strong nose that went with her strong chin. Her hair, in the sunlight—well, but he had no words for it.

He smiled at her, one of the genuine smiles he bestowed on few people. She smiled back and his world tilted.

"Hello," he said.

"Hello," she returned.

Roddy took off talking. "You stood in at goal last

time, right? You going to play goalie again?"

"Not sure I want to play. I'd be happy with just a skate." Still looking at Maddie, Gilbert said, "Will you come skate with me? Just wait a minute while I strap on my blades."

She and her brother already wore theirs. She waited, head tipped to one side, watching him prepare, and held out both her hands. "All right. Come on."

They took off over the bumpy ice, hands joined, with Maddie skating backward. Gilbert, with a firm grip on her fingers, tried to steer her; she shushed her blades back and forth, making what, for lack of a better term he could only call headway.

"Hey, you're good at that," he said.

"It's fun. Let's go faster!"

They did, working up a ripping speed down the shining expanse of the river. Hands still joined, they spun in wide circles, both of them laughing in joy. They fit one another, Gilbert thought. And he wanted to kiss her so much it hurt.

When at last they halted in a spray of ice, they were both breathless.

Keeping tight hold of her hands, Gilbert said, "You're amazing, do you know it?"

"First time a man's ever told me that."

"You must be seeing the wrong men."

"I'm not seeing anyone, if that's what you mean." Beautiful color flooded her cheeks and turned them pink.

Gilbert pulled her toward him. "Glad to hear that. Would you like to be seeing somebody?"

"Maybe. Depends on who it is." For the first time, her gaze fled his. "Though my life's a bit of a mess right now."

"I'm pretty good at helping people out of messes. What sort is yours?"

"I got in trouble at work. Serious trouble." She wrinkled her nose. "So I didn't get paid for my hours last week. A friend—a friend lent me some money. I paid the rent and that didn't leave much for feeding Roddy."

"I'll bet he eats his share."

"He does, and most of the time he eats my share too." Her gaze touched his fleetingly and he saw her agony.

His throat went tight. "Listen, if you need to borrow some money, I can help. I don't spend much on myself and have a bit put aside."

She looked stricken. Her eyes filled with tears. "Oh, that's real nice of you. You don't even know me."

"Sure feels like I do."

"I might make off with your money and you'd never see it—or me—again."

"That won't happen. Anyway, I want to see you again." He squeezed her fingers. "Lots of you." He felt certain of that, right down to his toes.

"Gilbert?"

"Yeah?"

"Is that your first or last name?"

"Last, but it's what people call me."

"Why don't they use your first name?"

"I hardly ever tell anybody what it is, my real first name, I mean." Had she heard what Stewie called him before the scratch game, last time? If so, she quite likely didn't remember, and she might as well know everything up front. It could make a difference to her.

He drew a deep breath. “It’s an Indian name.” He added carefully, “I’m half Algonquin, from up in Canada.”

Her gaze never wavered from his. She nodded. “My parents brought me and Roddy over from Oban, in Scotland, when I was little.”

“So that’s where you’re from? I like your accent.”

“I’ve lost most of it.”

Gilbert spun her gently on the ice. “You haven’t.”

She sighed. “Anyway, what I really need is a job. The—er—unpleasantness at my workplace necessitates I can’t be there, at least for a while. And I can’t keep borrowing money I might not be able to repay.”

“Where have you looked for work?”

She wrinkled her nose again, in that way she had. “Where haven’t I looked? I thought I could get something scrubbing, but even those jobs are hard to find. All taken by steamies. I’ve nothing against steamies, mind. My best friend’s one. But even now when people have to pay them, they work for a fraction of what I need to earn.”

“Your best friend’s a steamie?”

“Yes.”

“How’d that come about?”

“We work—worked—together.”

“What skills do you have?”

“Nothing particular. I can work hard, lift heavy loads. I’m not a small woman, as you see.”

“Think you could shovel and barrow manure?”

“Sure. Why?”

“There’s a job going wanting at the stables, down where I work.”

“Do you know how much it pays?”

Gilbert told her. She stared. “That much, eh?” Just

like Mr. Crabbe had said. "And that's for how many hours' work?"

"I'm there about eight hours a day, sometimes longer. Sundays off."

"That's twice what I was earning at the laundry, and for fewer hours."

"Well, then, come talk to Mr. Philips. I've got to warn you, he's kind of a pillock. Doesn't care much about his horses. They're just—just things to him."

Maddie gave Gilbert a searching look. "But not to you?"

He shook his head. "They've got feelings, right? They get tired. No need to treat 'em mean. A soft touch goes a long way."

"Just like my boss at the laundry. He's a pillock too, and treats the steamies like they don't have feelings either."

"But they do."

"I believe so."

"So what do you say?" Gilbert gazed into her eyes. "Come work at the stables. I'd love having you close by." Probably he shouldn't have added that, at least not out loud.

But she shook her head sadly. "This Mr. Philips would never hire me. I can't see him hiring a woman."

Damn it, she was right. Reluctant to surrender the dream, Gilbert released her hands and eyed her up and down. "You know, you're pretty tall."

"I'm a right galumphing giant of a woman."

"Think you could fit into your brother's clothes?"

"Sure. Why?" Her eyes widened. "Oh no, you're not thinking—"

"Why not? Without all that hair, or with it tucked

into a cap—"

Gilbert pulled the hat off his own head. Very gently, he gathered her wild mane into his hands. It felt like silk, and tucking it into the knitted cap took all his will. He pulled the hat well down on her head.

Mattie's cheeks flushed again. "Are you saying I look like a boy?"

"No, not at all. I'm saying maybe if you kept your head down and didn't talk much, you might pass as one. Just for the wage."

She looked torn. Standing there with her eyes fixed on Gilbert, all her glorious hair hidden away, she did resemble Roddy enough to pass for his—well, brother.

"I don't know," she whispered. "What if I get caught? I'm already in enough trouble."

"Just give it some thought, all right? But don't wait too long or the place will be filled."

She questioned him with her eyes. "You really think I could pass?"

"Well, you don't look like a lad, to me." What would she do if he pulled her up against him here and now, and kissed her? He didn't suppose he should try.

"I'd never be able to keep Roddy from blabbing," she lamented.

"Maybe not. But," he spoke it like a vow, "you can trust me, Maddie."

To the end.

Chapter Eight

Maddie looked at herself in the wavy mirror that graced the communal bath room at their rooming house. She wore one of Roddy's rough woven blue shirts with a vest over it, to cover what there was of her bosom, and his pants which, to her embarrassment, fit her hips a bit too snugly. She'd cut her hair—braided it into a long plait which she'd then chopped off without mercy and stowed in her Ma's chest, the one that had come all the way from Scotland. It had been a bold move she'd bitterly regretted the moment she did it. If she had any claim to feminine beauty, it lay in her hair, and the sacrifice brought tears to her eyes.

Anyway, that was the whole point, wasn't it? She couldn't afford to show any feminine attributes.

And she certainly didn't, now. Peering into the spotted mirror, she saw she looked so much like Roddy it shocked her.

What man would even so much as glance at a woman who looked like a gangly boy? What chance did she have of finding love? But this wasn't about love, was it? Her existence had become all about survival.

People were going to mistake her for Roddy's brother, at the very least. Good thing she'd decided to say she was his cousin, newly arrived in town and looking for work.

Matthew MacGillicuddy—Matty, in case Roddy

slipped up and called her by name. Roddy was bound to slip up eventually, though she'd lectured him all last evening. He seemed to lose the threads of the scheme in his happy excitement.

"You're going to work at the stables with me? That'll be fun."

"Yes, but you have to remember it's your cousin, Matthew, applying to work there. Your male cousin, right?"

"Right, right. It's a secret."

"A secret, yes, just between us."

Searching the eyes of the young man in the glass one last time, Maddie figured she was doomed. Roddy rarely succeeded in keeping a secret. But if she could make a couple days' wages at or near Gilbert's rate, it would be worth the deception.

****

"I worked wi' horses back in Scotland, Mr. Philips," Maddie lied bald-facedly. In for a penny, in for a dollar. "Stables at a big house, till I decided to follow me cousins here to America."

"Do you have references?" Philips both looked and sounded like a pillock, just as Gilbert had said, but at this point Maddie didn't care.

"I did," she said. "A fine paper fr' the laird o' the place." She laid the brogue on heavy. "But it got washed over the side o' the ship wi' most my luggage."

"I see." Philips regarded her through narrowed, blue eyes. "This is just for mucking out and grooming, you understand. You know how to trim a hoof?"

Maddie nodded, hoping Gilbert would be able to teach her. She'd caught just a glimpse of him when she came in, down the stable row. It had heartened her.

"Well," Philips hedged, "I need someone right away, but no slackers, mind. You'd have to work hard."

"Give me a trial, sir, for a week maybe. If you find I don't work hard enough, you can strike me off." She didn't want anybody else snatching this place out from under her.

"That's an idea. Would you agree to go without any trouble, should I decide your work's not up to snuff?"

"I will, sir."

"No smoking around the horses, mind, or near the straw."

"I don't smoke, sir."

"And no pissing in the stable block. A lot of the fellas get lazy, don't want to walk down to the bog. They tend to just whip out their johns on the spot."

"I can guarantee I won't be doing that."

"All right. What say we give you that week's trial?"

"That's grand, sir. Excuse me, but what is the wage, just?"

Philips named a wage only slightly less than what Gilbert had quoted.

"Thank you, sir. When might I start?"

"Start now. See that pile of manure? And that cart? You fill one with the other and haul it away. One of the fellows will tell you where." He pulled out a notebook and pen before asking, "Matthew, you say? Matthew MacGillicuddy?"

"Yes, sir."

"Then get to work. And I don't want to see that cousin of yours hanging around here all the time. The boy's a halfwit. Understand?"

Maddie bristled but kept it from showing. "Yes, sir."

"By the time you're finished with the manure, the cabs will be coming in. Cool the horses down, groom them, and give them a feed, then clean and sweep out the cabs. They'll need to go out again."

"Yes, sir." She wondered when the horses got to rest.

"Look after my business and belongings as if they're your own."

"I will, sir."

"And don't make me regret this decision."

Philips stalked off. Maddie stood, torn between victorious glee at having fooled him, and chagrin that yes, she could pass for a young man. Now she just needed to manage performing the job.

****

Maddie swiftly discovered that shifting manure wasn't much worse than bundling up piles of filthy laundry and only marginally more malodorous. She had a bit of trouble at first, hauling the unwieldy cart, and had to ask directions three times before she located the massive pile at the end of the street, where she found she had to shovel it all out again.

No great hardship, that—she was used to heavy work, though her hands blistered before she finished. She dragged the empty cart back to Philips' stable, only to find Gilbert there, waiting for her.

She didn't know whether or not she felt glad to see him, at that point. She certainly didn't appear her best, and reeked of both sweat and horse shit. And in her heart, she wanted to look attractive to this man.

But he drew her into the shadows of an empty box

and grinned at her. “I see you got hired. Word’s all over the stables Philips hired a groom from Scotland.”

She told him, while demonstrating, “I laid on the brogue a bit.”

“Say that again.”

“I laid on the Scottish—” Maddie broke off and went silent. Gilbert had stepped right up against her, his body almost touching hers.

“That,” he whispered, “is the most alluring thing I’ve ever heard.”

“Really?”

“Oh, yeah.”

“But I’m standing here looking like a boy.”

“No, you’re not. You don’t look like a boy to me.”

Was it sheer gratitude that made Maddie lean in and kiss him? The assurance that at least one person still saw her as female, and attractive. She never knew, because the instant her lips met Gilbert’s, things heated up considerably. The taste and feel of him exploded upon her in equal measures, and she forgot trivialities like who did what.

Warm he was, so warm. She closed her eyes, the better to revel in the wonder of the contact. She longed to raise her hands and seize the front of his shirt—to pull him closer, of course—but she didn’t quite dare.

She wanted him to wrap his arms around her. He didn’t. Instead he leaned a hand against the wall on either side of her, where she’d ended up at the back of the stall. The only place they touched was on the lips. It did strange things to Maddie’s knees.

But oh, he made the most out of that single point of contact. He dove into her, wooing, persuading, sampling, and making Maddie feel more feminine than ever before.

She ached for more, to grab him by the shoulders and wrap her legs around him, to consume him from head to toe.

Instead, she stood and let herself be kissed.

When it ended, he withdrew—not far—and stared her in the eyes. There wasn't much light in the stall, certainly not enough to let her see his expression. But she had few doubts about what he was thinking, when he stepped up even closer, so their bodies—at last—came into contact.

Were they going to make love right here in this horse box, her first day on the job? Did she want that?

Maybe.

He drew off her cap, plunged his fingers into her hair and froze.

"You cut your hair off!" It came from him in a groan of protest.

"Well, yes, I had to. Can you imagine if my hat fell off?" She kissed him again, quick and hard. "Does it matter?"

What was she asking, exactly? Whether he felt attracted to her without the wild mop of hair? Whether they'd started something here, in the shadows, they'd eventually finish here, or elsewhere?

Whether they, henceforth, meant something to one another?

He groaned again. "No, of course not. But Christ, I liked your hair."

"I have it at home in my ma's chest," she told him earnestly.

"What?"

"My hair. I braided it up and saved it."

He started to laugh. Leaning one arm against the plank wall, he laughed till he doubled over, his dark head nearly touching Maddie's shoulder.

"What's so funny?" she asked, half annoyed.

"The hair in a chest. You offering it to me? No, thanks. I think I'll take what's left."

Once more, he plunged his hands into her hair, tangled his fingers in the corkscrew tendrils, and drew her tight against him. He kissed her with an intensity that eliminated any possibility of breathing.

How long could a woman exist without air? An endless expanse of time, so it seemed.

When this kiss ended, Maddie lay draped against Gilbert's chest, weak right down to her toes.

"Oh," she breathed.

"Is that a good 'oh' or a bad 'oh'?"

"Good. A very good 'oh.'"

"That's all right, then."

"I'd better get back to work."

"Not yet."

"What if somebody sees us?" Maddie fished inside her brain for a measure of sanity. "Mr. Philips said the cabs would be coming back soon."

"You're right." Gilbert sucked in a breath. "Maddie."

"What?"

"Just—Maddie." He caught her face between his hands and gave her a final kiss, searing enough to blister. Then, soft and dark as a shadow, he slipped away.

Maddie leaned back against the plank wall, feeling weak. She wanted the man. She wanted all of him from the top of his black head right on down.

She picked her cap up from the straw and fitted it back on her head.

What was she going to do about it?

Chapter Nine

"Will ya look at that fella skate!"

The call came across the frozen river, but Maddie, in full stride over the ice, didn't bother to turn her head. People called out all kinds of things, seldom at her.

Besides, after her long day's labor at the stable, she wanted to lose herself in the sheer bliss of just gliding. Eyes half closed, alone with the fiery ball of the sun on its way to set in the southwest, she needed to feel, not think.

Three days had passed since she took the job at Philips, and so far no one had twigged to her being a female. She didn't know if she felt glad about that, or insulted. The job had its advantages and disadvantages. She liked the garb, and skating in Roddy's trousers instead of her skirts felt marvelous and emancipating. But she stood in constant fear of discovery, or that Roddy would forget himself and blab. He still called her Maddie—fortunately those who overheard him took it for a diminutive of Matthew, used toward a cousin.

Most of them called her Mattie now.

And nobody here on the ice seemed to recognize her or connect her with the young woman who'd previously come out skating on the river. She'd even managed to wiggle her way into a pickup game once, when the men were shorthanded. The redoubtable Stewie had watched her skate before giving a hard nod of acceptance, saying only, "You're not funny in the head like your dimwit cousin, are you?"

She must be funny in the head, she thought now, to get herself in this crazy situation.

"Hey you, boy. Boy!"

Couldn't be calling to her, could he? Nah.

She glided away and caught a glimpse of a dark head, bared to the cold. That snared her attention, and no mistake. Gilbert had arrived and now stroked out in an effort to catch her, using his whole body.

Maddie smiled a little smile. She had to confess, she liked having him follow after her. But it made another danger in the workplace. After that first time they'd kissed, they'd done little more than exchange heated looks and, once, a swift brush of lips on lips. He wanted her; she could tell that much—wanted all of her, dressed in boys' clothing or otherwise. Yet if someone saw them together, it could wreck everything.

But, my, he made a fine sight skating after her with his broad shoulders set, the sun lighting his dark hair and his eyes fixed on her in a look that—

Funny how a single look from the man could set her pulse to racing and make her taste him all over again.

He fell into stride next to her. "Hello."

"Hello," she returned, careful to keep her distance. Not but she didn't long nearly all the time to touch him. But how would that look? She tucked her hands into the pockets of her coat, avoiding temptation.

Gilbert eyed the hat she wore, a knit one patterned in green and white, that Ma had knit for Roddy some time ago. He smiled the smile that put a spark in his dark eyes. "That looks good on you."

"Does it?"

"Oh, yes. Brings out the green in your eyes." Judiciously he added, "You'd look good all in green." His smile turned into a grin. "Or naked."

She gaped. For a good, decent man, he displayed a woeful tendency to come out with such statements, from the blue, as it were.

She lifted a brow. "How would you know, never having seen me in that condition?"

"I have a good imagination. And it's fixed on you most of the time."

"Well, you'd better unfix it. You keep looking at me that way, people are going to wonder."

"All right. But I have a confession to make."

Heaven help her.

He leaned close enough to speak in her ear. He had a tendency to do that too, and it made her shiver.

"I still love your hair—even though it's short."

Maddie flushed. Not knowing what to do with her emotions, she turned and faced him.

"Then catch me—if you can."

She took off, still facing him, skating backward. She'd learned the trick of it young, when her Da brought her out to skate, and she rejoiced in it.

With a whoop, Gilbert came after her, but they both knew he wouldn't catch her unless she let him. She was much too quick.

Back turned to the crowd of skaters, she flew, only to find herself once more the target of bellowing.

"Boy! I say, young man!"

The same voice that had called out before. He couldn't mean her? Oh, yes, he could.

She shushed to a halt and found she'd become the

center of attention. Everyone stared—the other skaters, kids without skates, men in business suits.

Men in business suits? Here?

One of them stumped toward her and Gilbert, stepping carefully over the bare ice. He wore a bowler hat that quite likely did nothing to keep his ears warm, a fine suit beneath a topcoat, and highly polished shoes. With her blades on, Maddie topped him by half a head.

He fixed intent blue eyes on her and said, "You there, that was some fancy skating. Best I've ever seen."

Maddie glanced around. "Are you speaking to me, sir?"

"Sure am. How'd you learn to do that?"

"Do what, sir?"

Gilbert poked her with his elbow. "I think he means skate backward."

"I do, my good man, I do. I've never seen the like. Son, what's your name?" he demanded of Maddie.

"MacGillicuddy, sir," she replied, phrasing it as she often heard males do. "Matthew MacGillicuddy."

"Well, MacGillicuddy, I'm Clive Brewster. Do you recognize that name?"

Mutely, Maddie shook her head.

"I'm the founder and operator of Buffalo's Best Beer—brewed right here in this city, and the finest beer on the Niagara Frontier."

Maddie shot an incredulous look at Gilbert and swept the staring faces, all around, with a second.

"No, sir. I'm sorry, sir."

"Doesn't matter." Brewster waved an expansive hand. "You've heard of me now, eh? You play hockey, MacGillicuddy?"

"Uh—" Maddie rolled her eyes like one of Mr. Phillips' horses. "I've played a time or two."

Mr. Brewster scrutinized her. "That's some accent you've got there, son. Where were you born?"

"Scotland, sir. Oban."

"How long have you lived in Buffalo?"

"Nearly three weeks."

Mr. Brewster gave a great laugh and nodded at his two companions, one of them much younger than the other two. "I guess that qualifies as a resident of our fine city, eh?"

The younger man stepped forward. He wore skates and proper sporting garb, like the fellows Maddie had seen practicing farther down the river. He scowled at her.

"Surely, Mr. Brewster, you're not considering putting him on the team?"

"Why not? Have you seen this boy skate? Backward, Rogers, backward! You know this game—can you imagine what a rover he'd make? Up the ice and back down again—the other team wouldn't know what hit 'em."

Rogers stared at Maddie in consternation. "But sir, I've already put a team together."

"Right, Rogers, but my fingerprints aren't on it. Now, this is a serious challenge from our neighbors to the north. I intend to win, whatever it takes. You're not going to get in my way, are you?"

"But sir, the team I've founded has been practicing together for some time. We have defensemen—good ones. We don't need some unknown boy from Scotland."

"He might have been born there, but he's a good

Buffalo lad now, and anyway, it's going to be my team. I have a coach right here. Harry?"

The other man stepped up. He wore a knit hat of his own, and an ill-fitting suit over a body built like a fireplug. His face looked like that of a guard dog stung by a wasp.

He too glared at Maddie from mud-colored eyes.

She started to feel dizzy.

"Sorry, sir, but I don't understand," she bleated.

"You want to play hockey?" the coach bellowed at her. "For real money?"

Maddie's Scottish blood kicked in. She narrowed her eyes. "I've got a job, but—how much?"

"Let's talk about that later, all right, MacGillicuddy?" Brewster put an arm around her and led her toward the shore.

"And you can keep that job, son. This would be done in your spare time. I'm getting up a hockey team, see, to play against a team from Fort Erie. That's across the water, in Canada."

"I know where Fort Erie is, sir."

"I'm calling my team the Buffalo Boilermakers. You ever played on a proper team?"

Maddie shot a panicky look at Gilbert, who trailed them. "No, sir. Not in earnest."

"This would be in earnest, MacGillicuddy, very much in earnest. There's going to be a series of five games—a tournament—and I mean to win."

To her surprise it was the coach, Harry, who spoke up in answer. "I been observing those practices, and while we were here I couldn't help noticing you, son. I ain't seen anyone to match your speed. Well, there was a girl, once, but she ain't come back lately. And that thing you do, stroking backward—"

"We could learn that," Rogers interrupted.

Harry glared at him. "Then you go do that, and learn all your friends. He can do it now. A thing o' beauty, the way he skates."

Maddie exchanged another disbelieving look with Gilbert. "But, sir," she protested, "I'm not a hockey player. I'm not even sure of all the rules."

"You'll get them down soon enough."

Another well-equipped player skated down the ice and joined them. He spoke in Clive Brewster's ear.

Brewster glared at the man. "So what if his cousin's a halfwit? MacGillicuddy, here, seems quick enough on the uptake."

"I suggest tryouts," Harry chimed in, "for anybody who wants to make the team."

Maddie shook her head. "I'm not trying out. Come on, Gilbert, let's go."

"Wait!" Brewster yelped. "There's a sign-on bonus. Ten dollars."

"What?" Maddie's eyes grew huge. With that, she could afford to pay Rita back and then some.

Brewster glared her in the eyes. "I tell you, Mr. MacGillicuddy, I intend to win this tournament, whatever it takes."

Chapter Ten

"What are you going to do?" Gilbert asked Maddie as soon as they were back at the stables. He felt uneasy about Brewster's proposition, but didn't know what to do about it. Apart from a few sweet kisses, Maddie had given him no indication she wanted him in her life.

He felt very certain he wanted her in his.

Either way, she sure wouldn't welcome him poking his nose into her business.

She gazed at him with wide eyes. "Ten dollars is a whole lot of money. Especially just for playing a game. A *game*, Gilbert."

"I know."

"I'd be able to pay back the people who loaned me their wages, and be good on the rent besides."

"Yes, but…" Gilbert shifted on his feet and tried to fathom how best to speak to her. "Hockey—the kind of hockey that man's talking about—is a rough game. You could get hurt."

"I'm pretty tough, you know."

"I know," he said unhappily.

"A big girl. I can take my knocks."

He wanted to touch her then, wanted it so much it hurt. He longed to pull her into his arms and tell her he didn't want to see her with bruises, or a busted head.

Instead he said, with considerable calculation, "You'd be taking a risk, putting yourself out in public that way. It gives you a better chance of getting caught—for being a woman, I mean."

"There is that. It's more exposure, and I don't like that part of it." Her eyes grew troubled. "I don't know what to do."

"Well, then." Gilbert calmed a bit. "You shouldn't make the gamble. Better safe than sorry."

"That's a good adage, yes." She waved a finger at his nose. "But I've another one. My ma always used to say, 'If you don't know the answer to a question, place it in the hands of fate. Let the answer come.' That's what my parents did when they were deciding whether or not to come to America." She stepped closer to him. "You're glad we came, aren't you?"

"Yes." The breath hitched in Gilbert's chest.

"Well, then," she echoed his words. "Maybe I should take the tryout. That coach seems like a real hard-nose, and I get the impression there'll be a lot of fellows trying. I probably won't make the team."

"And if you do make it?" Gilbert asked hoarsely.

"I can't possibly, can I?"

Gilbert didn't know. He too had seen her skate.

He edged closer. "I was kind of hoping I could take up some of your spare time. You get on that team, you won't have any."

She gave him a quick, hard, open-mouthed kiss and her eyes gleamed. "Good thing we work so near to each other, isn't it?"

****

Maddie sat at the wobbly wooden table in her rented room and stared at the small square of card Mr. Brewster had given her, with his name and direction printed on it. He'd placed the card in her hand as she left the ice, and told her with an intent stare, “You get back to me, MacGillicuddy, hear?”

She’d heard, and she’d made her decision. This morning she would walk all the way up to the brewery and tell Mr. Brewster she wanted to try out.

She meant to place this squarely in the hands of fate.

So far, as she well knew, fate had not been particularly kind to her. Losing both her parents had been a blow. There was Roddy—a trial to look after, and no mistake. There was the constant grind of trying to make a living. There was the uncertainty surrounding the situation with Mr. Trinedore, and discovery hanging over her head at the stable.

On the other hand, she had the possibility of earning ten dollars, just for signing on. And there was Gilbert.

Oh yes, there was. She scarcely dared think about him, for the way he made her feel—all ramped up, and at the same time weak and boneless. Strong, yet vulnerable.

He didn’t want her on Mr. Brewster’s hockey team. What would he do if she pushed ahead with it? Drop her like a hot potato? Would it put the blight on this fragile thing blooming between them?

The morning sun, coming through the soot-coated window, made her squint her eyes. She’d spent most of last evening lecturing Roddy about the ins and outs of the thing. If she got on the team, or even just tried out for it, he had to keep absolutely mum about her being his sister. She was a different person now, his male cousin, Matthew, from Scotland.

“But,” he’d protested, struggling to wrap his

troubled mind around it, "if you're Matthew, then where's Maddie gone? I miss her." Tears came to his eyes.

"I'm still here. You just can't tell anybody, because I'm Matthew now."

God only knew if he understood. Staring into the dawn, Maddie acknowledged she could well be heading straight toward disaster.

****

A short while later, ready to leave for the brewery, Maddie heard a knock on the room door. At once, her stomach tensed. Had Mr. Trinedore finally fingered her for flattening him? Had the coppers come to take her away?

That would be a firm answer come from fate, wouldn't it?

Feeling grateful Roddy had already left for the stables, she swung open the door.

And gaped in surprise.

Rita stood there, her corroded silver finish looking dull in the gloom of the hallway. For an instant, Maddie's brain refused to compute the automaton's presence. She'd never seen the unit outside the laundry, and certainly hadn't expected to see her now.

"Rita! Oh my goodness, how did you get here? Come in."

"I hope I do not intrude."

"Of course not. I'm happy to see you. At least, I hope you don't come bringing bad news."

"I do not think so." Rita trundled in and Maddie shut the door. "I do bring news, however."

"How did you ever get up all those stairs?" Rita's wheels were worn and wobbly, and the springs attached to them, which allowed her to raise or lower herself to surfaces with varying levels, barely operated any more. It must have been taxing, hauling her great bulk up all that way.

"I have become a bit overheated. I expect going down will be easier. I must confess I am pleased to find you here. I did not want to expend so much coal for nothing."

"Have you come for the money you loaned me? I'm afraid I don't have all of it yet, though I do have a chance of landing a windfall soon."

"I do not want the money I gave you back, Maddie. Please consider it a gift."

"Oh, no, Rita. I fully intend to repay you."

"I am informed one does not refuse a gift, especially from a friend."

"Especially from a friend," Maddie agreed softly. She pulled a chair out from the table and sat down. She knew all too well she couldn't invite Rita to sit.

"What's going on at Trine's? Is there news about Mr. Trinedore?"

"Yes, that is why I came. We had word late yesterday, and I felt you should know. Mr. Trinedore has been released from the hospital. He intends to return to the laundry next week."

Maddie clenched her hands together atop the table. "Has he told the police about me? Does he remember what happened to him?"

"It appears not. He sent an overseer, who was quite surprised to find we were all still doing our jobs. All the overseer told us was that Mr. Trinedore believes he suffered some sort of attack."

So he had.

"Whether he may remember more, once he sees you, remains to be seen. Edie said I should come and tell you Mr. Trinedore is due back. Also ask you what you want to do about your job at the laundry. If you wish to come back, you should be in place by the time Mr. Trinedore arrives, so he will not question your absence."

"Yes." Maddie bit her lip and thought about the risks involved in going back versus staying where she was.

"I miss you, Maddie," Rita squeaked softly. "Working at Trine's is only bearable with you there."

"Oh, Rita." Tears stung Maddie's eyes. "The thing is, I've got another job. I needed to, if I'm to keep Roddy, even with your help." A risky job. "It pays better than Trine's."

Rita seemed to sag where she stood. "Then you will not want to come back to the laundry."

"I don't know. Maybe after a while. I owe all of you so much for keeping mum about what happened. And I care about everyone there, especially you, Rita."

"I understand. Your concern must center on your brother's welfare, not mine." Rita brightened marginally. "Work has been some better with Mr. Trinedore gone. Otis has been running the laundry and doing a good job. But with Mr. Trinedore coming back, I did hope for your company."

Hope for. And some people insisted steamies had no feelings.

"Rita, listen to me." Maddie reached out and touched the unit's battered arm. "You deserve better treatment, all of you do. Go to the folks at the Automaton Liberation League. They're fighting for steamies' rights. Maybe they can set up some rules for the laundry and force Mr. Trinedore to comply, give you some protection so you don't get overused, and receive at least some basic maintenance."

"I could not possibly approach them, Maddie."

"Why not? They're automatons, like you."

"Not like me. They are mostly hybrids. They look like humans. I am nothing but an old, worn-out, rudimentary unit."

"That has nothing to do with it. And it's not your fault old Trinedore didn't give you decent maintenance." Maddie got to her feet. "Listen to me, Rita, you're as good as anyone. Better. You're my friend, and if you want me to go along to the Automaton Liberation League with you, to help with the talking, I will."

"Thank you, Maddie. I will consider it."

"Meanwhile, thank you for bringing me the warning about Mr. Trinedore. Please ask the others not to betray me."

"Yes, Maddie. Now I must get to work."

"Let me help you back down the stairs."

They descended together, a slow process that gave Rita a few new dents and caused Maddie a couple of bruises. At the bottom, Maddie enfolded the automaton in a fierce hug.

"Go safely, my dear, and be brave. Don't forget, you're still my best friend."

Chapter Eleven

"So you really did it."

Gilbert spoke from where he leaned against the wall of the first stable block, just where the lane narrowed.

Maddie had seen him there as soon as she came in—waiting for her?—with his arms crossed on the front of his old coat and a grave look in his dark eyes.

She paused when she reached him but said nothing.

"You told Mr. Brewster you'd go for it," he accused. "When's the tryout?"

"This afternoon, at four."

"You work later than that."

"I'm hoping Mr. Philips will let me go early."

"So this job's not very important to you, after all."

"It's important." She studied his face and added in a whisper, "You're important."

"Really?"

"Yes." Oh, yes. "Listen, Gilbert, why are you so set against me trying out for that team?"

"Because you have no clue how rough it gets. Because you could get hurt bad. Because," he straightened, "I might lose you, just when I've found you."

She looked at him standing there, foursquare, dark-eyed, and with the sun on his thick hair. "That won't happen."

"How do you know? You could get drawn into all this—big money and maybe a big name. You won't know me anymore."

"That won't happen," she repeated, gazing straight into his eyes, wishing she could tell him what lay in her heart. "Look, I probably won't pass the trial."

"You'll pass. I've never seen anybody skate as fast as you. And backward."

"I have to get to work. Don't want Mr. Philips mad at me."

She started past him. He whispered her name. "Maddie—"

Again she looked at him. "I wish you could be there, for encouragement."

For an instant he looked angry. Then he melted visibly. "I'll see what I can do."

****

"Tell me the rules one more time," Maddie urged Gilbert as they walked to the river, their blades slung over their shoulders, held by the straps. "I know you've already tried drilling them through my head." He had, this afternoon while he showed her how to trim a hoof and while they shared a quick cup of ginger beer, later. "I'm afraid when I get out on the ice I'll forget."

He shot her a look from the corner of his eye. He hadn't tried to kiss her once all afternoon, even when they were alone in the stables. When she'd aimed a peck at his lips, he'd pretended to be focusing on his tasks and stepped away.

Was he still mad? Would her playing hockey make him see her as less feminine? If only he knew how much of a woman he made her feel, like she could eat him up whole.

Maybe, she thought as the river came into sight, thronged with people, she should give the whole hockey idea up. But what about providing for Roddy?

This afternoon, she'd made sure her brother would stay distracted, running errands for Mr. Crabbe of Crabbe's Cabs. She didn't need Roddy messing things up. Which meant she must actually want to succeed in this mad venture.

She sighed and gestured toward the ice. "Look at all the people who showed up for tryouts, Gilbert. I don't stand a chance."

"Maddie—" At the edge of the river, he turned and looked at her.

"My God, Gilbert, if you look at me that way, folks are going to know I'm a woman. Else they'll start thinking strange things about you."

"I just want to say, 'Good luck.' Here, get your blades on. Nice and tight, eh? Want to wear mine? I think they're better."

"Are they?"

"When's the last time you sharpened yours? I did mine last night. There, take 'em. And pull your hat well down. Your hair's way too pretty."

"Gil—"

"Just go."

He didn't watch her push off onto the ice, but half the other people there did.

Mr. Brewster, with Coach Harry and a number of men in suits standing around him, turned and waved his hand. "Here he is now. Wait, gentlemen, till you see this young man skate."

"Mr. Brewster, Mr. Harry." Maddie nodded at the other men.

"These men, MacGillicuddy, are potential investors. If you make the Boilermakers, you'll get a sweater, hat, and some decent equipment. Meanwhile, are you ready to show us what you've got?"

"Yes, sir. What's the drill?"

"You can see the markers laid out, there. We're going to have everybody move down the length of the ice and circle those, demonstrating his speed and handling the puck."

"Puck, sir?"

Everyone stared. "That's right," said Brewster with a nervous laugh. "You've only played pickup, using a ball, right?"

"A ball made of rags, sir."

"We have a puck now—regulation, just like they use up in Montreal. On your way back up the ice, show us some of your fancy backward skating."

"I'll do my best, sir. Who else is trying out?"

"Who isn't? I think the only position we have open is goalie. Those boys used to have a decent goalie," Mr. Brewster indicated a knot of young men which included the verbose Rogers, "but he got hit in the head last Tuesday. Nobody else has the balls to step up."

"We'll find somebody, Mr. Brewster," Harry declared.

"Uh—" Maddie began, only to be interrupted.

"Mr. Brewster, we're ready to start sending men down the ice."

"You, MacGillicuddy, get in line."

This couldn't really be happening, Maddie thought as she joined the tail end of the serpent that curled around the marked area.

She'd never pass for a man in front of all these

other men. She'd never make the team. Compared to these fellows, she could barely handle a stick.

But watching the men skate down the ice, it became clear many of them couldn't play all that well, either. Some fell. Some lost the ball—puck—and most were painfully slow. Then came a group of young men all in a row who had the onlookers applauding.

Were they the ones Maddie had seen practicing before, in Rogers' group? To her eyes, they looked polished, even professional.

She could see Gilbert watching from the shore, could pick him out by his bare, dark head. He really should wear a hat. They were losing the light, and a cold wind quickly sprang up.

Suddenly she heard a steam engine cough to life. On shore, a big unit had been wrestled into place. Huge lamps, powered by the steam plant, came on. The auditions continued.

That sense of unreality touched Maddie again, making it easier to wait. None of this was truly happening, it simply couldn't be.

When her turn came at last, she merely switched off her mind.

And skated.

The stick Harry had put into her hand felt better than the broken board she'd used before. The puck, which looked like a flattened version of a ball, skittered obediently along the ice at her urging. All her tension flew away.

She floated down the ice, shot the puck at the makeshift goal, and swung back up the rink backward.

The crowd exploded.

Really? What was the big deal? Hadn't they ever

seen anybody do that before?

She made her way to the side and took a place next to Gilbert. He shot her one look—no more—and didn't say a word. They watched the rest of the tryouts to the accompaniment of the steam plant pounding away. One of the suits with Mr. Brewster kept making notes on a sheaf of paper.

At last, Maddie sidled closer to Gilbert and said, "We might as well leave."

"You'd better wait. If you still want a spot, that is."

She still wanted a spot. But she protested, "Those fellows from that other team will get all the spots. You could see they were the best."

Gilbert shot her another look. "You'd better wait."

So she did, standing in the cold till the dark settled over the water and the light shed by the steam plant made an eye-searing island.

At last everyone who'd queued up to skate had his chance. Mr. Brewster and Coach Harry put their heads together over the coach's papers. At length, Mr. Brewster waved his hand.

"All right, everybody gather round."

They did, making a dark blot on the shore while clouds raced in overhead.

Just let it be over, Maddie prayed, so I can end this and go home.

Brewster called, "Coach Harry Wilson and I have made our selections. These are tentative appointments, and we will name two backups for each position. The first name I read for each position will be the starter on the Boilermaker team. Everybody understand?"

Somebody yelled, "Get on with it!"

"When I call your name, step forward up here on

the left. We'll have some papers for you to sign and an advance on your salaries. All right?"

Not giving time for replies, Harry called out, "Forward, Belgrade Murphy!"

A big fellow, one of the well-equipped crew, skated forward. Gilbert gave a huff.

"Forward—Drane Rogers."

Rogers, Maddie knew—the snooty fellow who'd sneered at her the afternoon she met Mr. Brewster. Maybe she didn't want to be on this team after all.

"Darn it," she began.

Gilbert told her, "Wait."

"Forward—Leonard Leopold."

Leopold—not one of Rogers' regulars—stepped forward, grinning.

"Defense," Mr. Brewster raised his voice, "Ben Shandy."

This was another of Rogers' crew. Darn, they were going to take all the spots! Big and brown-haired, Shandy moved into place beside his buddy, looking a bit smug.

"Defense—Sean Culligan." Well, at least he wasn't one of Rogers'.

"See?" said Maddie to Gilbert, surprised at how disappointed she felt. "I told you I wouldn't get picked."

"Still one spot open," Gilbert replied quietly.

Mr. Brewster peered at the sheet of paper in his hand. "For the position of rover—Matthew MacGillicuddy."

Maddie's mouth fell open and stayed that way.

Gilbert gave her a push. "Better get up there."

She heard very little after she joined the line at

Brewster's side, standing half dazed while the list of extras was read.

She came to miraculously when Mr. Brewster said, "The only position empty right now is goalie. If anyone wants to try out—"

"I know someone."

All heads turned to Maddie.

"A goalie," she blurted. "A real good one."

Brewster looked interested. "Oh, yeah?"

"He another Scot?" Rogers asked derisively.

"No, he's—he's not."

"Name him," Brewster said expansively. "I'll give him a trial on your say-so."

Maddie craned her neck, trying to sight Gilbert in the crowd. Was he still there? "His name's Gilbert. See that fellow on the shore, with the dark hair?"

Shandy sneered at the sight of Gilbert. "A damned half breed. It figures."

Brewster turned on him. "There'll be none of that on my team, Shandy. You want off?"

"He's half French, from Canada," Maddie explained quickly.

Coach wagged his eyebrows. "Some good hockey players from up that way."

"He a resident of Buffalo now?"

"Oh yes, sir, for years and years."

Mr. Brewster waved Gilbert onto the ice. He skated out reluctantly, even as Maddie asked herself whether she'd done the right thing—from his point of view.

Gilbert, baffled, stopped and stared from one to the other of them.

"You want a place starting as goalie, son?" Brewster asked gruffly and without preamble. "If you do, it's yours."

"You haven't given him a trial," Rogers protested. "You don't even know if he can skate."

"Don't need to skate. He just has to stand in goal. You able to take your knocks, Gilbert?"

Gilbert opened his mouth, looked at Maddie and shut it again.

Maddie asked quickly, "Does the goalie get the same pay as the rest of us?"

"Sure. You go sign those papers, and you'll get your ten-dollar signing bonus. My advice is, don't drink it all in one place."

Chapter Twelve

"You're mad at me," Maddie accused. Gilbert felt rather than saw her steal a glance at him as they walked back to the stables, side by side, both with ten dollars in their pockets.

He returned, "Shouldn't I be? You volunteered me for something I might not want to do."

"You played in goal before. I thought—"

"Do you know how many times goalies get hit in the head? In the face? In the knee? I get hit in the knee, I won't be able to work my regular job. What then?"

"I—didn't think. I wanted you to earn all that money. And I figured if you were playing goal, at least we'd be on the ice…together."

That struck him down silent, like a slap. She wanted to be near him? Could that truly be the reason?

She hurried on, "You could have said no."

"I couldn't."

"You didn't have to sign."

He thrust his hands into his pockets and jiggled the coins he'd been given. "If I said no, then we couldn't be…together. On the ice." She'd move away from him, into fame, maybe. Why should she even look at the likes of him then?

They stopped walking and turned to face each other, not touching—just two buddies walking back from a game.

Gilbert wished he understood what lay in Maddie's eyes, but he hadn't a hope.

He turned and resumed walking.

"Don't be mad," she begged.

"You shouldn't have done that." They were back where they'd started.

"You're right, I shouldn't. Let's talk about it."

"No."

"No?"

"Not tonight. I've got all this money in my pocket. I'm going to take Brewster's suggestion to heart and get drunk."

"No, you're not."

"I'm not?"

"Not tonight."

They'd reached his berth in the stables. She jerked him inside and left her hand on his arm. Earnestly, she stared into his face in the gloom.

"You're spending the night with me."

"What?" He goggled. "Have you lost your mind?"

"Maybe. But I don't think so." She kissed him, the kind of kiss a pal didn't give another—not ever. They melted into each other there in the dark, even while Gilbert's mind screamed at him.

Not a good idea.

Her tongue wooed his, tangled with it, and drew it inside her mouth in a manner that invited other intrusions of a similar nature.

Somehow, he broke the kiss. "Why?"

"I want you," she gasped. "Can't you tell?"

"Yeah."

"Well, then, I've decided I'm going to have you."

"But I mean, why tonight?"

She went quiet, her gaze still clinging to his. "Things might get crazy after this."

So they might.

"I want to make sure…make sure…" She withdrew a bit. "But if you don't want to—"

"I didn't say that."

"If I'm not woman enough, or something—"

"My God, Maddie." He thrust his hand inside her shirt, slid it up and cupped her breast. "You're all woman. I can't believe those fellows couldn't see it."

She dropped her head back and groaned. "Don't stop."

"We can't do this here. It'll be your job, if we get caught. Where?"

"It'll have to be your room. I can't take you back to mine. Roddy's there."

"No. My place is a pit."

"I don't care."

Gilbert thought furiously, weighing ways and means. And consequences. Her breast remained cupped in his hand, the heat of her an added persuasion.

"All right," he said, the only answer available to him. "But won't Roddy wonder where you are?"

"I'll stop by, tell him it's—it's something to do with the hockey tournament. Change my clothes." She caught his face between her hands. "When I come to you, I want—I want it to be as a woman."

Seemed she wanted a lot. Gilbert began to hope he could live up to it all.

"Where's your room?" she breathed while rubbing her lips over his, which turned out to be the most arousing thing he'd ever felt.

"Carolina Street." He told her the number. "Second

floor."

"You go ahead of me."

Still, they couldn't manage to part, there in the shadows. They clung together, bodies making full contact, Gilbert's hand still inside her shirt.

At last he stirred and released her reluctantly. "Don't want anybody to catch sight of us here."

"Right. I'll meet you at your room."

Gilbert wondered, even as he slipped out, whether she would, or if, once they parted, sanity would return.

****

Back at his room, he tried to prepare, not entirely sure how. The place looked grim and shabby. But, he reminded himself, if she came here she wouldn't be paying attention to the place.

Him. She came for him.

That set him to tingling so he could barely think straight. He still felt annoyed over her volunteering him for the goalie position, but a bit mollified by her confession she'd done it to keep him close by.

There hadn't been anyone important in his life, truly important, since his pa died.

He washed in the basin and thought about that. Maddie MacGillicuddy mattered. She mattered so much it shook him.

But she'd never show tonight. He'd wind up pacing this floor for hours with a stiffy he couldn't control.

That thought was interrupted by a soft scratch on his door. He opened it and lost any hope of breath.

She wore a dress—a pretty dress—and her head lay bare, the short hair loose in a blossom of squiggly red curls. She pushed past him and came in, her cheeks flushed, and shed her coat.

"Look at you," he murmured.

"I wanted to look completely different from the man who works at the stables, just in case anybody saw. And—I wanted to look different for you."

"You're beautiful." For a moment, Gilbert could think of nothing else. Then reality kicked in. "What did Roddy say?"

"Not much. I told him to keep the door locked and that I wouldn't be back all night." She quirked an eyebrow. "I do assume I'm staying all night? Just—I figured once wouldn't be enough."

Gilbert's knees went soft—unlike the rest of him. He shook his head wildly.

She frowned. "Is that a 'no' once won't be enough or 'no' I shouldn't stay the night?"

"First. The first."

She nodded, and her fingers moved to the buttons that ran down the front of the dress. There seemed to be an awful lot of them, and they—or what lay beneath them—consumed all Gilbert's attention.

But he moved forward and seized her arm. "Wait. Let me look at you."

Color pounded up through her freckled skin as he gazed at her. Stepping still closer, he touched a freckle with a reverent forefinger. "Are these all over you?"

"Yes."

"I'd like to see."

"That's what I'm trying to do. If you'll stop gaping at me and let me get my clothes off—"

"That's a pretty dress."

"It belonged ta my ma, her Sunday best." Maddie's brogue had thickened. "It's one o' the few things I ha' left o' hers. I wanted ta look my best."

"I understand." He drew her into his arms, and the hunger rose up to swamp him. He pushed it down far enough to ask, "You ever done this before?"

"Yes. But not like this. I never—never wanted it like this before. You?"

"The same." He gazed into her eyes, full of warm, honey-colored light. "I never imagined wanting anybody this much."

"Then for heaven's sake, do something about it."

****

Maddie lay on her back in the bed, staring at the lumpy, gray ceiling while Gilbert counted her freckles—with his tongue. It was, she decided judiciously, the single most arousing experience of her life.

But wait—maybe not. The first time, when they'd given themselves to one another in a shower of heat and urgency, had been pretty darned arousing. She hadn't known it could be like that or imagined her body could explode with such magnificent power—that she could want to give so much to him.

Or feel so fragile and, at the same time, so cherished.

The very idea made her smile.

She should have been ashamed of the wanton way she'd behaved right before she broke into a thousand quivering pieces. Intimacy—this kind of intimacy, when you let a man in, and *in*, with no barriers—took things to a different level, crossed a line of no return. The desire for more pleasure had a woman lying stark naked while a man touched—and licked—her everywhere he pleased.

He reached the freckles splashed across one breast

and paused to give them extra attention. Maddie arched her body and made a sound of wordless approval.

She swore she felt him smile.

He released her nipple from between his lips slowly, with a delicate caress, and stretched up to gaze into her eyes. She became lost, suddenly helpless, adrift on a dark sea.

She touched his cheek with wondering fingers. "I think your eyelashes are longer than mine. You have bonny eyes, Gilbert."

A spark of humor appeared in the black depths, but he spoke seriously enough. "Nobody has eyes prettier than yours. And you taste so—damn—good." He dropped kisses along with the words, on her lips, on her shoulder and cheek. "I'd like to taste you everywhere."

Oh, so that was the light of devilry she saw in his eyes… Maddie, who'd only ever been treated to a quick bang and fumble, wondered just what he meant, since his lips had already been all over her.

As if he could read her mind—as if he had license to it, with the rest of her—he reached down to the tangle of red curls between her thighs, and inserted a finger. When he drew it out again, he brought it to his mouth, and tasted.

Maddie's eyes widened. "Oh."

"Would you say no?" he asked. "I've never wanted to do it with anyone else. But—"

The thrill started deep inside Maddie's belly—the place he'd touched—and worked its way upward, heating as it came.

Whispering, she told him, "My body belongs to you, tonight. Do what pleases you."

"And pleases *you*. Maddie, it's all about you."

Nothing had been all about her, not ever.

The light in his eyes brightened. “Bend your legs,” he told her gently, “and part your knees for me.”

Maddie did.

Chapter Thirteen

"How am I ever going to keep my hands off you?" Maddie asked Gilbert as she fastened the buttons on the front of the blue dress. "At the stables, or out on the ice?"

Gilbert turned his head and looked at her. He felt like a new man—he'd never been sure till now what that phrase meant. But he knew he'd been changed by their night together, by the searing heat and intimacy of it.

He now knew how Maddie MacGillicuddy tasted, inside and out. He knew the feel of her when he plunged inside and the way it felt when she shattered all around him.

Who would have thought sex could be like that?

But with the coming of morning, reality streamed in just like the sunlight. Last night had been madness, a really good madness. Now he had to return to work and deal with the fact that she'd volunteered him as goalie for the Boilermakers.

Still, just looking at her made his legs seize up and caused physical pain. Her hair stood out all around her head in silky red tendrils. Her eyes held the memory of all they'd shared.

He sucked in a breath—somehow—and tried to put the desire away from him. It sure didn't help when she stepped up close and ran her fingers through his hair.

"Gilbert, I wish—"

What? She wished what? That they'd get naked and do it all over again? That they might somehow have, together, a night that would never end?

He made a wordless sound that best translated to, "Um?"

"I wish I could be beautiful for you."

The last thing he'd expected. Emotion nearly closed his throat. "My God, woman, you are beautiful."

"I wish I was small and fragile for you—dainty and feminine."

"You're the most feminine woman I've ever known. Couldn't you tell I thought so, last night?" He'd worshipped her with his hands and with his tongue. "Didn't you feel the way we fit together? So—so perfect."

"Yes. But now I've got to dress in Roddy's clothes again and pretend to be a man, and go out on the ice to play that rough game. And take my knocks. Being with you—it makes me want to stay a woman."

He caught her hand and pressed a kiss into the palm. "You'll stay a woman for me, Maddie. In my heart, you will. I only hope I can hide what I'm thinking when I look at you. Probably, I'll get hit in the head with that puck and killed, so it won't matter."

Her eyes pooled with concern. "Could you really get killed?"

"Well, sure. Why do you think nobody wants the position, in spite of the pay?"

"Then I don't want you doing it. You have to quit."

"I already signed the paper. It says if I quit, I have to pay back double the bonus they gave me. Where would I get twenty dollars?"

“I don’t care. If it really is dangerous, I don’t want you anywhere near it.”

“Hush.” He kissed her. “I want to be on the ice. With you.”

Then he could keep an eye on her, maybe take off the head of anybody who tried to hurt her—he would be armed with a stick, wouldn’t he? Far better than the agony of watching from the sidelines.

“I never should have volunteered you.”

“Never mind.” All his anger had burned away in last night’s heat. “Let’s see what the practices are like. It might not be safe for either of us.” If she dropped out, so would he.

“But, Gilbert, only think of the money we might earn!”

****

Money got a man only so far, Gilbert thought later that same afternoon, as he endured his first hockey practice. *Endured* seemed the right term—the two forwards, Rogers and Leopold, peppered him with shots nonstop until he felt like a punching bag.

Of course, this was just practice. When the tournament started, it would be the team from Fort Erie, apparently called the Freighters, who would be firing at him.

Brewster had given them a long lecture about it. Today’s practice was for getting used to their new equipment. Tomorrow they’d face a team put together from players who’d applied to be in the Boilermakers, mostly Rogers’ former lot.

There were other teams, Brewster said, in the area. Eventually, as lead-up to the tournament, the Boilermakers would face them all.

Gilbert liked his new equipment. He had bumper pads for his shins and more for his forearms, a quilted pad that covered his chest. He had a great big wooden stick. And best of all, decent skates that laced on, in place of his scuffed boots.

They fit well.

He wished he had some kind of protection for his head. And his face. He'd already been hit in the face once—he could feel a massive bruise come up despite the cold—and in the head several times.

Coach Wilson seemed happy when he got hit in the head, so long as he kept the puck out of the net. But damn, that puck was a hard bastard.

Maddie had skated by twice and paused to ask if he was all right. The second time he told her, "Get out of here."

"Why?"

"It don't look right."

From his station at one end of the rink, he'd watched her fly over the ice. Nobody there could touch Maddie for speed. And when Rogers—without question the cockiest of the lot—tried to copy some of her maneuvers, he fell on his butt. No one laid a check on her, for which Gilbert felt grateful, though he expected that would come soon enough from players of opposing teams, when they faced them.

He had the decided conviction they were going to earn their pay.

Afterward, when the big lights turned off and the steam plant shut down, he and Maddie lugged their equipment back to the stables, not looking at each other.

"You sure you're all right?" she asked him finally.

"That slap shot you took to the face looked like it hurt."

"It did hurt."

She forced some brightness into her voice when she said, "One good thing, I overheard Mr. Brewster and Coach both saying you had the makings of a good goalie. Grand reflexes, Coach said."

"It tends to help the reflexes when you're trying to keep from having your teeth knocked out."

She turned to face him. "If you hate it so much, quit. I don't want to force you into anything."

Gilbert stared in horror. "Are you crying?"

"Maybe."

"Cut it out. What if the fellas see you?"

"It's too dark."

"No, it isn't."

She fought for control. "Everything rests on me being a man. But I don't want to be a man when I'm around you."

"Shush! You're just tired." God knows, they'd barely slept last night. Gilbert thought about what they'd done instead and his groin tightened.

"I'm not sure I can do this," she quavered.

"You can."

"Drane Rogers hates me."

"He's just jealous 'cause you can skate better than him."

"But I don't shoot as well." They resumed walking.

"Nobody shoots as good as him."

"What about the guys from Fort Erie?"

"Unknown quantity."

"They've got to be good, if the brewery over there has challenged Mr. Brewster."

"Don't borrow troubles."

"Funny—my ma used to say that."

"So did my pa, though he said it in French."

They'd reached Stanley's stables. Gilbert set his equipment down in a pile.

Maddie backed him into Jessop's empty box. "You can speak two languages?"

"Well, sure. Pa and I mostly spoke French."

"No wonder your tongue's so clever." She kissed him, hot and hungry. "Can we be together tonight?"

He wanted it—every inch of him did, some inches downright demanding. But he said, "I don't think so."

"Why not?"

Very gently, hands on her shoulders, he moved her away from him. "What about Roddy?"

"He was fine last night. He will be again."

"Not a good idea, Maddie. You're tired, and I'm tired and pretty bashed up."

"Never mind. Like I said, I'm not about to force you into anything you don't want to do."

"It's not that I don't want to. It's just...we're handling an awful lot right now. Why complicate everything even more?"

She flung at him, "I didn't think warmth and passion, and c-comfort were complications."

"I didn't say—"

She ran from the box, leaving all her equipment behind, and Gilbert was left cursing under his breath.

****

"Maddie, are you sick? Roddy's face, big, pale, and freckled, hung above Maddie's cot like a troubled moon. "You staying home from work today?"

Work. The stable. Gilbert. Maddie groaned. "No. Why would you think that?" She never missed work.

"'Cause you're always up way earlier than this. And your eyes are all red."

She'd cried herself to sleep, stifling her face in the sheet so Roddy wouldn't hear. The funny part was, she didn't quite know why.

Gilbert. The Boilermakers.

He didn't want to be on the team. He didn't want her.

She ached for him.

She wanted to touch him, tangle her fingers in his hair. She wanted to taste him, longed for the way he smelled. She wanted the bliss of joining her body with his.

But having had her for one night, he didn't want her again. How utterly humiliating was that?

Well, she wasn't a woman to beg. If he wanted her to stay away from him, she would. If he wished to concentrate on hockey, she could manage that too. She'd done harder things.

Hadn't she?

Well, maybe not. Keeping away from Gilbert would be—well, no skate on the ice.

Chapter Fourteen

"That's four games in a row. I'd say you're coming along."

Mr. Brewster pointed to the chart on the wall with satisfaction. The team, including the extras, had met in the back room of Buffalo's Best Brewing, on River Street, which had become their unofficial club house. Out back, just above the harbor, workers constructed the regulation rink where the rest of their games would be played. It had permanent steam-powered lights and boards painted bright blue to match their sweaters.

The players, despite their recent victories, looked sullen, each sunk into his—or her—separate seat, not looking at one another. Heck, Maddie felt sullen.

More than two weeks had passed since she'd slept with Gilbert. Since then, their relationship had been careful and restrained—distant, she guessed she should call it. No touching. No stolen moments in the shadows at the stable. He hadn't even come by to help with her work.

Hell, she'd gone and spoiled everything. And she didn't even know how.

"Next up for us to play are the Rochester Ramblers. They're a good team, damn good. That means we need to fix our flaws before we face them."

"Flaws?"

Coach took it up. "There's gonna have to be a lot

of hard work and some changes, or certain people are gonna get replaced." Deliberately, he focused on each of them in turn.

"Rogers, your scoring's pretty good—damn good, in fact."

Drane Rogers flashed a cocky smile, which quickly died when Coach went on, "But you've got to work harder on guarding the puck. Too many giveaways."

Coach glared next at Gilbert, who sat with his dark head bowed and his hands dangling between his knees, and studied him a moment before he switched his gaze to Rogers' crony, Shandy.

"Shandy, I want to see you block some shots. You're a defenseman, for God's sake. Your job's to keep shots from reaching Gilbert. You afraid to get kissed by the puck?"

Shandy looked indignant for a moment, then shook his head ruefully.

Coach switched his hard gaze to Leonard Leopold. "Leopold, you're slow. No two ways about it. And your stick-handling needs improvement. I don't see something better from you in the Ramblers game, we'll need to talk about it."

Leopold looked crestfallen.

"MacGillicuddy." Coach fixed his cold eyes on Maddie, and she wondered if she, too, were in trouble. She'd been working hard, but tripped up a lot.

"Nobody can fault your skating. But you need to handle the puck better, and God damn it, you've got to remember the rules."

"I know, Coach. I'm sorry."

"You're not stupid, are you?" Coach asked.

"Like his cousin," Shandy muttered.

"No, Coach. I'll work on it."

"I have a complaint about MacGillicuddy," Rogers put in. "Not only doesn't he know the rules, I don't think he understands play. As rover, he's only supposed to jump in on offense when needed, but he keeps trying to grab the puck and score ahead of me. Why can't he be like Culligan"—the other defenseman—"who does a grand job keeping to his zone, playing defense?"

Brewster took it up. "I've got no problem with MacGillicuddy's play. If he's good enough to skate in and get to the puck ahead of you, so be it. That's what makes him so effective on the ice. He's everywhere at once, puts extra pressure on the other team. That's what a great rover does, Rogers."

"He should funnel the puck to me," Rogers insisted. "Scoring's my job."

"A scoring chance is a scoring chance, no matter who initiates it."

Rogers refused to give it up. "They're gonna steal the puck from him, and score on us—a good team like the Ramblers will."

"I don't see him making turnovers, because he's fast, and he keeps out of their way." Coach yelled. "Are you the one who's thick, Rogers?"

"No, Coach, but—" Rogers stole a look at Maddie and buttoned his lip.

"What about me, Coach?" Culligan asked. A big fellow, he had a broad face that screamed Ireland.

"Like Rogers says, you're doing all right, son."

"I'm not in danger of getting cut, then?"

"You just keep working hard and don't worry about it."

"One more thing I want to mention," Mr. Brewster

lit in again, "and that's morale. I've never seen a more miserable group of men. You'd think you were slated for hanging instead of being handed a chance for fame and fortune. Danny," he spoke to one of his assistants, "hand out the beers."

Danny, tall, narrow, and a bit of a sycophant, hurried around handing out brown bottles.

"What's this?" Maddie asked.

"What's it look like? Buffalo's Best brew. The team that drinks together plays well together."

Culligan grinned crookedly and yanked the cork from his bottle, using his teeth. Leopold quickly followed suit and took a mighty swig.

Gilbert gave his bottle a judicious look and did likewise.

"I don't drink, Mr. Brewster," Maddie ventured.

Rogers stared. "There you go—I knew there was something wrong with him."

Maddie flushed. Not wanting to seem different from the other fellows, she cracked open the bottle and cautiously sampled the brew.

"Now," Mr. Brewster declared, "it's my considered opinion this team is too tight. Every man's out there playing his own game, not playing together. It's also my opinion a good beer can fix anything."

"And this is a grand beer, sir," Culligan chimed in. "Buffalo's best."

"I want this team to be a *team*, damn it," Mr. Brewster declared. "The Boilermakers. If you fellows can't manage that, I'll find others who can."

The players looked at one another unhappily.

As if I don't have enough trouble getting along in the stable where everybody picks on everybody else,

Maddie thought sourly. Now I have to play buddy with this lot.

It seemed all she did was play at what she wasn't, darn it all.

She watched Gilbert toss back his head and chug down a long drink, and she tried not to make it obvious how much she admired the strong line of his throat.

The beers continued to go around while Mr. Brewster berated and encouraged them by turns. By the time they left, Maddie felt unsteady on her feet.

She fell into step beside Gilbert as they started away. He'd downed three beers—she'd counted. Might it be a good time for her to approach him?

"So," she asked as they slipped off into the shadows, "you think I'll get cut?"

"No. Leopold might."

"Would you be happier if I did get cut?"

He didn't answer.

She bumped his shoulder with hers, as one fellow might do to another—any excuse to touch him. He kept walking.

"Gilbert," she said softly, "are you going to stay mad at me forever?"

"I'm not mad. I'm worried and I'm frustrated and—I still want you, damn it."

"There's a solution for that."

"Is there?"

"Why don't I stay at your room tonight?" Maddie could hear the yearning in her own voice. "We can do anything—anything you like."

"Oh, God."

"Get it all out of our systems."

"Will we? Thing is, Maddie, I don't think I'll ever

get you out of my system."

"Really?" Her heart thudded and her skin flushed.

He shook his head sorrowfully. "Don't expect so. I go to sleep wanting you—when I sleep—and wake up wanting you even more. Nothing seems to help."

Maddie stopped walking and turned to face him. "Touching me will help. And me touching you. What do you say?"

"It's a bad idea. Really bad."

"I'll stop home first, make sure Roddy has his supper. Then—I'll come dressed as a woman, so nobody suspects."

"You realize if we get discovered everything blows up. Everything."

"I know." She swallowed hard. "We won't get discovered."

He groaned.

"You go ahead, Gilbert. I'll be there soon."

****

"Oh, my God," Maddie yipped when Gilbert took his shirt off. He didn't take it for a cry of admiration. "You're nothing but one big bruise! Look at your chest."

Gilbert had no desire to look at it. The chest protector Brewster had given him didn't help much against a puck traveling full bore. His skin showed patterns of deep blue, purple, mottled red, and yellow-green.

"Oh," Maddie gasped, "my poor darling."

This is more like it, Gilbert thought as she threw herself at him, crooning and soothing, with her hands all over him.

"You might have some bruises too," he suggested.

"Let's see." He knew the beer had gone straight to his head. He'd had nothing to eat since breakfast and shouldn't have chugged all that down.

He peeked inside her unbuttoned blouse—she'd been halfway done with undressing when she caught sight of him—and placed his hand there, against her warm skin.

"Oh, and your poor bruised face," she lamented, before she kissed his cheek and chin.

He caught the back of her head with his free hand, burying his fingers in the wealth of her hair. "You want to make me feel better?"

"Yes, oh yes."

"Anything I want, you said."

Her eyes met his; he saw a promise there, a wicked one. She whispered against his lips, "Anything."

"Might take all night to make me feel some better."

"Good thing we've got all night."

They fell backward onto his bed, her on top, him below. Once again their eyes met. Would she know without words just what he craved?

She kissed him, taking her time with it and doing a thorough job, before making her way open-mouthed downward over his battered chest and lower, ever lower. She conquered the buttons on his fly with eager fingers and, when he surged forth, met him with her lips.

So—she could read his mind, after all.

Chapter Fifteen

"Hey, Injun—yeah, I'm talking to you."

Gilbert turned, the shovel with which he'd been busy mucking out still in his hands, as the cry penetrated the shadows inside the stable. It seemed he always had an implement in his clutches these days, a shovel, a pitchfork, a hockey stick. He now knew how to use them all equally well.

A week had passed since his night of indulgence at Maddie's hands—and lips. Life had moved on since then; practice had continued. The Boilermakers had met and defeated the Rochester Ramblers and another team from somewhere down state.

None of it had made Gilbert crave Maddie MacGillicuddy any less. It felt like torture being around her and not able to touch. His mind seemed caught in a permanent storm caused by remembering the events of their last night together, and chafing at his restraints.

It almost felt like a relief, hearing the taunt and getting a chance to show some anger.

Carl Mueller it was, a fitting target for Gilbert's frustration, and him with a weapon in his hands. On the ice, he'd learned that a hockey stick could indeed become a weapon, one he no longer hesitated to use. When the opposing team's forwards came at him too aggressively, he treated them to a vicious poke or swipe, always managing to make it look accidental.

Damned if he was going to be the only one getting bruises.

On the ice, a player had to be careful. Here on his own turf, not so much.

He slanted a look at Mueller. The craven idiot had not come alone, but stood backed by two of his cronies, Strone and another unsavory customer called Trask.

"You must be bored, Mueller, what with having lost your job and all," he called back.

"What d'you know about it, Injun?"

"Well, I've noticed boredom's what makes you go looking for trouble. Did you forget you don't work here anymore?"

"I ain't forgot nothin'. I remember that you're the one cost me my job."

Gilbert walked to the door of the stable, where the three stood, keeping the shovel in his hands. Glancing down the way, he could see Maddie sweeping out farther along; she had her eye on them.

"You managed that yourself," he told Mueller, "beating on Mr. Philips' horses and whipping one of them to death. Don't blame me."

"We're supposed to stick together, have each other's back," Mueller retorted. "Right, fellas?"

"I'm supposed to have your back, when you shout insults at me?"

"Seems you've always been a damned outsider," Mueller sneered. "And now I suppose you think you're hot shit, eh?"

"Why would I?"

"Playing goalie for this new team, the Boilermakers. Everybody knows a tree stump could stand in for goal."

Gilbert's temper raised another notch. "Oh, yeah?"

"Yeah."

"Well, what's it to you?"

"I figure you need taking down a peg, me and the boys do." Mueller cracked his knuckles. "So we came down to take care of it. We get done here, they'll have to prop you up in that goal."

Gilbert gave no outward sign of his rage. His fingers tightened on the handle of the shovel. "You figure that, do you?"

"Yup."

"And it'll take three of you to handle me, will it? Big men." Gilbert spared a fleeting thought for the Boilermakers. Their next big game was tomorrow—if he got too busted up to stand in goal, Mr. Brewster wouldn't be happy.

But, what the hell, it would feel good to smash his fists into some faces.

The three spread out in the doorway. From the corner of his eye, Gilbert saw Maddie start toward him, broom still in hand.

He wanted to keep her out of it. If Maddie got hurt, the Boilermakers were done.

He raised the shovel like a hockey stick ready for a cross check. "Come on, then."

They attacked him in a cluster; he had one clear glimpse of Mueller's face twisted in hate before he crashed the handle of the shovel across his nose. Mueller screamed and went down like a stone. The other two leaped on Gilbert, one from either side, the first landing a blow to the side of his head that rocked his senses.

The second fellow—Strone—began to pummel

him in a similar fashion. Mueller struggled up from the ground and pushed his way in, to fasten his fingers around Gilbert's throat.

"He's mine!" Mueller shouted, and Gilbert, already off balance, went down under his weight. His head hit the packed dirt floor hard enough that he saw stars.

He brought his knees up, planted his feet in Mueller's groin and heaved. Mueller let out a wail, but refused to let go.

"What the hell?" someone cried.

One of the two men holding Gilbert down swayed under a solid blow to the head from behind. His eyes closed and he fell to the side.

Gilbert had a brief glimpse of Maddie's face—scarlet with outrage—before she hauled Trask out of the way and slipped her broom handle over Mueller's head from behind, across his windpipe.

Bracing herself, she used all her strength, and pulled.

Mueller flew backward and landed on his backside. Quickly, he scrambled up on his feet and faced Maddie, his shoulders hunched.

Outmatched in weight if not in height, armed only with her broom, she looked far too vulnerable for Gilbert's liking.

If Mueller got her down beneath him and felt what lay under her rough clothing, well…the jig would be well up.

With a wordless roar, Gilbert laid hold of Mueller's collar and hauled him off balance. Mueller stumbled and fell to his knees. Gilbert clouted him once on the top of the head, and he collapsed in a sprawl.

Maddie puffed out a breath and looked at Gilbert in

consternation. "I could ha' taken him." Her Scottish accent had thickened considerably, and her chest rose and fell.

Others of the stable workers had come running, wearing avid expressions, their eyes and ears all over everything; Gilbert couldn't show the extent of his concern.

"What's going on here?" Mr. Philips, newly arrived, came pushing in. "Brawling in my stable? And what's he doing here?"

He aimed a kick at Mueller, still on the ground. "I thought I fired you."

Mueller groaned and hauled himself up. "I came for justice." He gestured wildly at Gilbert. "It's the Injun's fault I got struck off."

"I fired you because you didn't take good care of my stock. Now get out of here before I call the coppers on you for trespassing."

He glared at the other two men. "What are you doing here? Do you want to be out of jobs also?"

"No, sir." Strone put his cap back on his head. Trask merely slunk away.

"Make way, make way!"

The call cut across the confusion and turned heads. A large steam-powered lorry came backing into the brick area in front of the stables, scattering the curious from its path. Accompanying it on foot was Gilbert's employer, Robert Stanley.

People watched open-mouthed as the rear doors of the lorry were hauled open by two brawny men. Inside was revealed…

Gilbert blinked, and blinked again. Even though he'd been forewarned by Stanley, he could scarcely believe what he saw. The others, not prepared, gasped and exclaimed.

"What the heck's that?"

A horse. A big, silver one, gleaming dimly from within the confines of the lorry. To Gilbert's eyes it looked oversized, but that might have been due to the setting.

No. When one of the delivery men—for such they were—entered the back of the lorry, the horse's height became apparent. The size of a Clydesdale it was, with graceful pumping hooves and a sculpted mane and tail. It stepped regally down the ramp the workers fitted, so highly polished its sides reflected the surroundings.

"A mechanical horse," one of the onlookers exclaimed. "It's a God-damned steam-horse."

So it was. In fact, as it approached Stanley's stable block, Gilbert saw little trails of steam coming from its nostrils, similar to what a real horse emitted into the cold air.

"What do you think, Gilbert?" Mr. Stanley asked proudly, before he did a double take, looking at Gilbert's face. "What's happened to you? You're bleeding. Haven't been fighting on the job, have you?"

"I didn't start it, Mr. Stanley."

"I should hope not. We have important matters at hand. I thought we'd give the new horse Jessop's stall. And you can help me come up with a name, eh?"

"Jessop's stall, sir? But what about Jessop?"

"I'm retiring him. Or, rather, sending him to the boneyard. It's all the same, right?"

"The boneyard, sir?" Gilbert stiffened and his stomach turned. "But—he's worked so hard for you. And there's still some life in him."

"Not much. And we won't need him, with this beauty in place. Now son, I know you've been nursing old Jessop along for me, but I'm sure you'll agree this is more humane than forcing Jessop to continue working."

"Mr. Stanley—after all those years of service Jessop's given you, surely he deserves to be retired, really retired."

"He's a broken-down old horse, not worth the feed. This fellow, here, will show you how to maintain the mechanical, supply it with water and coal. No more currying—you just wipe it down with a cloth. Finest automaton built, fresh out of the shop down on Chippewa Street. This can run all day and all night if need be." He looked around at the gawking crowd. "Gentlemen, you are looking at your future."

Gilbert, feeling far more battered by Mr. Stanley's words than by Mueller and his cronies, sincerely hoped not.

Chapter Sixteen

"Maddie, I am so very happy to see you!"

The squeaky voice came from behind Maddie and stopped her in the act of leaving the door of the rooming house, dragging her hockey equipment behind her. She needed to get to the rink early tonight for practice, and that meant not stopping back here later. She would have to take everything with her, and quite likely skip having any supper, in order to make it.

Yet the words spun her around and brought a surge of gladness to her heart. The last person—if person she could be called, and Maddie felt she could—she expected to find behind her on the street was Rita. Yet there the battered unit stood, gazing at her with those empty, sculpted eyes.

Happy, Rita said. Not a word often employed by your basic steam unit. And Rita did not appear, by any stretch of the imagination, happy. Rather, her condition had deteriorated visibly since she'd come to visit Maddie last time, the finish gone more extensively to rust, the corrosion on her rubber digits painful to see. To be sure, everyone said steamies couldn't feel pain. Maddie wasn't so sure.

Rita's voice whined. "How different you look, dressed like that."

"Yes, I know. I'm still the same *me*," Maddie assured her, wondering even as she spoke the words whether they were true. "I'm just wearing…work clothes for my new job. But my goodness! It's odd seeing you away from the laundry."

"I bring news I thought you would want to know."

Maddie sobered. "From Trine's?" Was she still in danger because of what had happened there? It seemed so distant now, so impossible that she'd truly knocked Mr. Trinedore down and risked prosecution. She'd moved on so far since then. Yet Rita, faithful Rita, still came, out of duty, friendship, or concern.

"Let's go somewhere we can speak," she told the unit. Not back up to her room—the stairs were much too difficult for Rita to negotiate on her broken-down wheels. "Come on, there's a café just down on the corner."

"Café? I cannot go there." Rita appeared appalled by the suggestion. "I go nowhere except the laundry and sometimes on errands. And I am…rusted and broken and…" Shame seemed to suffuse her. She stopped speaking.

"It doesn't matter. You're with me. You're my friend." Neither did it matter if Maddie was late to the stables, this once.

Yet people stared, when they entered the busy café. Rita's wheels squeaked, and she rumbled behind Maddie, who made for one of the few vacant tables. Rita, as she knew, could not sit down. She ushered the unit into the corner behind the table, then glanced around to find them the center of all attention.

Turned out, though, all the notice wasn't because of Rita.

"Look," she heard someone say, "it's Matthew MacGillicuddy. From the Boilermakers."

"Hey, you're Mattie MacGillicuddy!"

A waitress appeared and gazed at Maddie a bit dreamily. "Oh, Mr. MacGillicuddy, I admire all the members of the Boilermakers so much! But I think you're the most handsome, by far."

Maddie blushed—a strange sensation, since she rarely faced admiration of any kind and least of all from another woman. Stammering, she ordered a cup of tea for herself, and tried to ignore the rest of the stares.

"What is it?" she asked Rita, as soon as the waitress moved off. "Is something wrong at the laundry?"

"Yess. Yesssss." The wail turned heads again. Maddie placed a soothing hand on Rita's chipped and dented arm.

"Is it Mr. Trinedore?" Had he remembered what Maddie had done, at last? Would he now send the coppers after her, ruin the tournament and all her hopes for the future? Hope for her and perhaps Gilbert having a better life…

"He is back. Back in charge of the laundry. It was so much better when Otis was in charge. Otis is very fair and not cruel like Mr. Trinedore. Otis allows all of us rest time, the humans so they can take a break, as he says, and the rest of us so our machinery can cool down. My joints no longer function well, and a great deal of friction ensues. It is most…" Rita hesitated before she supplied the word, "uncomfortable."

"I'm so sorry to hear that. Now that Mr. Trinedore's back, he doesn't let you rest?"

"No. And even though we are working more hours under Mr. Trinedore, we are getting less done. The laundry operated very efficiently indeed, beneath Otis."

"I see." Too bad, Maddie thought, the steamies and human workers couldn't purchase the laundry outright. That way they'd receive the profits of their hard work. But life didn't work that way, did it?

The waitress brought Maddie's tea. She took a scalding sip.

Someone edged up, a notebook in his hands. "Mr. MacGillicuddy? I'm the owner here, sir, and I'd love to have your signature, as one of the Boilermakers, to pin up on the wall of my café."

"Oh." Maddie stared at him, dumbfounded. "Why, sure. Be happy to." She accepted the book from him and carefully wrote "Matthew MacGillicuddy."

"Thank you, sir. And your tea's on the house." The café owner glanced at Rita, seeming a bit stymied. "And anything your…er…friend requires."

"We're fine for now, thank you."

The man moved off in the wake of the waitress. Rita waved her hands in distress.

"Rita," Maddie said, "tell me what's wrong. Has Mr. Trinedore remembered me thumping him? Is he coming after me?"

"No. Mr. Trinedore does not even remember that you ever worked there. He remembers very little since he returned. He gets the orders all confused, and when he tells us to do something, he will often then tell us over again. I think there is something wrong inside his head."

In Maddie's opinion, there had always been something wrong inside Trinedore's head, or at least in his cold heart. She didn't say so.

Rita announced baldly, "He is planning changes to the laundry. It is already unbearable without you there,

Maddie. Especially since Mr. Trinedore's return. I have come to ask you to return to work there. I am sure it will be safe for you, since Mr. Trinedore does not recall what has happened, and no one else has spoken a word of it. We have all kept your secret most loyally."

Secrets, Maddie thought. The bane of her existence. She closed her fingers on Rita's arm.

"Oh, Rita, honey, you want me to come back?"

"Yes, very much I do."

"Darling, I'm not sure I can."

"But, Maddie, as I say, it is safe for you now."

"Yes, and I appreciate that. But it's not just my safety that concerns me. Yes, that's why I left in the first place. But it's as I told you when you came to see me at my room. I have another job now, a better one that pays more. Going back to the laundry…" Could she bear to go back? To the steam, to the never-ending, back-breaking labor, the heavy vats and the lye that made her eyes water? To old Trinedore's casual abuse, and the misery of her fellow sufferers? To being a woman, downtrodden and powerless?

She didn't think she could. Yes, maybe she had changed.

"I remember what you said. I do not forget. But I cannot bear it there without you, Maddie. And I thought—I hoped for the sake of *friendship*, you might return."

"Oh, Rita." Tears flooded Maddie's eyes. She blinked them back manfully. Many eyes still rested on her, here in this place. Could she let them catch the big, bad hockey player weeping in the company of a battered steam unit?

Yet Rita's battered state only made her plea the

more eloquent. Maddie knew that Rita seldom complained, and she never asked for anything. The fact that she came here now, doing both, shook Maddie to the core.

"All of us steam units left at Trinedore's," Rita lamented, "are in terrible condition. Each of us needs repair. Our damages make us slow and clumsy." Rita paused before continuing in a squeak. "Mr. Trinedore no longer has any patience with us."

No longer? The old pillock had never possessed very much with the units, with any of them. Things must have got much worse, indeed.

"He says production is down, even though it was up while he was recovering. When Otis tried to tell him that, he became angry and threatened to shut Otis down." She waved her hands again in distress. "He threatened to shut all of us down."

"He won't do that. He can't. He needs workers." And cheap workers, at that.

"He plans to replace us one by one. Edie heard him talking about it to another man, in his office. The man—a visitor—says the new steamies being manufactured are twice as efficient and burn less coal. He told Mr. Trinedore he's throwing his money away, running us. And paying us."

Oh, heavens, Maddie thought. Old Trinedore had often threatened to send his units to the scrapyard when they didn't move quickly enough to please him. But this sounded like a whole different proposition, and perhaps not an idle threat.

Retirement for units such as those at Trine's equated shut down, which in turn equated death. No one else would buy them, save for scrap. No one would use them. End of the line, much the same as for Gilbert's ancient cab horses.

She did not know what to say. Having labored so long beside Rita, she could feel the unit's very real distress. Despite that, she couldn't help thinking it might be time for the old units at Trine's to stop struggling to keep up despite their damaged and poorly maintained mechanisms. To stop striving toward the impossible demands Mr. Trinedore set, to stop accepting his abuse.

"Maddie," Rita beseeched, "please return to the laundry, and help us. You always stood up for the weakest of us, human and machine alike."

She had, and look what it got her. A life pretending to be a man.

"Rita, I don't think I can return. Even if I did, what could I do for you? Mr. Trinedore will never listen to me, especially if he has this idea in his head of buying new units."

Rita began to wail, turning heads once more all over the café.

"Hush," Maddie begged. "I can't return to the laundry, but I may be able to help you another way. Maybe it's time for you to leave Trinedore's."

"And die?" Rita asked piteously.

"No, no, of course not. I'm thinking the lot of you could club together and start your own laundry, on your own terms. That money you lent me—I should be able to pay all of it back soon. And more, if all goes well."

"I've told you, I do not want the return of that money. It was a gift given in friendship."

"And I'm ever so grateful for that. But you need it now, Rita."

"Even that money, returned, will not be enough to fund what you suggest."

"I know it. But what I'm saying is, I may be able to help you, help all of you at Trine's. Rita, have you heard about this hockey tournament?"

"Yes, Maddie. I believe everyone in the city has heard of the hockey tournament."

"Well, I stand to make a fair amount of money if our team, the Boilermakers, wins. I'm hoping to make a new start for Roddy and me, if I can." With Gilbert? Maddie could only pray so. "But there should be enough if, as I say, we all club together, to save the lot of you, and get you all out of that place."

"Oh, Maddie, you would do that for us?"

"I surely will, if I'm able."

"I thought you forgot about me. I thought you no longer cared."

"Don't ever think that, Rita."

"I feared that once you got out into the world and away from what you always called the *hellhole* of Trine's, I would no longer matter to you."

There it was again, a word like *feared* creeping into Rita's vocabulary. Was it just verbiage she'd assumed, like *hellhole*? Taken on by hearing it in common usage? Or did she truly fear, hope and dread?

Questions like that one fair divided the city, even the way this hockey tournament looked to unite it. Suddenly, Maddie felt she stood at a crossroads, facing fundamental change in a way she'd never imagined.

"You matter to me, Rita," she assured the unit. "You're my friend. And I'll help you if I'm able. If you want to hope for something, please hope the Boilermakers win the tournament."

Chapter Seventeen

"Gilbert, pay attention. Or do you want me to put Turner in? That's the second goal you've let by!"

Maddie, some distance down the ice from Gilbert, shot Mr. Brewster a look. He seemed unusually tense this practice, possibly because the big game against the Fort Erie Freighters fast approached. He'd taken to threatening everybody with replacement and, since he'd just hired a back-up goalie, that included Gilbert for the first time.

Maddie had her doubts about Turner, a big, sandy-haired fellow who worked days unloading cargo on the docks and had a head like a square block of wood. He might stand in goal, but Maddie didn't see him reacting very quickly. A goalie had to be smart, like Gilbert.

Not but, she had to admit, Gilbert did seem distracted. He'd been off ever since the arrival of that big mechanical horse, three days ago.

She knew he'd pled hard to his boss, Mr. Stanley, for Jessop's life and won, at least temporarily. She'd overheard him telling Mr. Stanley he'd pay for Jessop's feed himself, till he found a place for the horse to retire. Not the easiest prospect, she supposed. Old, broken-down cab horses were a dime a dozen in the city.

She skated past the goal and paused, pretending to scrutinize her skate. Today's practice match against another local team had no real importance. Still, there were enough onlookers that Brewster wanted to make a good showing.

“You all right?” she asked Gilbert in a low voice.

He stared at her. He looked none the better for his battering at Mueller’s hands. Plus he’d taken a tremendous shot to the shoulder earlier, during the first period. She wondered if that bothered him.

He shook his head. And what, she wondered, did that mean?

“MacGillicuddy, get moving!” Brewster bellowed. And the practice game dragged on.

When it ended, Brewster called them all over to the rink side for an impromptu meeting. The rink at the brewery had been completed—they no longer had to practice out on the river, and a wall had been built up to keep out the wind. But the buzz of the lights and the throb of the steam plant proved a constant annoyance, at least to Maddie.

“Listen up,” Mr. Brewster called as soon as they gathered. “That was a sloppy practice game and we’re lucky we won. We have no room for sloppy players on this team. Do you know what’s at stake in the upcoming tournament? A whole bunch of money and my reputation, as well as the fine name of Buffalo’s Best. We have to win, no ifs, ands, or buts. That being said, Leopold, you’re out.”

“What?” the big forward yelped.

“Coach and I gave you a chance to improve. You didn’t. Enough said.”

One of the backups pressed forward. “That mean I’m in, Mr. Brewster?”

“No, Cannell.” A cunning look crossed Brewster’s face. “I have a new man coming in.”

"From where, Mr. Brewster?" asked another of the backups, Jordan.

"Never you mind. All you need to know is he's going to be a first-class player, and the leg-up we need, so long as the rest of you fulfill your potential."

"But, Mr. Brewster," Leopold protested, "I've worked hard."

Maddie noticed Gilbert looked up sharply at that.

Brewster just shrugged. "You'll be paid for your time, Leopold. That's the way it goes."

Gilbert grumbled, "Seems there's no reward for hard work—or loyalty."

"You got a problem, Gilbert?" Coach glared at him. "You want to be replaced?"

Gilbert merely shook his dark head once more, looking mutinous.

"I'll say again, I want a better attitude among you players. I want the Boilermakers to be a real team. That's why when our new member gets here, you're all going to give him a big welcome, right? And show him your best."

The members of the Boilermakers eyed each other.

"Sure, boss," Rogers spoke at last. "Whatever you say."

****

"What's eating you?" Maddie asked as she and Gilbert took their usual walk home, dragging their equipment. "You sure you're not hurting?"

"No more than usual."

"If you're worried about Coach putting Turner in, don't be. In my opinion, Turner's an empty threat. He doesn't ha' the brains God gave a stump."

"A goalie doesn't need brains," Gilbert retorted.

"Don't you know that? He just needs to keep the damn puck out of the net."

Maddie stopped walking and turned toward him slowly. "Gilbert, if you're still so unhappy playing hockey, maybe you should quit. I wanted us to do this together, but it's your choice."

"Choice?" He stared at her, by the light of a smoky steam lamp. Above the city, thin starlight shone from the cold sky; Maddie could smell the river, and coal dust, and Gilbert's sweat.

"There's no choice in any of this," he told her with real anger. "I've got people sneering at me on a daily basis—I even heard Rogers call me 'half breed' under his breath. I've got a damn, big mechanical horse in my stable, crowding out one of my best friends."

"Best friend?"

"Jessop. Yeah, I suppose it's pretty stupid for a fella's friend to be an old horse."

"I don't think it's stupid at all," Maddie said softly.

Ignoring her words, he barreled on, "But you don't understand. We've put up and shut up and suffered together, Jessop and I. All these horses suffer. They endure. I get that. I've spent my life enduring too. And now, but for me paying Mr. Stanley off, Jessop goes to the boneyard. How fair is that, eh?"

"Not fair."

"And how am I supposed to keep paying for his feed if I quit the team?"

"I don't know."

"And to top all that off… To top all that off, I can't stop wanting you. Every time I look at you, every time you skate past me out there. But I can't touch you. I can't even let it show. It's driving me out of my mind."

"I see." Maddie drew a long breath. "I want you too. Maybe we need to do something about it."

"Like what?"

"What do you think? We need another night together."

"Yeah, sure, right! We tried that before, didn't we? You said it would cure us, but it didn't. We're supposed to be buddies, team mates. If you keep coming to my place, people are gonna put two and two together. One glimpse of that hair—"

"You think so?"

Gilbert tossed his hands in the air. "I don't know what to think anymore."

"Well, then, maybe we can't take a chance on spending the night together. But nothing says we can't grab a quick dose of the medicine we both need."

"What are you talking about?"

"In the stable. The night cabs are all out. We could stop by there and—"

"You're crazy. There are always attendants. All we need is to get seen there together!"

"So? We're attendants too, right? Expected to be seen there. I happen to know that McNamara, at Stanley's, spends more time outside smoking and gossiping with the other fellows than anything else. There will be several empty boxes."

"It will never work. We'll get nabbed for sure."

"Not if we keep quiet. Do you think you can make love to me while keeping quiet, Gilbert?"

Now he let out a breath. "We've got about half an hour before the first cabs are due back. Come on."

****

As Gilbert swiftly discovered, the need to maintain

silence merely served to make the encounter with Maddie more arousing. In the deepest shadows of a vacated box, he found his other senses heightened, including those of touch and taste.

He'd never made love to a woman who wore trousers, or rather who wore trousers and a man's shirt, now wide open down the front. He'd never had a woman run her lips all down his body while he stood half clad in his hockey sweater, and while she slipped in utter silence to her knees in the straw. He'd never had her address him most generously there before climbing back up his body and capturing his groan of bliss in her mouth.

Quick the encounter might have been, but intense as silent lightning. After, he stood straining his ears for sounds of the errant McNamara, Mr. Stanley's night man, clasping Maddie against him and almost shaking with love for her.

He loved her. How could he have failed to know it? He should tell her, make this more than a fumble in the dark. He should declare his need and devotion—that was what a man did—but he wasn't sure she wanted all that from him.

He didn't know if she felt the same.

Had she knelt in the straw and taken him in her mouth because she loved him? Or because she wanted to keep him on the team? An absurd question, on the face of it—what woman would go to such lengths to get her way? Headstrong, confident Maddie MacGillicuddy wouldn't. Anyway, he'd tasted desire, hadn't he?

She must care about him.

Yet caring about somebody did not equal *love*.

"Feel better?" she murmured, the merest breath of

sound.

He captured her face between his hands, his fingertips twined in the springy silk of her hair. He kissed her slowly, hoping that would tell her what he felt.

When it ended, she whispered, “Keep that up, and I’ll want you all over again.”

All right, so she did want him. He could accept that. But was he just a stand-in for her need, the way he stood in goal?

“Maybe,” she suggested, “we need to do this regular, every night after practice.”

His pulse leaped raggedly. “We’ll get caught for sure.”

“The taste of you just might be worth it.”

Love, as well as desire? Damned if Gilbert could tell.

He sighed. “Now we have to get away out of here.”

“You go first. If McNamara sees you, say you were dropping off my equipment. If he sees me, I’ll tell him I’ve come to pick it up here.”

Gilbert nodded helplessly.

She leaned in and kissed him, one last, fierce kiss. “And dream about me.”

He knew he would.

Chapter Eighteen

"I am Nilsson, Nils Nilsson. I am hockey player. Good to meet you, team mates!"

The members of the Boilermakers stared at the new arrival with nearly identical expressions of amazement. Whatever Maddie had expected of Leopold's replacement, it wasn't this. A player from some other team, perhaps, experienced and scarred by battle. Someone tough and tempered.

In some inexplicable way, Nilsson looked brand, sparkling new. Though he couldn't be, of course—he appeared to be in his mid to late twenties and towered on his blades, quite fully grown. It was just that she'd never seen anyone else like him.

She exchanged incredulous glances with Gilbert, Rogers, Murphy, and Culligan before sizing Nilsson up again.

She had to admit he made one heck of a first impression—tall, strongly built and with a mop of yellow hair that, since he stood hatless, spilled with abandon across a noble brow. His eyes looked blue as the sky over the lake, and his face—well, had it not been so strongly made, it might actually be considered *pretty*.

Not so much as a bruise or a scrape disfigured it. And at this point, even Rogers, who was generally careful about his looks, bore abrasions.

Maddie snorted to herself. That wouldn't last long.

Nilsson wore one of their Buffalo's Best sweaters—blue as his eyes and with the picture of a beer bottle embroidered on the front—and a big grin, wide as his face. He shook hands with each of them, introducing himself over and over again.

"I am Nils Nilsson. I am hockey player—the best!"

Finally Mr. Brewster placed a hand up—way up—on Nilsson's shoulder and said jovially, "All right, son. They know you're a hockey player. That's why you're here, right?"

"He's got an accent," Murphy pointed out.

"Yeah, he does," Rogers agreed. "Where are you from, Nils Nilsson?"

"I am from Buffalo," Nilsson replied happily.

"Like hell you are," said Culligan.

"Come on, boys," Mr. Brewster interrupted. "Most people in this city have an accent of one sort or another. Just listen to MacGillicuddy. Doesn't mean you're not from this city."

Rogers narrowed his eyes. "But there's a residency requirement, right?"

"Oh, yeah?" Murphy asked. "How long you lived here, Nilsson?"

"All my life." Nilsson seemed pleased about it, judging from his persistent smile.

Gilbert shot Maddie another look. In his dark eyes she saw an emotion beyond disbelief. Was that consternation?

She thought—for the thousandth time since it took place—about their encounter in the stable last evening. Just remembering what had taken place between them, recalling the heat and taste of him, made her lightheaded with desire.

Hell of a way to begin practice.

"So," Murphy challenged, "where are your parents from, Nilsson? Mine came from Cork, and I'm proud of it."

Nilsson's smile did not waver. "My forefathers came from Sweden. Many good skaters there. Folk grow up on skates and skis."

"Enough conversation," Brewster declared. "Nilsson, go show 'em what you got."

Rogers leaned his head toward Maddie, where she and Gilbert stood side by side. "I've never heard of a Nils Nilsson, have you? And I'm up on most the players on the local teams. Even the pick-up players."

"Something funny about him," Maddie said.

"He's too pretty." Gilbert shot Maddie another look, but it was Rogers who nodded.

"Damn right."

He truly was, Maddie thought, narrowing her gaze. Nilsson's fair hair, longer than hers since she'd chopped it off, and longer than most men wore their hair, streamed and fluttered as he sped down the ice. His pale skin glowed.

But damn, no one could deny the fellow was quick and could handle the puck.

"There you go," Coach roared when Nilsson completed his circuit of the ice. "And he's hard to check as a brick shithouse. That's the standard I want all of you to meet. Now, out on that ice and get working!"

****

Nilsson truly was as hard to check as a brick shithouse, so Gilbert had to admit. From his place in the net, he'd watched everybody try—everybody except Maddie, of course, who only threw a check during games, and then just when she had to.

Even Gilbert had taken a shot at the big Swede in passing, when he went out to retrieve a puck. Nilsson's only reaction had been another big smile.

When their practice opponents showed up, a team from down Binghamton way, things got more serious. The Brigadiers had some big galoots on their team, but even they couldn't force Nilsson into the boards.

Gilbert began thinking better of Brewster's selection. Nilsson was tough, fast, and showed impressive scoring abilities, even if he was, in some vague, inexpressible way, annoying.

Gilbert just didn't like the way Maddie looked at the fellow—as if she couldn't quite believe what she saw.

The Boilermakers beat the Brigadiers five nothing—a shutout for Gilbert, and Coach was mightily pleased with him. Nilsson scored four of the goals, the other an empty-netter Maddie shot from way down the ice.

After the game, while Mr. Brewster lavished praise on Nilsson and congratulated himself on hiring him, Rogers edged back up to Gilbert and Maddie.

In a low voice, he said, "Nilsson claims he's spent his whole life in Buffalo. Somebody has to know something about him. He can't just spring up from nowhere, right?"

"Right," Maddie said.

"I'm gonna ask around. You two fellas do the same. We've got to hang together in this."

"Hang together?" Gilbert questioned. Rogers had

never wanted to get friendly with them before. Now they were suddenly supposed to be a united front?

A team?

"There's obviously something…well, wrong about him."

Maddie snorted. Gilbert could only wonder what that meant.

Later, while walking home through the cold, windy dark, he asked her, "Well, what do you think of the new guy?"

She shrugged.

"He's pretty, isn't he?" Gilbert asked sourly.

That swiveled her head. "What do you mean, asking that? You setting your eye at men now?"

"No."

"Is that what being with me has done to you? I seem so much like a man, you've started admiring?"

"No, God, no. Not me. But he is pretty. I thought you might think so."

"You think I'm attracted to Nils Nilsson?"

"Well, yeah."

"Gilbert, I'm attracted to you, so attracted I can hardly stand it, and he couldn't be less like you if he tried."

"Well, but—"

"I spent the whole third period wondering how I could get you alone so we could do what we did last night."

"You don't say." Gilbert brightened. He also began to ache.

"I do say. I'm thinking an empty stall again."

"We're gonna get caught, I'm telling you."

"I don't care. I'm desperate for another taste of

you."

That miraculously dissolved Gilbert's weariness and had him up, rampant. "Uh—"

"Of course if you don't want to risk it—"

"Did I say that?" He longed to grab her, right here on the street. But how would that look, two brawny hockey players engaging in a sudden clinch?

"Good thing McNamara's a careless bugger," he commented. "But ya know, if we keep it up, we do stand a good chance of getting caught."

She leaned closer. Her eyes gleamed wickedly in the light from the corner street lamp. She whispered, "You think you can keep it up?"

"I know I can."

"Then come on."

Lugging their heavy equipment, they fairly ran. When they reached the stables, they could see McNamara well down the block, talking to another worker and tipping a flask.

"Thank God," Gilbert breathed.

"How long till the first cabs get back?"

"Not sure."

"We'd better hurry."

Bliss, so Gilbert decided some short moments later, lay in being propped against a wall, his hair catching on the rough planks that lined it, while Maddie "saw to him," as she so sweetly put it. In fact this sort of bliss could well kill a man, but the woman wanted what she wanted, and he damn sure wasn't about to tell her different.

Madness, he thought even as he hauled her up into his arms and kissed her, whispering as soon as he could speak, "My turn."

"But I—" she gasped.

"You just stand there, MacGillicuddy, and don't make a sound."

Oh yeah, they were sure as fire going to get caught.

Chapter Nineteen

"Maddie, I want to come and watch your practice. Why can't I?"

"I told you, Roddy, now that we're using the rink behind the brewery, Mr. Brewster only lets certain people in to watch."

Newspaper reporters, for one thing. Yesterday there'd even been one from Fort Erie, come over on the ferry. Mr. Brewster wanted news about the team—and his new star forward—to reach far and wide.

Nobody on the team felt very happy about it, especially Rogers who, officially or otherwise, had considered himself the star prior to Nilsson's arrival.

"But I came before," Roddy protested.

"Before it moved from the river. Lots of people were there."

"It's lonely with you gone all the time, Maddie. And you're always late getting home from practice."

Maddie flushed with guilt. She was late because she'd been lingering in the stable with Gilbert, doing sweet, naughty things, the very thought of which made her feel warm.

"I'm sorry, Rod. It'll only be for a while. Once the series against the Freighters is over, things will go back to normal."

"No more games?"

"I don't think so."

"No more practice?"

"Why would there be? Mr. Brewster only put the team together to beat the Freighters. So, when it's done, win or not, it's done."

"Plus it will get warm out, right? And the ice will melt."

"Yes." And what would she do then? No more pretending to be a man, at least during practice, and having to sneak away when she wanted to take a pee. No more putting up with the other fellows whipping theirs out. Why, yesterday Murphy, Culligan, and Shandy had engaged in a contest for distance. Only Gilbert, busy fixing his equipment, and Nilsson, seemingly oblivious, had failed to participate. Oh, and Rogers of course, who wouldn't stoop to such antics.

And no more snatched meetings with Gilbert in the dark at the stable. Oh, how would she bear it? Their steamy sessions had turned into a habit. But no walks home together after practice equaled no chance to duck into the darkened workplace.

She'd need to go to his room if she wanted him. And she did want him.

"I don't like being here alone, and the fellas at the stables still call me names when I'm there, like *dummy*, *blockhead*, and *halfwit*," Roddy confessed.

"They're wrong, you understand. You know lots of things."

"Maybe. Maybe not."

"Talk to Mr. Crabbe. Maybe you can stay with him while I'm at practice."

"I guess so."

Maddie gave her brother a hug. "It won't be much longer. And remember, like we said—don't tell anybody I'm a girl, and your sister, instead of your cousin."

"I remember."

Maddie arrived for work just in time to see Gilbert leading the big, mechanical horse, who'd been named Piper, out from its stall. The immense animal, which had a high sheen, gleamed in the morning sun and tossed its head proudly, almost like a real beast.

She caught Gilbert's eye. "What's going on?"

"There's a glitch, a malfunction. It went lame last night."

"Lame?" she echoed in surprise.

"Something wrong with one of its feet. I think it's a spring, see?"

Sure enough, the machine's left front hoof hung loose when lifted, and smacked hard against the hock when it came down.

"It shouldn't have broken already, should it? I mean, it's brand new."

"Mr. Stanley's run it hard—it's had no rest and has operated almost continuously since he got it."

Maddie stared. "Does it need rest?"

"Everything needs rest." Gilbert scowled. "These fellows have come from the factory to see what's wrong."

He led the horse forward to join Mr. Stanley who, Maddie now saw, stood with three other men. They bent to examine the machine's hoof. Gilbert, all the while, held Piper's harness in his hand. As if Piper were a real horse, he ran a comforting hand up and down the machine's contoured nose.

Maddie fairly melted with love. Who could resist giving her heart to a man like that, who would risk himself in goal to pay for the keep of an old horse, and who even had it in him to care about its mechanical replacement? A man in a thousand, was her Gilbert.

Her man?

She stood watching while the workers from the factory inspected and discussed the mechanical unit. They did so gently and with care, and a certain amount of respect, a fact Maddie also admired.

She knew she should get to her own station and start shoveling out manure, but she stood on while the workers fiddled with a switch under the unit's sculpted mane. The machine went still, and they set about disassembling the hoof. Gilbert took a cloth from his back pocket and began polishing the horse's silver hide.

"Damn shame," someone spoke beside Maddie.

She turned and found Mr. Crabbe standing there, with Roddy behind him. The old man, wizened and bent with arthritis, was barely half Maddie's height, and the morning sun showed his age mercilessly.

"What's a shame?" she returned.

"Putting a thing like that in front of a shabby black cab. It's a travesty, it is."

"You think so, do you?"

"Don't you? That piece of machinery's far too fine to waste here. An engineering marvel, it is. Why spend it giving complaining customers a ride?"

"I guess Mr. Stanley thinks it's a way to make money. No feed."

"Just coal," Mr. Crabbe confirmed.

"And it won't get too old to work."

"But this unit's already broken down. That's the trouble with these automatons. People think they can abuse 'em with no ill effects. Nothing stands up to abuse—nothing. There always comes a reckoning. Just like in this city now, the mechanicals are asking for a reckoning. They want their rights."

"Yes," Maddie agreed uneasily.

"Take those three repairmen, there." The old men nodded at the fellows working on the mechanical horse. "Only one o' them is human. Can you tell which?"

Maddie gave Mr. Crabbe a close look. "How do you know that?"

Mr. Crabbe chuckled. "I happen to know who they are. From the factory down on Chippewa Street, where the hybrids are building others of their kind."

"Oh."

"And dogs and horses, and the sweet lord knows what else."

Maddie shot him another look, wondering how he felt about that. "Is that so wrong?"

"Not up to me to say what's right or wrong." Mr. Crabbe returned Maddie's stare. "Just remember, *young man*, all may not be what it appears."

****

"Mr. Crabbe told me two of those workers today—the ones who fixed Piper—were automatons. Hybrids. Could you tell?"

"No." Gilbert's voice sounded husky. They lay in one another's arms, half dressed and in the hay at the back of Piper's empty box. The workers, automaton or otherwise, had replaced the spring in the unit's hoof and it had gone out to pull the cab without complaint.

The two of them had never done this before, lain together following one of their desperate stable sessions. But they'd spent themselves on one another so completely, Maddie had been unable to rise.

Now she reached out and touched Gilbert's cheek in the near dark. "Will you tell me something?"

"Which of those workers was human?" He stirred in the hay. "They all looked human to me. Maybe old Crabbe's imagining things."

"I don't think so. Haven't you ever seen those hybrid policemen? And there were those prostitutes last year. Men went to see them and paid good money."

"Umm?" Gilbert's fingers, which still rested on Maddie's breast, stirred in a caress. "Foolish idiots. Not so lucky as me."

"So you're happy with my company?"

"Happy doesn't describe it, though I still say this is risky."

"Risk is part of what makes it so exciting." She leaned in and kissed him, long and luxurious. "Now, hush and tell me something."

"I can scarcely do both, hush and tell you something."

"What's your name? Your first name, I mean. You never did tell me."

He stiffened. "Never mind."

"No, but Gilbert, I want to know." Didn't he understand she wanted to possess all of him, had already memorized the way his eyebrows grew and even that mole on his chest? She wanted to consume him, body, mind, and spirit.

"I never use it."

"Why?"

He moved again, uneasily this time. "We'd better get out of here."

"Not just yet." She rolled over on top of him. By now, she knew what he found irresistible. "You're going nowhere till I feel you inside me."

"Erg?"

"And that's not gonna happen till you tell me your first name. I've already told you all my secrets."

She felt him smile. "That's 'cause you like to chatter after we make love."

"And you don't. You like to make me dig for information—like your first name."

"It's Algonquin."

"Your name?"

"Yes."

"Algonquin Gilbert?"

"No, I mean my mother was Algonquin, from way up in Canada. She gave me an Indian name."

"You said that much before. So?"

"So I already have folks tossing insults at me on a daily basis. The last thing I need is to trot out an Indian name."

"I'm not asking you to trot it out. Just tell me. We keep each other's secrets, right?"

"Yeah."

"Anyway, I don't think being called Indian is an insult."

"It is, the way they say it."

"What was your mother like?"

"I don't remember her."

"She died when you were young?"

"No, she took off when I was about three. Her and my pa didn't get along, and she went back to her own people."

"Why didn't she take you with her?"

"I don't know. Didn't want me, I guess. Luckily, Pa did. He was a great father, brought us here for a new start. Supported us by work with training horses, and died in a boating accident, some time back."

"I'm so sorry."

Gilbert shrugged.

"What was his name?"

"Jacques. Jacques Gilbert." He gave it the French pronunciation—Jill-*bear*.

"But your name's not Jacques?"

"It is not."

"Well, then." She kissed one corner of his mouth, then the other. "You can make me force it out of you, but I warn you, I intend to be merciless."

"Huritt."

"What?"

"My name's Huritt."

"Oh! What does it mean?"

"Not sure. Pa always said it meant 'handsome,' but I don't believe it."

"I think that suits you right well."

"Don't tell anyone, all right?"

"I'll only use that name when we're alone together." She wanted to tell him then how she loved him—she longed to whisper the words over his skin, shower him with them, the most intimate gift she could bestow. But she didn't know if the confidence would be welcome—after all, they'd never spoken about forever.

Instead she whispered, "Huritt, can I please have you inside me?"

It seemed she could.

Chapter Twenty

"Nobody has any information about our friend Nilsson. No one who knows anything about hockey's ever heard of him." In a huddle with Maddie, Shandy, Culligan, and Murphy, Rogers growled the words. "He says he's Swedish, but then he turns around and claims he's always lived here. How can that be?"

Maddie felt Rogers' frustration. At least he'd dropped his air of superiority toward the rest of them. United in their dislike of Nilsson, they'd at last become a team, but probably not the way Coach or Brewster had intended.

"He's got that funny accent," Murphy pointed out, which was pretty rich, given Murphy's thick brogue.

"So has MacGillicuddy," Rogers pointed out. "So do you, Murphy, come to mention it."

"Aye, but I was born here, right in the upstairs garret where my parents still live. It's just I speak the Irish at home with them."

"It might be the same for Nilsson," Maddie suggested. To be fair, she couldn't say she actually disliked Nilsson as much as the others seemed to. With that smile of his, and his perpetually sunny nature, she found dislike impossible. But she didn't blame Rogers or the others for their aggravation. Something about the man felt off.

"It's feckin' suspicious," Culligan agreed, "nobody

havin' heard of him. But by Patrick's beard, the man can shoot a puck."

"And skate," Rogers agreed, his gaze following Nilsson, who even now swooped across the ice. "And have you noticed he's always where he's supposed to be? In position."

"I have, that." Murphy nodded. "That's what makes it so easy to get the puck to him."

"Then he scores," said Shandy in bitter wonderment.

"Aye."

"And," Culligan gathered steam, "he's never in a bad mood. He doesn't get discouraged, no matter how much Coach hollers."

"It ain't natural."

Gilbert skated up from goal and joined the huddle. "What are you talking about?"

"The new freak," Shandy told him. "Anybody know where Nilsson goes after practice?"

Maddie's body jerked involuntarily in response to those words, *after practice*. She knew where she and Gilbert usually went.

"He has a room up on Connecticut Street," Rogers supplied the answer. "I followed him."

"With his family?"

Rogers shook his head. "It's a rooming house for gentlemen."

Culligan snorted.

"Maybe," Murphy posed, "we should take him out to a bar, get 'im drunk and loosen his tongue, get 'im talking."

Rogers snapped his fingers. "Good idea, Murph. We'll do it tonight. MacGillicuddy, why don't you invite him?"

"Why MacGillicuddy?" Gilbert demanded.

"Nilsson's friendliest with him. Why, Gilbert—do you want to ask him, instead?"

"Not me." But Gilbert looked at Maddie unhappily. She widened her eyes at him. In the face of the searing intimacy they'd been sharing, he couldn't still have doubts about where her interest lay.

"Come on, you lot!" Coach bellowed. "Our first game against the Freighters is in two days. You just gonna stand there gossiping like girls?"

****

"Hey, Nilsson, the rest of us are going out for drinks after practice, to celebrate—well, to celebrate the start of the tournament. Would you like to come?"

Maddie made the invitation off hand, the way one fellow might ask another, without much interest.

Nilsson looked plenty interested, however, though he replied, "I do not drink, MacGillicuddy."

"You don't? Really?"

"No, I believe in healthy living, good for the body and good for the mind."

"Ah." Maybe that explained why he looked that way, fairly brimming with health and vitality. Because he truly did, now that she saw him up close. And Gilbert was right about something else—the man could scarcely be better looking if he tried.

"But," he added, showing his beautiful smile, "I will come along for the camaraderie."

"Well, that's good, then." Maddie, who was giving up time alone with Gilbert for this, hoped they'd at least get something out of him.

"Thank you for the invitation, Mattie."

"Right. Come on."

Clancy's tavern had the sole advantage of being close by. A rough place with a big, plank bar and questionable whiskey, it was already crowded with unwashed humanity, most of it Irish, when they arrived. Since two of their number claimed membership in the Irish race, it seemed a logical choice.

"I do not drink," Nilsson announced again, when Rogers ordered the first round. The others all stared at him as if he had sprouted six extra legs and dropped from the ceiling.

Culligan clapped him on the shoulder. "How do ye manage such a rare feat, me fine fella?"

"Sorry, friend?"

"How d'ye get through life wi'out the help o' good ale or whiskey?"

"Let alone endure the hits out on the ice," Shandy put in sourly.

Nilsson beamed. "I am very good at taking my knocks. Indeed, my family say I was made to take them."

"Tell us about your family," suggested Rogers, leaning on the bar next to the big Swede. "I mean, the rest of us are a pretty tight team, but we don't know much about you."

"My family members are very dear to me. I owe them everything."

Gilbert asked, "Will your folks come to the games, once the tournament starts?"

"I am certain they will come to watch," Nilsson assured him.

"What's your father do?" Rogers pressed, narrowing his eyes.

“He is a craftsman, and makes wonderful things with his hands. My mother is very beautiful. She was from Landskrona, in Sweden. My father, he came from Stockholm. I know all this, me,” he boasted.

“I’ll bet they’re proud of you, your folks,” Murphy suggested.

“Very much proud.”

He was actually a nice fellow, Maddie decided, and took a big gulp of her ale. Kind of sweet, and so earnest. She really couldn’t say what it was about him that bothered everybody so much.

“When we win this tournament…” Culligan began.

“And we will,” Murphy put in.

“Sure. What’s everybody going to do with the money?”

Rogers answered immediately, “I’m thinking of starting my own professional team. Any of you lot want on it, just let me know.”

“You think your cut will be enough to cover that?” Gilbert asked.

“Maybe not, but it’ll make a good start.” Rogers, too, gulped down some ale.

“What about you, MacGillicuddy?”

“I want to make sure my cousin’s all right, if something happens to me.”

“His cousin’s simple,” Shandy told Nilsson in a loud whisper, and Maddie glared at him. Culligan added, “Just sayin’.”

“That is a worthy aspiration,” Nilsson declared. “One should always think of family. You, Culligan?”

“Well…” Culligan looked suddenly sheepish. “There’s this young lass I’ve been after courting. I’d like for us to marry.”

“Also a worthy aspiration.”

“I’ll be sending most o’ my winnings home,” Murphy confessed. “Want to bring my little sister and brother over.”

Maddie blinked at the big, burly forward in surprise. Not so different from her, after all.

Shandy boasted, “I’ve got plans, big plans. I’m thinking of starting a brewery, maybe turning out hard lemonade. God knows, this town can consume all the hooch it can produce.”

Everyone looked at Gilbert. “What about you?” Culligan asked.

“I want to buy a horse.”

They all stared. “You starting up your own cab company?” Rogers asked.

“No.” Gilbert didn’t smile. “I want to buy him so I can retire him in comfort. Otherwise, he’s gonna end up in the boneyard.”

“Crazy,” Culligan shook his head. “But each to his own, eh?”

“Each to his own,” Rogers repeated the sentiment. They all—except Nilsson—drank to it.

“So, Nils, old boy,” Murphy said then, “why don’t you partake o’ the water of life?”

“I am sorry?” Nilsson tipped his head.

“Whiskey,” Murphy clarified, “or at least a good pot o’ ale.”

“It is not healthy. You will all regret this, come tomorrow. And we must be at our best, for the tournament.”

“We’ll be at our best,” Culligan vowed. “Just so’s MacGillicuddy here keeps skating backward and you, Nilsson, keep scoring.”

"So I will," Nilsson assured them. "It is what I do."

****

Nilsson edged up to Maddie at the bar, as she collected a batch of drinks to carry back to their table in the corner. He leaned close to her ear and said, "MacGillicuddy, I know your secret."

"Huh?" Her head felt a little foggy from the ale. She should have left for home hours ago. A measure of guilt and concern for Roddy dominated her mind. But Roddy was a grown man, wasn't he? And she was already giving up so much for his sake. The right to be a woman. The freedom to kiss Gilbert in public, like she wished. Being in his company and pretending he was just her buddy was torture.

"Here." She thrust two drinks at Nilsson. "Help me carry these."

He gave her his matchless smile. "Sure thing, friend." He winked, which made Maddie blink at him.

"Hold on a minute, what did you say? You know my secret? What secret?"

Nilsson paused with a pint in either hand. He gazed straight into her eyes. "The fact that you are—"

"Wait! Don't say it." A wave of heat and distress swept over Maddie, in a scorching blush. "How did you guess?"

"I did not guess. I discerned. I am very observant."

"Oh, God."

"I noticed, first, how you look at Gilbert. It is unusual, though certainly not impossible, for one male to look at another in that manner. So I decided one of you might not, in fact, be male. And since his beard has thickened during the course of the evening's adventures and yours has not yet made an appearance—"

"Enough. Shh! I've—I've never had much of a beard," she said truthfully. "It's the red hair. But I'm sure you'll agree I'm too big and tall to be a woman, right?"

"Many women in Sweden are, in fact, tall. I believe the same is true of Scotland."

"Uh—please, Nils, don't tell anyone. I'll lose my place on the team."

"Will you?"

"Women aren't allowed to play. And with the tournament starting the day after tomorrow, that would spoil everything."

Nilsson's eyes looked bright and interested. "Does Gilbert know?"

Maddie felt sick. "Yes. But no one else, understand?"

"Of course I understand. It is the nature of a secret, *nej*? Are you and Gilbert lovers?"

She glanced at their table. Gilbert watched her and Nilsson together, his gaze intent. He couldn't possibly still think she was attracted to the big Swede, could he? Not after the kind of things they'd been doing together.

She said, "Yes. But you can't tell anybody that, either. Do you promise?"

Nilsson laid his hand solemnly over his heart. "Promise." He looked amused. "And maybe someday you will learn a secret about me, and you will keep that, also."

"Sure I will," Maddie agreed desperately. "We're friends, right?"

"Buddies," Nilsson agreed, and gave her a wide smile.

Chapter Twenty-One

"What do you mean, he knows?" Gilbert stared at Maddie, his stomach lurching with alarm. Already nervous about the first game of the tournament tomorrow, and unhappy about the close words he'd seen Maddie and Nilsson exchanging at the bar last night, he didn't need to hear this.

That pretty boy Nilsson *knew*.

"How?"

"He guessed." Maddie spoke the words out of the corner of her mouth as they donned their equipment for practice.

"How?" Gilbert repeated.

"Something about the way I was looking at you, apparently."

Gilbert choked, scandalized.

Maddie shrugged. "I'm not used to beer. It must have relaxed me a bit too much."

"So now what happens? He goes to Mr. Brewster? We're out?"

"On the ice!" Coach bellowed. "Drills!"

Gilbert groaned. He hated drills. Coach wanted everybody to be able to hit the goal with the puck—even with their eyes closed. Sometimes he blindfolded them before making them shoot pucks at the empty net, over and over. It got worse when he put Gilbert in net to stop the shots. Rogers had a hard shot, or so he'd thought till he started getting in the way of Nilsson's. The man shot like a cannon.

No wonder their opponents' goalies rarely stopped him.

"Talk to you later," Maddie said, and took the ice.

Gilbert stood for a moment, armed with his pads and big stick, and watched her. It seemed like she transformed when she hit that surface, became free, like someone released from a cage. All strength, grace, and speed, her body flowed and she came into her own.

She was becoming good at handling the puck too, getting a lot of scoring opportunities. She might have been born for the position of rover, moving back and forward, up and down the ice. She could skate in, grab a chance at a goal, and return to her zone skating backward, fending off attackers all the way.

Priceless.

He watched her and the other members of the team, including several of the second stagers, fire pucks at the empty net. It seemed he spent all too much time watching Maddie these days. She had him on a lead, a short one.

His eyes narrowed when he saw Nilsson skate past her and give her a big smile. His euphoria died. *Nilsson knew she was a woman*, a woman warm and passionate enough to give searing kisses in the dark, to deal out lovemaking hot enough to strip a man's skin from his bones. Would the big Swede make a move on her?

What might Maddie—if flattered—do then?

While Gilbert believed that Maddie cared about him, and reasoned no girl would do the things she did with him if she didn't care, he suspected that desire was desire, and might drive a woman to the same lengths as a man. Love—love was something else again. Neither of them had spoken that word.

Not yet.

Now, with this damn tournament upon them, probably wasn't the time.

"Gilbert, get in there!" Coach roared. Time to go under fire, he thought as he skated off to his goal.

It might be easier if he got hit in the head and didn't survive.

****

"Are you all right?"

Faces swam above Gilbert—there seemed to be an awful lot of them, all looking concerned. They came and went like the waves of Lake Erie, hitting the shore, and voices faded and roared in turns, sloshing against his ears.

"Can you hear me?"

"That was a hard shot, and right to the noggin."

"Better call the quack."

Gilbert's head hurt, and he could feel cold coming up from under him, spreading through his back. He seemed to be lying stretched out on the ice—laid out just like when Maddie finished with him, in the stable.

Maddie.

A flash of red caught his eye. She was there among the crowd of worried faces.

"How many fingers am I holding up?"

That was a damn foolish question, but Gilbert complied by answering, "Twelve."

Someone said, "Well, that can't be good."

Mr. Brewster's face swam into view. He had a stogie clamped in the corner of his mouth and worry in his shrewd eyes.

"Son? You just lie quietly a moment. Doc's on the way."

"The hell with that." He didn't want a doctor—they tended to let folks die and then charge for the service. The one who'd pronounced Pa dead had sent a bill, afterward. It had taken Gilbert weeks of labor to pay the bastard off.

He struggled to sit up. Strong hands assisted him.

"There. He's all right."

"He's bleeding." Maddie's voice.

Rogers asked, "Gilbert, you gonna be able to play? First game's tomorrow."

An Irish voice suggested, "We could put Turner in."

Dead silence met the proposal. Sounding desperate, Coach said, "No, we need Gilbert. Gilbert, the Fort Erie team comes in tonight. You gonna be with us?"

A Swedish accent. "Perhaps we should allow him to rest a minute."

Gilbert sat with his head spinning, wondering if he was going to be physically sick right there on the ice, in front of everyone, and weighing up what would happen if he said he couldn't play. Then, assisted by still more hard hands, he heaved his way to his feet.

"There you go!" Mighty slaps on the back almost knocked him down again. "He's tough, our goalie. Can take his knocks."

The story of Gilbert's life.

"Coach," Maddie said, "maybe he should sit down till the quack gets here."

"Good idea. Gilbert, you're benched for now. You others, practice your passing."

"Don't want the quack."

“I don’t care what you want, son. On the bench.”

Gilbert sat and, a bit blurrily, watched the drills start up again. Everything looked confusing. He wondered why Coach had so many men on the ice and why pairs of them moved in tandem.

Suddenly Maddie appeared in front of him. She had two heads.

“You sure you’re all right?”

He wasn’t, actually, though the sight of her—of them—helped. He wondered how it would be if all three of them, him and the two Maddies, met up in the loose box later. Holy hell!

He told her, “I’m a little sick to my stomach.”

Two Nilssons skated up and leaned on the boards in front of Gilbert. Dandy, there was one for each Maddie.

“I am sorry,” the Nilssons told Gilbert earnestly. “I’m afraid I fired the shot that hit you in the head.”

“Congratulations,” Gilbert told them. “It was a real whopper.”

“Coach,” Nilsson called, “goalie says his stomach doesn’t feel so good.”

“What’s that got to do with his head?”

“Never mind,” Brewster hollered. “Somebody bring him a Buffalo’s Best while he’s waiting for the quack. Good beer can fix anything.”

When the quack finally showed up, though, near the end of practice, his examination of Gilbert caused him to look concerned.

“Don’t like the look of him,” he declared while everyone else stood around in a worried knot. “Needs rest. He shouldn’t play hockey for at least a week.”

“Not play?” Rogers bleated.

Coach threw his hands in the air. "Well, there goes the tournament."

Gilbert stared in surprise. He wasn't that good in goal, was he? Or maybe Turner was just that bad.

"I'm all right," he said. At least now, since drinking the beer, he only saw one doctor, and one of everybody else.

"Hear that?" Brewster asked the doctor. "He says he can play. Doc, the tournament starts tomorrow. There's a fortune riding on it. And the reputation of our city."

The doctor snapped in reply, "You think I don't know that? I have a dollar riding on you to win. But he's got a big old bandage on his head, see? The Freighters get a load of that, they'll target his head like a gong."

"He can wear his knit hat—that thing he calls a tuque," Rogers said. "No one will see the bandage."

Another secret, Gilbert thought. Then he remembered old Jessop, in his temporary box. Mr. Stanley said he had another mechanical horse on order. Another Piper. When it arrived, Jessop would have no chance of remaining in the tight quarters of the stable. Gilbert needed enough money to rent him a permanent berth in one of the liveries. Hopefully, he could buy Jessop outright. Crazy idea, sure enough, but…

He shoved the gawkers aside and got up on his skates. "Let me between those pipes."

"That's the spirit." Mr. Brewster beamed. "But practice is over, son. You go home and get some rest. Be here tomorrow afternoon, right?"

"Right," Gilbert replied. He had a lot riding on it.

****

"I'm going to stay with you tonight," Maddie told Gilbert as they made their way home after the practice.

"Eh?" He looked at her. "Not sure I'm up to—well, our usual."

Usual, Maddie thought, and her lips twisted. Was that all she meant to him, what it had become—a regular? Oh hell! Well, what had she expected, throwing herself at him the way she had?

"I didn't mean that, Gilbert. Doc says you have concussion. You shouldn't be alone."

"Why not?"

"If you fall asleep, you might not come round again."

"You don't say."

"And I—" Maddie sucked in a big breath. "I couldn't live with that. God, Gilbert, you scared the life out of me when you took that shot off Nilsson and went down so hard. Just like a steer at the slaughterhouse. Your eyes rolled right back in your head."

"Like when they kill a horse. You ever seen them kill one?"

"No."

"It's an awful sight."

"I can imagine."

"One minute they're standing there, looking at you with all that intelligence—recognizing you, right? Next, they're gone."

"Gilbert—"

"I don't want that to happen to Jessop. Might sound stupid to everybody else, but we're friends, him and me."

"Doesn't sound stupid."

"I want to buy him, give him a good retirement.

That means I need to play."

Maddie sighed. "I understand, and it's real admirable of you. But Coach says the Freighters have some hard shooters. They're a big team." She expected to take some crippling body checks and possibly be on the receiving end of what Rogers called *boarding*. There were penalties for boarding, if the person getting shoved didn't have the puck. But she doubted that would alleviate the pain much.

"If you should get whacked in the head again—"

"I won't. Got good reflexes."

He'd *had* excellent reflexes. Maddie wasn't so sure about that, now.

"I just never saw that shot of Nilsson's coming. In fact, if he hadn't apologized, I wouldn't have known what hit me."

"He's quick, and he has a heck of a shot when he snaps it. He's really sorry he hit you."

Gilbert's eyes slid in Maddie's direction. They still didn't look right to her—almost as if they moved independently of each other. In fact, he didn't look right, paler than she'd ever seen him under his tan.

"You been cozying up to him?" he asked.

"Gilbert, you can't still be jealous of Nilsson."

"Can't I?" he grunted.

"He and I are just friends. Anyway, I need to keep him sweet, don't I? Since he knows the truth about me."

Gilbert swayed violently. "Just so long as you don't keep him too sweet."

"I'll ignore that comment, since you're not in your right head. Come on, let's get you home."

Chapter Twenty-Two

"Look at 'em. They're huge!"

The comment rolled from between Murphy's lips in a rich brogue rife with wonder. Quite the pronouncement, Maddie thought, from a man who topped six feet by close to half a dozen inches and had a neck like a bull.

But lord, it was the truth. The Fort Erie Freighters filed into the rink for warmups the way stampeding bulls might. They looked like freighters, even the smallest of them, who happened to be the goalie, bigger than Maddie.

She looked doubtfully at Gilbert, who stood beside her. To her eye, he still looked pale. He wore his blue knit hat pulled down well over the bandage on his head, and he appeared bemused.

Not a good sign in a goalie. Gilbert's skill, as she'd already observed, lay in the fact that he was quick and he anticipated the path the puck would take. He seemed able to know where a shot would go even before he moved to meet it—self-preservation, maybe.

Except for that shot of Nilsson's.

Nilsson seemed to be the only one of the Boilermakers feeling relaxed and positive today. He skated up and down in front of their bench, barely giving the oversized Freighters a glance.

The rest of her team mates, including the backups,

looked slightly sick. If one of the starters got hurt, the backups would be for it. She'd overheard Coach tell Mr. Brewster that if that happened they might as well resign themselves to losing.

Yes, well, she couldn't afford to lose. Just this morning, Roddy had got in a scrap at the stables with someone who'd called him the town idiot. Roddy was smart enough to know when he'd been mocked, all right. And now he'd decided he could throw a punch and answer back those who insulted him by battering them.

This morning, Roddy had given as good as he got.

She glanced at the stands. Roddy was here somewhere in the crowd. But it was a very large crowd, its members having streamed in from both Buffalo and Fort Erie.

She wanted to win so she could get Roddy out of the stables, maybe set him up in an apprentice trade.

"Look at the size of that forward," Culligan groaned. "A real bruiser."

Yes, and Maddie could already feel those bruises, the ghosts of ones to come.

"Take heart, fellas." Rogers threw one arm around Maddie's neck and the other around Culligan's. "We can win this. Yeah, they're big, but are they fast? We've got MacGillicuddy and Nilsson. And Gilbert," he added grudgingly.

Culligan replied, "I appreciate your confidence, old son. But those bastards look mean."

"So? Are we scared of mean? We're from Buffalo, for God's sake. They don't know mean till they've been on our streets." He lowered his voice. "Look, we only have to win three games. Three out of five—that's it.

And we bring home all the bacon."

"Me, I love bacon," Murphy said decidedly.

"Three games," Rogers repeated. "Nilsson, you with us?"

Nilsson turned his head and flashed his big smile. "Where else would I be?"

"Now, that's what I like to see—a united team." Coach stumped over. "It took you lot long enough to come together, but I think you've finally done it. Rogers, I couldn't help but hear your encouraging words to your team mates. Mr. Brewster told me to give you this."

They all stared as Coach shook out a blue Buffalo Boilermakers sweater. It looked the same as the others, except this one had a letter "C" on the left front shoulder.

"What's this?" Rogers asked.

"You've been promoted to captain—and well deserved. Now get out there and lead your team mates to victory."

****

Gilbert winced as he watched Maddie get smashed off the boards—again. The Freighters were hard fore checkers, back checkers, and cross checkers. Everybody, with the exception of Nilsson, had been knocked off his—or her—feet multiple times. Gilbert didn't know how Maddie withstood it.

He, himself, had been smashed into the pipes, forced back into his net, and smacked in the shoulders repeatedly. Fortunately, he hadn't yet been hit in the head. Still more fortunately, the assault had resulted in only one goal.

He felt there should have been a penalty called on

the play that pushed him into the net, and the goal denied. But there hadn't been, and now, part way through the second half, the Boilermakers were losing.

The Freighters had scored three times—the questionable goal and two others that the biggest of their three enormous forwards had blasted by Gilbert with blistering velocity. The Boilermakers had scored only once—a similar shot from Nilsson. Nobody else had managed a shot on goal due to the Freighters' fierce checking ability.

They used their size to full advantage and so far hadn't given Maddie, Rogers, or Nilsson much chance to make a weapon of their speed.

At least, Gilbert thought as he watched Maddie get up from the ice more slowly than she should, his double vision had settled down and he saw only one of her.

"Maddie!" A voice hollered from the stands. It sounded like Roddy. Fortunately, everybody would assume he yelled "Mattie!" at his cousin.

Maddie shook herself like a spaniel coming out of the rain. The ref glanced at her and turned his back.

Nilsson swooped by her and said something. Then he went in and put a massive hit on the Freighters' forward, who'd just got control of the puck. The fellow went down, Nilsson's shoulder to his gut, and Rogers stole the puck. The action moved up the ice.

Rogers took a shot that the Freighters' goalie—a stoic individual with a bald head—managed to stop. The play came back the other way, Maddie skating backward in front of it, defending furiously. Gilbert braced himself.

He had to stop whatever came at him. A two-goal deficit they might overcome. Three—well, he didn't think they had time for that.

He got into his crouch, sending up a swift prayer he wouldn't get smashed in the face. The Freighters' forward shot—high, arcing over Gilbert's shoulder. He leaped, making an acrobatic twist in the air, reached back, and stopped the puck with his hand.

Even over the pounding of his heart, he heard the crowd roar.

A chant started up: Gil-bert, Gil-bert!

Well, how about that?

Nilsson swung by and retrieved the puck, giving Gilbert one of his smiles in passing. Incredible endurance, the man had. Gilbert had seen him get checked a dozen times, and hit in the ear by the puck once. Nilsson barely showed a red mark on him.

Nilsson moved the puck down the ice toward the Freighters' goal with Murphy, Rogers, and Maddie in train. He took a shot that hit the Freighters' towering defenseman, stationed in front of the net, in the side of the head. The fellow dropped like a stone.

Well, Gilbert knew how that felt.

They waited while the man was dragged off the ice by the heels. Another much smaller defenseman came on in relief. He looked nervous.

"Come on, fellas!" Rogers shouted. "We've still got a chance."

The next few minutes passed in a hectic blur. The Boilermakers, applying full pressure, took five shots on goal, one of which—Maddie's—went in. When the buzzer went, though, they were still one goal short of a tie, and fully short of a win.

Gilbert, battered, soaked with sweat, and utterly exhausted, couldn't believe how disappointed he felt—

disappointed and angry. They should have won that, could have won it. Looking at his fellow players, he saw his feelings reflected in their faces.

While the Freighters celebrated and the fans, a heavy proportion of whom had taken the ferry across from Fort Erie, cheered wildly, the Boilermakers huddled at Gilbert's net.

"Never mind," Nilsson, still cheerful, said and bopped Gilbert on the head. "We will win the next match."

"That we will," Rogers agreed, his hair soaked with sweat and bruises rising on his face. "We've got their measure now. Gilbert, you did a grand job. The rest of you did, also. Nilsson, you're a beast out there."

"I am not, actually," Nilsson told him seriously. "I am a Swede. Hockey player."

They all laughed. "Yeah," Rogers agreed, "and a damn fine one."

"Think that big forward o' theirs will be back for the next game?" Culligan asked worriedly.

"Two days? No doubt about it." Rogers stared around at them. "But we'll be ready, right? We're Buffalo's best."

Coach waved an arm at them. "All right, get off the ice."

While they stripped the equipment from their battered and aching bodies, Coach regaled them with all the things they'd done wrong during the game. Then he told them all over again, with extra profanity. Then he praised them mightily.

"Rogers, I like the way you kept pressing. You were a real leader on the ice. Gilbert, you got cheated on that one goal, but the stops you made were bloody brilliant. The Freighters should have had half a dozen more on us. Culligan—you really stood tough. Shandy, I saw some real smart moves from you out there. A brick wall, you were. Murph—I like those body checks you were throwing. More of that next time. MacGillicuddy, you were all over the ice, and you took some fine hits. That goal of yours—a killer."

Gilbert eyed Maddie. Unlike the rest of them, she could only strip down so far. He'd have to find out later the extent of her bruises. Despite his bone-deep weariness, his interest stirred.

He loved what she had beneath her sweater.

"Nilsson…" Coach turned to the blond Swede. "What can I say? Keep shooting like that, and we have a chance of taking the tournament."

"Do we, though, Coach?" Culligan asked rather plaintively. "Do we really have a chance?"

Coach glared at him. "You'd damn well better believe it. This team's gonna win. And don't you dare take the ice with any other thought in your mind."

Chapter Twenty-Three

"Oh, God, I hurt." Maddie stretched her body gingerly in the bed and gave a bone-deep groan. Beneath the sheets in Gilbert's room she lay naked, and felt far sorer than she could ever remember.

Last night, when they'd arrived here after the game, it had been too dark to see the full extent of her bruises. Now she lifted the sheet, peered at herself, and made a soft sound of distress.

Not good. But tomorrow afternoon she had to be ready to do it all over again.

Still grumbling, she propped up on one elbow and looked at the man who lay beside her. Against the pillow, his hair looked like black feathers, his eyelashes two thick fans. A magnificent bruise bloomed at his left ear. He slept the sleep of the exhausted—or dead.

They'd been far too beat—literally—to do anything other than fall into bed when they reached here last night, and sleep. Even Maddie's fingertips hurt from being bashed against her stick. But now, with the early morning light, she wanted him.

At least, the spirit was willing. About the flesh, she couldn't say.

She dropped a kiss on his abused ear and he stirred. A groan came from him that rivaled her own.

Maddie wondered how many lovers in this city could compare hockey injuries. She bet the two of them were unique, and rightfully so.

“Hey, handsome,” she whispered. “We’re supposed to be at work soon. And at practice after.”

He opened his eyes, and she lost all her breath. By heaven, what gorgeous eyes the man had, deep as midnight. And how she loved him—helplessly, like a woman past saving. Whatever had happened last night on the ice, she felt all woman now, here with him.

They gazed at one another for the space of twenty heartbeats before Gilbert croaked, “Are you all right, Maddie? You took some awful hits last night.”

“I know. Look.” She lowered the sheet and showed him her left breast, which was both cut and bruised. “That took the full brunt when I got smashed into the boards in the second half.”

Gilbert sat up like a shot. “Maddie—” Very gently, he brushed his fingers across her skin. “I don’t want to see you hurt this way. You have to quit—”

“I can’t, Gilbert.” To Maddie’s dismay, her eyes filled with tears. “I need to get Roddy out of the stables before he breaks somebody’s head and winds up in jail. But for that, we have to win. Do you think we can win the next game?”

She longed desperately for him to say yes, but she knew him for an honest man—which was probably why he hadn’t told her he loved her. What man would tell a big, galumphing female who bore hockey injuries that he loved her? So she watched his eyes for the truth.

“I don’t know, Maddie. I hope so, but the Freighters are pretty tough.”

“Tougher than I expected.”

“Yeah. If we do win, it’ll take all of us playing at our best. And I think you should pull out. You shouldn't have to accept that kind of punishment."

"You telling me, Huritt Gilbert, I'm not strong enough?"

"I'd never say that. You're the strongest woman I ever met. But just look at the state of you!"

"No worse off than you, with your wonky head. I'll just have to keep out of their reach."

He cupped her cheek with his hand. "You pull out, Maddie, and I'll keep playing and give you the money to get Roddy a new start, if we win."

"You just said we can't win, without all of us."

He looked chagrined.

Fiercely, Maddie blinked her tears away. "I guess we knew what we were getting into when we started all this."

"Wish we hadn't started, now. Maddie, promise me if you get hurt again you'll quit the team."

"You can't ask that of me, or tell me what to do, Huritt Gilbert."

"I'd never try to tell you what to do. And stop calling me that."

"Of course," she said, her gaze dropping to his mouth, "you might be able to persuade me." Of just about anything, though she sure wouldn't admit that.

"How much time do we have before work?" he wondered.

"Long enough."

He kissed her and, with mutual groans, they sank back beneath the sheet.

****

"Good news!" Mr. Brewster called as soon as they got out on the ice for practice. "I know all of you are feeling beat up and discouraged after yesterday's loss, but take heart. You've now achieved underdog status, and this city loves an underdog. In fact, this city always backs an underdog. Bets on you lot winning are up, and we've received some unexpected support."

"From whom, sir?" Rogers asked.

"Some of you may have heard that the boilermakers in this town—many of them automatons—have recently formed a union. Because of our name and yesterday's plucky performance, they've offered a bonus for a Boilermaker win in the tournament. The money's being donated by the members themselves, and they'll be in the stands to see the rest of the games."

"Cheering, I hope, *sor*," Culligan put in.

"I don't doubt it. The thing is, men, it's a pretty pot of money—enough to set each of you up for the future. This could change your lives."

"How much?" Rogers narrowed his eyes.

Brewster named a sum that stole Maddie's breath.

"That could buy me and Rosie a house," Murphy said.

"Indeed," Brewster agreed. "But, boys, first you have to win."

They all forgot their bruises during that practice. Eyes on the prize, they played better than they ever had, making connections, completing passes, and putting up a flawless defense.

Afterward, Brewster beamed. "I think you're ready for the Freighters, boys."

Murphy growled, "Bring 'em on."

****

"I'm very sorry." Mr. Crabbe looked up at Maddie earnestly, his aged face troubled. "I tried my best to ride herd on Roddy, but he slipped away from me. And the next thing I knew he was down the laneway scrapping with them fellows, the ones who always taunt him. Somebody called the coppers, and the rest is history."

"They hauled him away?" Maddie exchanged an incredulous look with Gilbert. They'd swung by the stables after practice as usual, only to find that all hell had broken loose while they were on the ice.

She sighed. "Not your fault, Mr. Crabbe. You were kind enough to keep him company, but it's not your job to keep him in line—it's mine, and his sister's, of course." And she'd fallen down on that job.

Mr. Crabbe gave her a sharp look. "His sister's, yes. But your practice is important. The tournament's important, the way I understand it. The pride of the city's at stake."

"Yes. I guess I'll have to go down to the station house and see if I can bail him out."

"I'll go with you," Gilbert volunteered.

"You sure you want to?"

He shrugged. "We'll have to walk. Doubt we'll find a cab this late."

Mr. Crabbe chuckled. "There are cabs all over this place. I'll send you in mine, free of charge."

They received considerable attention down at the station on Delaware, still dressed in their hockey sweaters as they were. One of the coppers outside gaped at them and said, "Hey, I know who you are. Look, Danny, it's some of them Boilermakers—the hockey fellas. You're the talk o' the town, d'you know that?"

"Uh—well," Maddie said, "maybe you can help me, then. I'm here to see about releasing my br—

cousin. He was picked up for brawling." And wouldn't Ma be mortified by that? As a matter of fact, Ma would be mortified by any number of things that had happened recently.

"Sure, let me take you right in," the helpful copper offered. "You can see our new captain. My name's Dennis, by the way. It's an honor to have you here. Hey, everybody, look who's here!" he announced as they entered the big main room of the station. "It's two of the Buffalo Boilermakers!"

Chaos erupted. Smiling men in blue uniforms gathered around Maddie and Gilbert; everybody wanted to shake their hands.

One officer said to Maddie, "I was there last night, MacGillicuddy. You took some terrific knocks, didn't you? Got to say, you look bigger on the ice."

"It's the skates," she told him hastily, making sure to lower her voice.

"That makes sense. Say, you boys are gonna win tomorrow, ain't you?"

"Bet on it," Gilbert said.

"We already did—took up a collection and all went in together for the Boilermakers to win it all."

A taller officer, with bright green eyes, stepped up. "You are all fine players, but I have to say my man's Nilsson." Did he wink at Maddie? But why would he?

"Nilsson's a grand player," she said gruffly. "Don't know what we'd do without him."

The green-eyed officer emitted a strange grinding sound.

"Here," said Dennis. "Let me take you in to see the captain."

The captain's office proved to be small, the

desktop buried in paperwork, and the captain himself turned out to be a strapping fellow, surprisingly youthful—also ridiculously handsome in a very Irish way, with red hair and impossibly blue eyes.

"Cap'n Fagan," Dennis said, "these are two of the Boilermakers come for—well," he stared at Maddie, "I forget why you've come."

"Thank you, Dennis. I'll take it from here," Captain Fagan said.

Dennis went out and shut the door behind him. The noise died to a dull roar.

"It's a pleasure to be after meeting you," Captain Fagan said. "Please sit down."

Maddie half fell into a chair. Gilbert remained standing.

Maddie said, "I'm here about my cousin. His name's Rodney MacGillicuddy and he was taken in today for brawling, down at Crabbe's Cabs."

"Ah, yes." Fagan's blue gaze inspected her swiftly. "Funny thing, the young man in question"—he looked at a paper on his desk—"indeed, one Rodney MacGillicuddy, kept asking us to call his sister, Maddie, to come and fetch him."

"Uh—" Maddie flushed. "Right. She can't come 'cause she's out at work. Works down at Trine's Laundry." And why had she said that, to a copper, no less? She could have bitten her tongue.

"I see. Your cousin was taken in for battery upon two men. One's been sent to the hospital."

"Really?"

"The other man got cleaned up and went home."

"Is—is Roddy all right?"

"A few bruises. Said he didn't need a doctor."

"All right, well, how do I get him out of here?"

"Won't be tonight, I'm afraid, Mr.—"

"Also MacGillicuddy."

"Mr. MacGillicuddy." Another sharp glance from the keen eyes. "He'll have to go before the judge, who will set a fine."

"A fine?" Maddie's heart sank. "But, sir, it's his first offense."

"He seems unwilling to admit he's done anything wrong."

"Captain Fagan, sir…" Maddie leaned forward. "You may have noticed that my br—cousin is a bit, well, different from the rest of us. The fellows at the stables, where we both work, ride him mercilessly, and call him all manner of things, like 'halfwit.' Just lately, he's discovered he can answer them with his fists. He's a big lad, sir—like me."

"Rough and tough, eh?"

"Something like that."

Fagan glanced at Gilbert. "Thing is, Mr. MacGillicuddy, now that he has discovered he can answer people back in blows, I'm afraid he'll keep it up."

"Oh no, sir, I'm sure he won't. His sister and I will both talk to him about it. And she—she's working on getting him out of the stables, and into a better situation."

"I see. Well, let's give him a night in the cells to teach him a lesson, eh? Tell his sister she can come and collect him in the morning."

"Uh, his sister, sir? But she works—"

"I'm sure she can manage it, if she wants him out."

Maddie shot a hopeless look at Gilbert. "Yes, I'll

tell her, sir."

Outside on the dark street and well away from the station, Maddie began to cry.

"Don't do that," Gilbert begged.

"I can't help it. He's going to be so miserable in there all night."

"He's a big boy. Maybe time you stop protecting him so much."

"He won't understand, Gilbert."

"He'll figure it out. That's what battering folks gets you—locked up in a jail cell. Not saying it isn't tempting, all the same—there's people I want to batter."

She stared at him. "Like who?"

"Never mind. Better stop with the crying. It just doesn't look right for a big, tough hockey player to go sniveling on the street."

"What are we going to do all night? I doubt I'll get any sleep for worrying about Roddy—and the next game."

"You come stay with me. I'm sure we'll think of something."

Chapter Twenty-Four

"I promise, Maddie, I won't do it again." Roddy, pale of cheek and red of eye, looked wholly abashed, and utterly convincing.

Maddie had come to pick him up in her best dress, battered face screened by one of her mother's hats and a judicious application of face powder. It emerged that the helpful Captain Fagan, no longer on duty, had made sure Roddy had a cell to himself so none of the other prisoners could pick on him.

Amid her worry and embarrassment, Maddie felt profoundly grateful for that.

Since she wanted to attract as little attention as possible, she went alone to get Roddy and lectured him all the way home.

"What were you thinking? Did you know I had to pay a fine? It's cut into the money I was saving for—well, for something better."

"I'm sorry, Maddie. You look pretty. Is that Mam's hat?"

Pretty? Surely that was a stretch. "Yes. But you listen to me, now."

"I'm listening."

"Mr. Crabbe could have got in trouble, since he was looking after you. Do you want to cause difficulties for him?"

"No. But, Maddie, Pa always said we should stick

up for ourselves. He said we're as good as anybody else."

"That's right."

"I got sick of those fellas always calling me names. It's not right. I'm as good as anybody." He grinned unexpectedly. "Especially wi' my fists."

Well, damn, Maddie thought. Maybe Gilbert was right and she should let Roddy make more of his own mistakes, and seize his own victories.

She paused outside their rooming house and hugged him. "You just be careful, all right? I have to get inside and change. You go ahead to work."

"I will, Maddie. Can I have some breakfast first?"

"Sure you can. And a good wash. Will you be at the game later?"

"Sure thing."

"Just remember, Roddy—I'm a fella there, just like at the stables. Your cousin."

"I won't forget."

****

"So, old fella," Gilbert told Jessop as he brushed him down, "you can see everything's at stake. Not just the game and not just winning, but what might come after."

A mad idea had entered Gilbert's brain. If he earned enough money in the tournament—and he just might—he could buy a plot of land outside the city. There was open land in West Seneca, which sounded like a good place to him, and even farther south in Eden or Holland. It would be a good place for horses—old, broken-down retired ones. A good place for a family.

He might ask Maddie to marry him.

It was one hell of an idea, terrifying in its audacity.

He was all too aware he hadn't even told her he loved her, not yet.

But he did.

He was also aware he'd done pretty much everything wrong when it came to her—jumped into exchanging all that heady pleasure without benefit of a courtship. The complication of the hockey tournament hadn't helped. He'd put the cart—er, cab—before the horse. How could he make it right, now?

And how could he propose to a woman who went around doing her best to *not* be a woman? Should he ask her to marry him when they were alone? In bed together?

No, not that.

He had to convince Maddie he valued her. He'd never met a woman like her, or dreamed there were women like her.

He caressed the old horse's neck. "Yeah, Jessop, if you could see your way to wishing me luck, it would be welcome."

Jessop raised his lip and blew air by way of reply. Did the old fellow know how near he stood to the boneyard? Only he, Huritt Gilbert, stood in the way. If he got hit in the head during tonight's game—killed—he didn't have to ask what would happen to Jessop, and to all these highfalutin plans he was making for the future.

He leaned close and spoke into Jessop's attentive ear. "Just hope for a win."

****

The stands were packed to overflowing, and more folks stood all around the boards, even behind the goals. Gilbert could tell the Fort Erie supporters from the Buffalo ones by the names they screamed toward the ice and at each other. Many of the Buffalo supporters wore blue. Those from across the river had on red, like the Freighters' sweaters, which were a loud, gaudy cherry color. The game hadn't even started yet, but Gilbert had already seen two fistfights among the onlookers. The air fairly vibrated with hostility and excitement.

A chill chased its way up Gilbert's spine as he watched his team mates buzz around on the ice like so many hornets, waiting for the puck drop. Even that was a big deal tonight.

Mr. Brewster stepped out on the ice along with a squat, florid-faced man in a blue flat-cap. Brewster made a speech about the support the team had been offered by the Boilermakers' union. By the time the squat man—head of the union, so Brewster said—dropped the puck, the whole place was at fever pitch.

Settle down, Gilbert told himself. Get comfortable in your goal. But could he? The previous games had taught him to rely on his reflexes. If he tensed up too much, he tended to let the puck in. But it was hard not to get tense as he watched Maddie skate up the ice.

Culligan liked to stay on his patch and remain close to Gilbert in goal. Shandy was like a wolf on the prowl, skating back and forth, guarding their zone. Maddie ranged far and wide, forcing her way into the play, trying to score—and opening herself up to the Freighters' savage checking.

Could speed and skill win out against brutality? Seemed like they were going to discover just that.

Unfortunately, the Freighters' towering forward—called Billington—was back. The play skirted around the Freighters' net, where Rogers took a shot on goal. The Freighters recovered the puck and moved down ice.

Gilbert saw them coming at him, Billington in the lead, with the puck on his stick. Billington evaded Shandy, and Culligan moved in, half blocking the net.

Gilbert narrowed his eyes. He couldn't let a goal in this early, he couldn't, he couldn't—

Billington shot. The puck came at Gilbert with tremendous velocity and hit him in the chest with a kick like a draft horse. Somehow, instinctively, he corralled the rebound and directed it to Nilsson, who appeared in that miraculous way he had and swooped away with it. Gilbert felt rather than saw Maddie give him a look before she skated off again.

The crowd screamed deafening approval. Once more Gilbert heard his name chanted. But he couldn't breathe. Broken rib? Surely not. Just the shock of taking that hard impact.

He was going to have purple bruises on top of the yellow ones.

Culligan shouted something at him. The crowd screamed too loud for him to tell what. At the other end of the ice, there came a flurry. Nilsson's stick went up in the air, as did Maddie's and Murphy's.

"Whoo-hoo!" Culligan hooted.

The Buffalo crowd stamped their feet; the players on the bench bashed their sticks against the boards. The Boilermakers roared.

They had scored.

A grin spread across Gilbert's face, and the pain from his bruises promptly disappeared.

"Come on, Jessop," he whispered. "This is for

you—for you and Maddie."

****

By the middle of the second half, the score stood two-one Boilermakers, and Maddie felt wildly optimistic. Every member of the team was playing at his best. Rogers—who'd scored their second goal—wore a look of determination. Murphy was checking like a fiend. Shandy and Culligan guarded their zone ferociously. In net, Gilbert had been an acrobat, allowing only the one goal that had dribbled in after ricocheting off a Freighter player. The crowd loved him.

In fact, the union members in the crowd made so much noise, Maddie could barely hear herself think.

The Freighters, getting desperate, were playing stupid, taking a lot of warnings and penalties, mostly for boarding. She had been smashed into the boards repeatedly—once she'd seen stars, and not the kind she saw when Gilbert kissed her.

For an instant, there amid the ordered chaos, she longed for it, the two of them alone somewhere dark and quiet, the bliss of skin sliding against skin, the sheer ecstasy of it when he plunged into her.

Then the rink went suddenly and uncannily quiet.

Skating up, she immediately saw why. In horror, she watched Nilsson sway on his skates, reeling from a blow in the back of the head, delivered by Billington's stick. For an instant he wavered, like a tree about to fall, before crashing to the ice.

Nilsson, down? But he never went down! She'd seen him take hit after hit, check after check, and somehow keep to his feet. He couldn't be down!

The referee blew a whistle. Play suspended.

Maddie darted forward while the Boilermaker fans surged to their feet in the stands and howled for a penalty.

High sticking, yes. But that didn't matter—only Nilsson's welfare did. The team gathered around him. Coach came out onto the ice.

Nilsson lay flat on his back with his eyes—unnaturally blue—wide open and staring upward. Maddie doubted he could see much. The steam lights were too bright, and anyway, he wore a terrible, blank look.

Could he be unconscious, with his eyes open?

"Nils?" she called. "Nils?"

He couldn't possibly hear her amid all that racket, yet the blue eyes swiveled in her direction.

Coach bent over him, an alarmed expression on his face. Looking for blood? From where she stood, Maddie couldn't see any. But, no. Coach said something to Nilsson and—wonder of wonders—Nilsson sat up. There was no blood on the ice.

A penalty was called, and Billington was escorted away. With help from Coach and Mr. Brewster—from where had he come?—Nilsson skated a few feet.

"All right, Boilermakers, let's capitalize on this."

"But is he fit to play?" Murphy bleated. "Should he be on the ice?" At Nilsson he bellowed, "You all right, man?"

Nilsson gave his wide, merry smile. "Top form."

Well, hell, Maddie thought. The man must have a head like a rock.

The Boilermakers scored during that penalty—Maddie herself put the puck in the net—and during the two that followed. Gilbert allowed no more goals, and when the final score stood at five-one, the union members in the stands threw their tools on the ice in apparent approval.

The Freighters moved off, looking sheepish. Most of the Boilermakers team stayed on the ice, enjoying the adulation of their supporters and helping to gather up the tools. Maddie, who saw Coach order Nilsson off to the changing room, decided to follow him.

Heck, somebody should. The man had to have a concussion. The team quack should be called, and Nilsson shouldn't be alone till he got there.

She did find him alone, though, sitting on one of the rough plank benches with his hands raised to his head.

"Here," she called when she stumped in on her blades. "Are you sure you're all right?"

Suddenly he didn't appear to be. In fact the whole darned scene looked wrong in a way Maddie couldn't identify. Nilsson's face had gone blank again, his eyes too vacant and wide.

He'd lifted half of his hair aside.

And right up off his head.

Horrified fascination took Maddie forward, the desire to know how a man's hair could come away from his head like that. Had Billington's blow partly scalped him?

But if so, surely there'd be blood.

She got a good look at Nilsson's head as she stepped up. Not at all what she expected. No blood. No scalp—just a smooth metal surface beneath the flowing, yellow locks, now dented and laid partly open.

Wide open, so Maddie could see the mechanism beneath.

Chapter Twenty-Five

"What the heck is that?" The words burst from Maddie and caused Nilsson to slew around on the bench. For an instant that seemed to last forever, they stared at one another.

Maddie demanded, "What the hell are you?"

But she knew the answer even before the question left her lips. There was only one thing Nilsson could be: an automaton—one of the hybrid ones, so difficult to tell from humans.

Unless you got a glimpse inside one's head.

"Shh," Nilsson said. "Do not tell. No one can find out."

"You're a ringer on the team." Had to be. The papers she'd signed had clearly stated the members of the Boilermakers must be *men*. Of course, that pretty much disqualified her too, didn't it? If anyone ever looked under her sweater, it would be the same as looking under Nilsson's hair.

No wonder he was so fast, though, so difficult to check, and had such a hard shot. She'd heard these things had the strength of four men.

No, not a *thing*. He was still Nilsson, her team mate. And friend.

"My God," she breathed. "Does Mr. Brewster know?"

Nilsson nodded. His hair flopped disconcertingly.

"Coach knows also. But no one else can be allowed to find out. I will be forced off the team." He added weightily, "Just like you."

I have a secret. One day you may know.

"Well, but…" Maddie faltered. "It's cheating."

"I am hockey player. I was created to play hockey."

"And you want to keep playing. I understand that. No—don't nod again. It makes my stomach feel queasy."

The whole thing did, the very fact that Nilsson was a machine. What about that smile? The hint of humor she sometimes caught in his eyes?

He was a machine. One built to play hockey.

She waved her hands. "Are you—broken? Your head—"

"My artificial intelligence does not seem to be damaged. The automatons who crafted me designed both an inner and outer shell to provide extra protection, since there have been dire injuries in the past. We learn," he said simply. "We improve."

"I'm glad." Maddie glanced at the door. "People will be coming. You'd better put—put your hair back down, and cover the wound. Are you able to operate like that?"

"I will need repair." He looked at her earnestly. "You will not tell? Not anyone? You promise? A promise, as I have been instructed, is a powerful thing."

"It is."

He added with cunning, "I promise to keep your secret if you will keep mine."

Well, damn. She wanted to tell Gilbert. She trusted him. And yet—she knew Gilbert had ambiguous feelings toward Nilsson. And it wasn't her secret, after all.

If her secret did get out, her reputation would be ruined along with any chance of starting a new life.

Nilsson said, "Please. I want to continue playing hockey."

"Here." She bent over him. "Let me fix your hair."

She was still busy smoothing the silky yellow locks when Gilbert came in. He had removed his skates in the rink and so approached quietly, catching Maddie and Nilsson in what no doubt appeared to be an intimate clinch.

He glared. "What are you doing?"

"Checking this wound on Nils' head."

"Aren't there doctors for that?"

"The doctor is on the way," Nilsson assured him. "Meanwhile, MacGillicuddy wished to see if I am bleeding."

Gilbert had no chance to say anything else. The rest of the team, including the backups, filed in, and Coach along with them.

"All right, men. Great game! That is the way I want to see you play. We do that two more times, we'll put the Freighters away and win this tournament."

Culligan said, "They're going to come back even harder next time."

"But they're reckless," Coach declared, "and they take stupid penalties. We can capitalize on that."

"Coach is right." Rogers took it up. "They spend all their time looking for ways to put us in the boards, while we're looking for ways to score. We've got brains on our side. I saw some smart plays out there tonight, especially from MacGillicuddy, Gilbert, and

Nilsson." Rogers blinked at the Swede. "You all right? That was one hell of a shot you took."

"Yeah," Murphy agreed. "I couldn't believe it when you got up again."

"Doctor's on the way," Mr. Brewster declared before Nilsson could answer. "In fact, I think I hear the ambulance now."

"I'll walk him out, sir," Maddie volunteered.

Nilsson swiftly agreed. "Yes, my team mate MacGillicuddy is a good fellow to take me out."

The ambulance was, in fact, an ambulance—backed up to the rear doors of the brewery. But Maddie thought she recognized two of the attendants as the workers who'd dropped Nilsson off his first day—no, not Nilsson but Piper, the mechanical horse.

She had to believe it then, that Nilsson was an automaton. But she turned to him in concern and said, "I hope you'll be all right. Are you sure you'll get healed—er—mended?"

He lowered his head to hers. "I am certain. Will you keep my secret? Tell no one."

She thought about Gilbert and the suspicious look in his eyes. "So long as you tell nobody about me."

****

The suspicious look in question met Maddie in full later, when they reached Gilbert's room and once more peeled off their uniforms.

"So," Gilbert asked with an edge, "do you mind telling me what was going on back there?"

"I already did tell you. I was looking over Nilsson's wound, trying to see how bad it was."

"I've inspected Culligan's injuries plenty of times, and Murphy's. I never caressed their hair like I saw you doing." Gilbert's breath hitched. "But maybe that's because I'm not *attracted* to them."

"How many times do I have to repeat it? I'm not attracted to Nilsson."

"That's not how it looked."

"I know how it must have looked. But he's just a team mate who took a hell of a wallop." Swiftly, she sought to change the subject. "As did you. I saw you stop that shot during the first half. Off with the sweater, and let me see."

He did not comply. "Maddie—I don't like it. You and him. You say you're not interested, but what if he is?"

Maddie bit her lip. She wanted to tell him the truth, so much she trembled. Or maybe that was just exhaustion.

"Gilbert, you're going to have to trust me, and trust what I tell you. Nils isn't attracted to me, and I'm attracted to you. Understand?"

She stepped up and kissed him, the kind of kiss that should leave a man with no doubts, the kind she'd wanted to bestow each time she looked at him, all evening. "I'm on fire for you, can't you tell?"

Dark eyes troubled, he said nothing.

"Gilbert, Nilsson's only interested in me as a friend. As a friend, I was concerned about him. I'm glad he can keep playing, aren't you?"

"Sure, I'm glad. And again, I'm not. Tell you the truth, I'd just as soon have him out of the picture."

Maddie experienced a wave of annoyance, or maybe it was frustration. "What kind of attitude is that?"

"He's dangerous, Maddie. He knows about you.

What if he starts raving while he's at the hospital and spills the beans that you're a woman?"

"He won't. Honestly, Gilbert, I didn't think you were this stubborn and purely pig-headed."

"Must be the ignorant savage in me, eh?"

"I didn't say that!"

"You don't have to."

"I didn't think it either, not ever. You're one of the smartest and finest men I've ever known—"

"But you don't respect me enough to give up your cozy 'friendship' with Nilsson."

"What's so cozy about it?"

"You needn't shout."

"I feel like shouting."

"I followed you out and saw you whispering together before he got in that ambulance. I saw the way you looked at him."

"Oh, did you?"

"I'm not blind, so don't try and lie to me."

"As if I would." But she was lying, she realized, at least by omission. She couldn't tell Gilbert that she and Nilsson now shared another secret.

He glared at her. "I can see the guilt on your face."

Maddie flushed.

"See!" he accused. "You always get all red when you're fibbing. You fibbing to me?"

"No," Maddie fibbed, and blinked harder.

They did not make love that night. Instead they lay in the same bed, backs firmly turned toward one another. Maddie listened to Gilbert snore softly and wondered how he could sleep, given his anger. She couldn't drop off for hours, and when she did at last fall into a doze, she had troubling dreams.

She rose before first light and left for home, wondering if she'd ever sleep in Gilbert's bed again.

Chapter Twenty-Six

"Maddie?" The word, issuing in a whisper through Gilbert's lips, went unanswered. He lay for several moments with his eyes closed, remembering the hard words they'd exchanged last night, and aching in both body and spirit.

His chest hurt with every breath. His heart hurt far worse.

He opened his eyes and saw the bed next to him lay empty, the covers thrown back. Gone. Got up and left him without so much as a word.

She'd never done that before. They always parted from here reluctantly, with kisses and many times more lovemaking. Her lips all over his aching body. That mischievous light in her eyes.

Had he lost her?

Well, but a man could expect some loyalty, right? To not walk in on his woman making eyes at another man—a pretty boy—and with her hands all over him.

He had to admit, if grudgingly, that Nilsson was more than just a pretty boy. God, the fellow could take his knocks. And Maddie might well have been checking the wound on his head, like she said.

But she'd done it so…tenderly.

Just remembering that scene brought the ire back up in Gilbert's blood and made his chest hurt worse.

The heck with that. If she wanted that flaxen-haired

hunk of Swedish muscle with his big smile and skilled hands instead of a half-Algonquin Frenchman, there was nothing Gilbert could do about it. He needed to concentrate on winning the tournament and making a place for Jessop and others of his kind.

Maddie didn't come near him at the stables that day, which made his chest ache even more. It was pretty unusual—generally she stopped by half a dozen times if only to, as it seemed, smile at him.

Now she kept away, which meant he didn't see her till practice that evening.

A lot of other people did stop, though, to congratulate him on last night's game. He heard no taunts of *injun, injun* now. They all had good things to say, showering him with lavish praise and encouragement for the next game. One boy even wanted him to sign his name on a scrap of paper. He wrote *H. Gilbert*, with *Buffalo Boilermakers* underneath.

The first thing he saw when he walked into the changing room behind the brewery was Maddie, in another huddle with Nilsson. They had their heads so close together, the red hair nearly touched the yellow.

Gilbert gritted his teeth and turned his back. He'd told her, hadn't he? She knew it bothered him, and still she cozied up to the big Swede.

At that moment, he wanted nothing more than to quit the team, to walk away and not look back at either Maddie MacGillicuddy or the Boilermakers. But damned if he'd let those two deprive him of his share of the winnings when the Freighters went down.

Coach started off practice with a lecture. The tournament had been designed with a day off between games.

"This gives us a chance to lick our wounds, but it also gives the Freighters a chance. You are the better team. That screams aloud, on the ice. You have the skill, the speed, and the endurance."

Culligan laughed. "Did you see the Freighters' rover before the last game, trying to skate backward like MacGillicuddy? He couldn't do it."

"I can't, either," Rogers put in ruefully, "and I consider myself a pretty good skater."

"As I say," Coach resumed, "we've got the skills. But they're a tough bunch of customers. And they'll be desperate, this next game. We'll have to lure them into taking penalties. And we'll need to hurt them any way we can.

"Murphy, I want you to complete all your checks. MacGillicuddy, you use your speed to keep out of their way. Gilbert, you'll have to be a brick wall."

Gilbert nodded miserably. "What about Nilsson?"

"Nilsson assures me he's well enough to play. Right, lad?"

Nils gave his big smile, looking none the worse for last night's blow to the head, about which Maddie had supposedly been so concerned.

"Rogers, you just be yourself. And don't let anybody take you out."

During the ensuing practice, Maddie kept away from Gilbert, stationed in his net. Normally, she skated by periodically, just to connect with him. Now she barely glanced in his direction.

Right, she had an angry on.

But, Gilbert noticed, she spoke to Nilsson whenever she had the chance. And every time she did,

Nilsson smiled at her. Well, to be fair, he smiled at everybody. But when it came to Maddie, Gilbert fancied his smile seemed that much warmer.

After all, Nilsson was the only one besides him, Gilbert—and, of course, Roddy—who knew Maddie was a woman. How could Nilsson help but admire her?

By the end of the practice, Gilbert felt more certain than ever that he'd lost her. She shot but one intense look at him as they left the ice.

Coach called him aside for a word. By the time he got to the changing room, Maddie had gone—the first time ever they hadn't walked home together.

Nilsson had gone, too. Together, Gilbert decided.

He went back to the stable—she wasn't there either, but he spent the next couple hours pampering Jessop, considered staying there the night, and eventually made his weary way home.

****

"Hey, you're MacGillicuddy, ain't you? The star defenseman for the Boilermakers. You're in this morning's paper."

"Am I?" Maddie, on her way to the stables with Roddy at her side, paused in spite of herself. The young man who'd hailed her in passing whipped out a copy of the *Courier* and flaunted the front page.

There was a picture of the team—made, she supposed, when she and Gilbert were still together, because they stood next to each other, strong and true. The rest of the members, with Coach, clustered around them.

A pang of emotion tore through her—grief, or maybe regret. They weren't together anymore, a fact that made her feel sick to her stomach. But hey, if he couldn't trust her when she told him how much she cared about him, and if he thought she'd so much as look at another man, what hope did they have?

"Well, how about that?" she said.

Roddy leaned closer to look. "You're famous, Maddie."

"It's Matt, right?" the young man with the newspaper asked. "Matt MacGillicuddy. We know all your names. Say, how do you skate backward like that?"

"Maddie shrugged. "I learned when I was a wee—uh—lad, in Scotland."

"Maddie's my cousin," Roddy put in, and winked.

The young man grinned. "You've gotta be real proud. The whole city's proud of the Boilermakers! Good luck at the game tonight. I'll be there with my buddies, if those union men leave us any room. You gonna win?"

Maddie touched a finger to her cap. "Depend on it."

The young man hurried off. A full day's work ahead before the game, Maddie thought—one without Gilbert. That made it hard to feel positive.

They passed Stanley's stable on the way in, and Maddie saw Gilbert there, already at work. His dark head rose and fell as he swept out, and she had a sudden, almost painful memory of his hands on her, strong but gentle.

Would she ever lie in his arms again? Would she ever come apart like that for any other man?

The day seemed interminable, even though Mr. Philips came by and sent her off to the game early. Even he had been infected with hockey fever.

The rink already buzzed with activity when she arrived. It seemed the Freighters had been making threats, bragging that the Boilermakers were nothing more than a bunch of sissies and they meant to flatten them during tonight's game.

"Bones will be broken," Billington was quoted as saying. "The Boilermakers should be afraid, very afraid."

Maddie might well have been, if she hadn't been so consumed by misery.

Gilbert showed up at the rink late, his mop of dark hair in disarray. Maddie had a mad desire to smooth it with her fingers, which she disciplined ruthlessly.

Mr. Brewster made a long speech about the importance of winning tonight's game, tipping the scale, and claiming the advantage. Then Coach spoke about them not being intimidated.

"Show no mercy out there, men. I know they're big and they're ugly, but being afraid will only give them the upper hand. I know you can take this game!"

Maddie glanced at Gilbert, who looked away from her. Nilsson nudged her with his elbow.

"You ready, buddy? This will be fun."

"Fun?"

"Hockey is the most fun there is."

Maddie lowered her voice and asked him, "Are you sure you're all mended?"

He knocked on the side of his head. "Good as new!"

****

To call that game challenging would be an understatement. By the start of the second half, Maddie considered hockey anything but *fun*. At least the crowd seemed to be having a good time—they roared and shouted and leaped to their feet repeatedly, making a deafening din. Every time Nilsson touched the puck, they chanted his name, and every time Gilbert made a save, they went wild.

Gilbert had made a bushel of saves. So far he'd been flawless, but so had the Freighters' goalie. Midway through that second half, the score stood at naught-naught.

Not for the lack of trying. Maddie had several good shots on net, as did Murphy, Rogers, and most of all Nilsson. They were running out of time. She'd been smashed off the boards repeatedly and had now almost run out of steam.

Nilsson, quite literally, hadn't. He alone, among them, remained fresh—though only Maddie, along with Coach and Mr. Brewster, knew why.

Despite all the hurt they'd dished out, the Freighters had been careful about taking penalties. Their hits had become sneaky and less blatant than before. But each and every one came with an ugly, threatening growl.

Now the Boilermakers had possession of the puck. Culligan, who'd recovered it after an unsuccessful shot on goal by the Freighters, passed it to Maddie, who started up the ice, accompanied by a mighty roar from the crowd.

Rogers trailed her on one side, and Murphy on the other. Maddie's mind raced. She could pass to Rogers, like he always insisted she should, or try to take a shot on her own. What would give them the better chance?

Suddenly Nilsson zoomed in, moving in that almost magical way he had, seemingly from nowhere.

He looked at her and tapped his stick on the ice.

Maddie, sailing at full speed, had no time to think. Her best goals came at full bore, but Nilsson had got himself into position and looked ready, and when he made that motion—that demanding tap on the ice—the results were usually good.

She dodged a check from a Freighters defenseman and made the pass. Nilsson received the puck on his stick with a delicacy beautiful to see, pivoted on one skate, and wound up for his shot.

It cracked off his stick like a bullet from a rifle and flew with blazing velocity. It cracked again when it took the Freighters' goalie in the middle of the forehead and dropped him like a felled tree.

Pandemonium erupted. The referee blew his whistle, which could barely be heard for the noise from the crowd. The Freighters' supporters threw objects at the ice, whatever they had to hand—most likely at the Boilermaker players.

Maddie skated forward and stood next to Nilsson, staring at the man stretched out in front of the Freighters' goal.

"Is he dead?" she asked, with a horrifying flashback to Trine's Laundry.

She didn't expect anyone to hear her in the midst of all that racket. But Nilsson had very keen hearing indeed.

He shook his head. "I do not think so. See—his chest is rising and falling."

Maddie couldn't see, and was given no opportunity to try. The Freighters' goalie, like others before him, got dragged off the ice by his heels, leaving a trail of blood.

The Freighters supporters screamed for a penalty. The referees went into a huddle with both coaches bawling at them.

Rogers skated up. "That was one hell of a shot," he said to Nilsson. "Must have busted his head like an egg."

Nilsson shrugged. "Unfortunately, I failed to score."

"That's cold, man," Murphy put in. "We might have just witnessed a man's death."

"He's not dead," Rogers confirmed Nilsson's opinion. "Wait up, here's the call."

One of the referees went to center ice and waited for the noise to die down enough for him to call, "No penalty!"

The stands exploded again. The Boilermakers exchanged glances, and the Freighters' backup goalie skated out on the ice.

He was a huge, black-bearded monster with shoulders like roughly carved boulders. When he got in position, he filled up most the goal.

Murphy snorted. "Now why didn't they play him in the first place?"

They soon found out. The new goalie, massive as he was, merely stood in one place and waited for the puck to reach him. He might stretch out a glove or his stick, but he never actually shifted position.

Maddie scored on him almost immediately, both Nilsson and Rogers a short while later. Before the time ran out, Nilsson scored again. The puck never even made it back to the Boilermakers' end, and they won four-nothing.

Afterward, the Freighters' coach and supporters

cried foul, citing the downing of their goalie and the lack of a penalty.

"Better hope your goalie's back by the next game," Coach retorted, "or that title's ours."

Chapter Twenty-Seven

"A word with you, Mr. Gilbert, if you please."

Gilbert was just leading Piper back into his stall at the stable, for refueling, when the two well-dressed men stepped up. He didn't know if the mechanical horse actually required a rubdown after his refuel, but Gilbert needed to fill every minute of every day here at the stable. That way he didn't have time to think about Maddie. Much.

She remained determined to avoid him. He'd barely set eyes on her since last night's game, and it didn't help that he still wanted her—in fact, that made it ten times worse.

But she must have made her choice and chosen Nilsson, the star.

He regarded his callers through narrowed eyes. One of them looked familiar; both made him feel vaguely uneasy.

"Yeah? What do you want?"

"A few minutes of your time."

"I'm working, as you can see."

"We can make it worth your while."

"I don't think so."

"We wanted to let you know, Mr. Gilbert, you're the best goal-tender we've ever seen, and we've seen our share."

"Not interested," Gilbert said, but it wasn't true.

That caught his interest, all right, and he gave the speaker a sharp look.

The man smiled. “Please, don’t be hasty. Why don’t you hear what we have to say? Let us buy you a drink in honor of your last great game.”

Before Gilbert could answer, the second suit stepped closer and said, “We’ll go somewhere quiet, where we can speak together. Because we’d like to make you an offer, Mr. Gilbert, one we’re quite certain you’ll want to consider.”

Piper lifted his head and, with a little puff of steam, knocked the man’s hat from his head. Gilbert laughed, but without much humor.

“What do you think, Piper?” he asked the mechanical horse. “Should I listen to what they have to say?”

With a glint from his silver hide, Piper nodded *yes*.

****

“What do you mean Coach wants to see me? Now? I’ll see him later, at practice.” Maddie stared at the apparition that lounged in the doorway of Mr. Philips’ stable block. Apart from the night they’d gone for drinks at Clancy’s, she’d never seen Nils out of uniform. She’d certainly never seen him like this, dressed in a handsome set of street clothes.

“He has sent me to ask if you will come talk to him and Mr. Brewster now, at the brewery.” For once Nilsson’s wide smile remained absent. “There is a complication.”

“Complication?” The lump that seemed to rest permanently at the pit of Maddie’s stomach heaved. Had she been discovered? From the very start of this she’d been waiting for that shoe to drop. Not now, she thought—not before the end of the tournament. Just give me a few more days.

And was this her, praying? She should know better. Prayer hadn't helped when her parents died, leaving her to make her own—and Roddy's—way in the world. It hadn't made Gilbert turn up at her door at any point this day, saying they had to mend things between them because he couldn't live without her.

As she couldn't live without him.

Just this—this automaton turned up.

She sucked in a breath. "Nils, did you *tell*?" She glanced down the lane, where Roddy swept the floor—the only person who might overhear.

"Tell?" Nilsson repeated.

"About me. That I am a…you know."

Nilsson cocked his head. For the first time since Maddie had met him, he didn't seem quite human—as if he processed the question.

"I did not *tell*. But I am afraid in my honesty I let something else slip. Deception is very difficult for me."

"What, exactly, did you let slip?"

"The fact that *you* know the truth about *me*. Mr. Brewster is very upset that you know. He said, 'Get him down here so we can talk to him.'"

"I see." Maddie's mind reeled. "Nils, you and I know I'll keep your secret—Mr. Brewster's secret."

"Yes, but you see, I cannot tell him *why* you will keep my secret or I would, in fact, have to tell *your* secret," Nils said earnestly.

Maddie set her shovel aside. "My God, what a tangle."

"Will you please come?"

"I'm working here. I don't suppose," she added,

eyeing his garb narrowly, "you work."

"I do not. Hockey is my sole job. It is my reason to *be*."

Just imagine, Maddie thought. "Yeah, well, nobody plays hockey for a living."

At last Nils' smile flashed. "I do."

"Tell Mr. Brewster I'll talk to him tonight."

"Too many people will be there tonight." Nilsson looked her in the eye. "He said if you were reluctant to come, I should mention the name *Rita*."

Maddie stared. She dusted off her hands and called to Roddy, "You hold the fort here for a few minutes, eh? I'll be back quick as I can."

****

"You look familiar." Gilbert scrutinized the men who sat facing him in the gloomy tavern, focusing on the one on the left. A light went on in his brain. "You work for the Freighters."

The two of them exchanged looks before the one on the left spoke. "Indeed, Mr. Gilbert, we do. My name is Ronald Lemon, and I'm the manager for the Freighters. This is my head scout, Jean LaPlatte."

Alarm bells sounded once more in Gilbert's head. "What do you want with me?"

A pretty waitress put a tall ale in front of Gilbert and smiled at him. "Say, aren't you the goalie for the Boilermakers?"

"Yeah," he conceded.

She gushed, "Oh my stars, you're so good."

"Thanks." He waited till she moved off before he said, "What's this all about?"

"You may recall seeing our goalie, Marchette, carried off the ice last night."

"Sure, I recall it. Is he all right?"

"Sadly, no. Mr. Marchette will not be able to play in the next game. Or the one after that, if there's a fifth."

Gilbert took a long draught of ale. "Is he dead?"

They laughed uneasily. "Of course not. But he's not seeing things as sharp as he might. Certainly, not as sharp as you do."

Blinded? Startled, Gilbert wondered. Oh, hell. "What's that got to do with me?"

Lemon leaned across the table. "Mr. Gilbert, we want to offer you the place of goalie on the Fort Erie Freighters team."

What? "But I'm on the Boilermakers team."

Lemon gave a sly smile. "Well, that doesn't mean you have to stay there."

A light went on in Gilbert's head. "You asking me to turn coat? What do you take me for?" What about all the hard work, what about loyalty?

To be sure, though, Gilbert thought with a pang, most his loyalty had been centered on Maddie rather than the team. He'd only taken the place of goalie in the first place in order to stay close to her.

"It's not turning coat, Mr. Gilbert."

"Turning sweater, then. You want me to take off the blue and put on the red."

"It's a matter of opportunity. A lot rides on winning this series."

"Hell," Gilbert said, "it's just a game."

"That's where you're wrong. Fort Erie and Buffalo are rival cities on either side of the mighty Niagara, as well as former enemies. Back at the start of this century, we burned Buffalo to the ground."

"So? Ancient history."

"It isn't, though, is it? Sure, things are friendly and peaceful now. On the surface. There's even talk of building a bridge someday. But at the moment, this is much more than a game. It's a matter of national pride. And, Gilbert, the mayor of Fort Erie wants to win. He's authorized me to let you name your price."

"Eh?" Gilbert stared.

"We won't win with our backup goalie. And it's our considered opinion we won't win while you're in goal for the Boilermakers. Come over to our side and we'll see you set right—no more working at that stable. Hell, we could even arrange to settle property on you, if you like."

"Property?" Gilbert's eyes widened.

"In Ontario, of course."

Surely this was the devil talking. Gilbert had never met the devil before, but he had to have a slick tongue like Lemon's, and similarly avid eyes.

"It's impossible," he said. "Even if I wanted to change sides, I couldn't. I signed a paper. And it's double the bonus I took, to get out of the contract."

"Nothing's impossible, Mr. Gilbert. The Freighters will be more than happy to pay the penalty and buy you out, so long as you sign on with us for the balance of the tournament."

Jesus, Gilbert thought, and tried to consider it fairly, without emotion. He found he couldn't.

He said, "Even with me in goal, you might not win. The Boilermakers are pretty good. MacGillicuddy and Nilsson—"

Lemon spread his hands on the table. "If we make a deal for you to come play for us, we'll stick to it whether the Freighters win or lose."

"You're kidding."

"I most certainly am not, son. The Boilermakers are good, yes, but we're betting you're the difference."

Gilbert's head spun.

"But even if I considered doing such a thing"—might he consider it?—"don't I have to be from Fort Erie to qualify?"

"You need to be from Ontario, yes."

"Well then, this is all a waste of time."

La Platte leaned forward in turn. "Mr. Gilbert"—he pronounced it Jill-*bear,* just as Pa had—"we have done some research on you. Quite frankly, we have checked the histories of all members of the Boilermakers, hoping to find a loophole as to why they could not play. Some—like Mr. Nilsson—have proved hard to trace. You, however…your father was, in fact, born in Quebec."

"So? You're not asking me to play for Montreal."

"Not yet, no, though there are some fine hockey clubs in that city. Your mother, now—" LaPlatte's pale eyes met Gilbert's, and Gilbert felt a chill.

"You're not telling me you checked into her?"

"We did. A member of an Algonquin tribe centered in Ontario."

Gilbert let out his breath in a big whoosh.

"You do, in fact, qualify to play for us, Mr. Gilbert, if you so choose."

Both men sat back and looked at Gilbert triumphantly.

A thousand thoughts poured through his mind. Thoughts of his father, his mother. Of honor and integrity and the way he'd striven to live his life despite his disadvantages.

He always tried to choose honesty. Yet this was a chance to sweep the disadvantages away, not just level the field but give him a leg up.

What would Maddie think of him, though? He could just imagine the look in her bright hazel eyes, disdainful and accusing.

But Maddie had dropped him. She was in tight with pretty-boy Nilsson now.

His hurt spoke for him when he narrowed his eyes and said, “All right, gentlemen, let’s talk terms.”

Chapter Twenty-Eight

"Rita," Maddie exclaimed with equal parts relief and dismay. "What on earth are you doing here?"

The battered unit Maddie had last seen at the cafe waved both hands in distress.

"Maddie, I have been purchased!"

"What?" Maddie stared from Rita to Mr. Brewster, who stood by sucking his cigar, with Coach at his side. "By this gentleman?"

Brewster took the stogie from his mouth and gave Maddie a catbird's smile. "It seems," he said carefully, "before taking your job at the stables, you worked at a place called Trine's Laundry, under the name of Madeline MacGillicuddy."

The ground tilted beneath Maddie's feet as her world tottered. She shot a look at Nilsson, who shrugged, the gesture almost human.

"I'm Matthew MacGillicuddy," she declared. "It's my cousin, Madeline, who worked at the laundry. You're getting us confused." In the face of their stares, she added, "I mean, look at me! Surely I'm too big and strong to be a woman."

"My dear, I don't care whether you're male or female. You're a damn fine rover, and the last thing I want to do is lose you from the team, at least not before we win the tournament. And we're going to win."

"Yes, Mr. Brewster," Maddie agreed, feeling sick

to her stomach.

"With both you and Mr. Nilsson on the team," Brewster added deliberately.

"Mr. Brewster, there's no need to—to blackmail me."

"That's a nasty word, Miss MacGillicuddy."

"But accurate. Why else would you bring Rita here? Is that why you purchased her?"

"Sit down. Let's all sit down and discuss this reasonably."

Maddie slid into a seat at the table, though Rita, of course, remained standing. She looked at Brewster unhappily.

He smiled at her again. "I thought this unit, with which you apparently had a close relationship during your last employment—I am happy to hear that, by the way—would make a fine gift for you, if we win the tournament."

"Gift?"

"I understand conditions at the laundry weren't…pleasant. Her liberation means something to you, I'll wager."

"We're friends," Maddie said, glancing at Rita.

"Just like you're friends with Nilsson, here?"

"Yes. But, Mr. Brewster, you can't bargain with people's welfare."

"Oh yes, I can, if it means winning. You know there's a big bonus in it for you if we prove victorious. As an added incentive, I would like to introduce a small matter your friend from the laundry let drop to me. It seems there was some slight unpleasantness there before you left—back when you were called Madeline MacGillicuddy. That incident, in fact, prompted your departure. Further investigation tells us the owner of the laundry, a Mr. Trinedore, doesn't remember who attacked him. As yet."

Maddie turned her eyes on Rita. Just imagine—all this time she'd lived in fear of Roddy letting slip the secret that she was a woman, cross-dressing as a male. Or Nils, who had, indeed, kept his word. And here it was Rita, whom she'd trusted implicitly, who'd let the twin cats out of the bag—not only that Mattie was, in fact, *Maddie*, but that she'd been responsible for Mr. Trinedore's injuries.

Rita waved her arms in distress. "I am sorry, Maddie. He tricked me. He said he already knew. And I am not designed to lie."

Maddie surged to her feet and put her arm around the unit. "It's not your fault, Rita. I'll bet he bullied as well as tricked you. He's a terrible man."

"I am not—merely a man motivated to win."

"I don't know why you think I'd want to play for you, given this."

"Maybe for the sake of these two friends of yours, or to keep out of jail." He pretended to muse. "I wonder what would happen to your cousin then. Simple, isn't he?"

Maddie narrowed her eyes. "You leave him out of it."

"I will quite happily do so, as long as you treat Nilsson like a regular hockey player and help us win."

"He *is* a regular hockey player, so far as I'm concerned. There was no need for all this. I would have been loyal to the team." Now everything had turned ugly and she felt soured by it. "There was no need to involve poor Rita."

"I like to be sure of my ventures."

"It is hockey, sir," Nils put in. "You can never be sure of anything."

****

"Where's Gilbert? He's late." Coach glanced at Maddie. "The two of you usually come in together."

"Well, we didn't today." Truth be told, Maddie felt a little concerned about Gilbert. She hadn't laid eyes on him, not even at the stables, and it really wasn't like him to be late.

What if something had happened to him? An attack by those thugs hanging around the stables, the ones who called him names and goaded him relentlessly, or even skullduggery on the part of the Freighters…who could tell? They must know how valuable he was to the Boilermakers.

She was miffed at him, yes, because he'd failed to trust her. That didn't mean she'd stopped caring about him. She cared so much it made her breathless.

How could she live without Huritt Gilbert in her life?

Mr. Brewster told one of his flunkies, "Get down to the stables and look for him. You know where he lives? Check there too. The rest of you, out on the ice for practice."

The next three hours passed in a blur. Maddie, skating with one eye on the door, missed multiple passes and had Coach bawling at her nonstop. Turner, standing up in goal, made a piss-poor substitute for Gilbert.

By the end of practice, Maddie's heart felt weighted with worry about him. Grateful to know Rita was keeping Roddy company, for at least Mr. Brewster hadn't attempted to hold her prisoner, she changed swiftly and headed off through the dark streets to Gilbert's rooming house.

A light burned in his window, but when she pounded on his door, he didn't answer. Not until she called repeatedly, "Gilbert, it's me," did the door open.

There he stood, dark hair mussed, only half dressed in a pair of worn trousers, browned torso on display. Maddie's heart stuttered and began beating double time. Heat flushed her skin.

"There you are," she said unnecessarily. "Why weren't you at practice? Everybody's looking for you."

"I know. They came here before, looking."

He swung wide the door, inviting her in. She entered the room and memory hit her in a staggering wave.

Not a large chamber, it was dominated by the bed, and otherwise populated only by a small table and chairs, and a washstand with ewer and basin. Gilbert's hockey gear sat in a pile in one corner. His clothing hung from pegs on the wall.

An empty bottle of beer stood on the table. He had another bottle in his hand.

Maddie inspected him minutely. "Are you sick? Hurt?"

He shook his head and shut the door.

"Then, what? Gilbert, what's going on? If Brewster's men were here, why didn't they find you?"

"I didn't want them to. Kept quiet and left the light out. Pretended I wasn't home." His dark gaze moved over her, feature by feature. "You look good."

Maddie knew she looked anything but—tired and sweaty, her hair a frizzy mop around her head. But what she saw in his eyes stole the last of her breath.

Heat, desire—and something more that she couldn't name.

Well, she wanted him too. Nothing new about that. She'd wanted him from the first time she saw him. Each time they'd touched each other had only amplified that need. Now it rose up, sharp-toothed as a rabid dog.

In an effort to exert control, she pulled out a chair and sat at the table.

"So what's going on? Why avoid Brewster's henchmen and skip practice?"

He set the bottle on the table. "Maybe I'm tired of Brewster."

Maddie nodded soberly. "I think the man's a rat. He's been putting pressure on me."

"What kind of pressure?"

"He's only gone and bought Rita—my friend from the laundry—and is pretty much holding her hostage, blackmailing me."

"Why would he do something like that? He must know you're playing your best."

Maddie couldn't tell him the reason, could she? Nilsson had kept her secret. She'd promised to keep his in return. But oh, how she wanted to tell!

Lamely, she said, "I'm starting to think he's the kind of man who just wants a hold on people. There's something else, Gilbert. Rita told him about the trouble I got in at the laundry, and that I'm a female. He doesn't care. He just wants to win this tournament."

Gilbert swore and looked away from her. "Tricked her, did he? That's rotten."

"I detest him. I'd quit the team if I could."

"Really?"

"I just wish the whole thing was over. Gilbert?" When he looked at her again, she asked, "You didn't skip practice because you and I—well, because we had that disagreement, did you?"

"No."

"I can't stand us being at odds. I mean, I don't like you being so suspicious of me either, but having you avoid me is far worse. Not seeing you at the stables or practice—" She stopped and swallowed. God, what had happened to her pride? It seemed to have dissolved the minute he opened the door.

"I can't stand it either," he said.

She surged to her feet and went to stand toe to toe with him, nose to nose. They gazed into one another's eyes and heat swept over her once more.

Before she could catch the words back, she said, "Then let me stay here tonight."

Chapter Thirty

"Maddie," Gilbert said, his voice hoarse with uncertainty and desire. "I don't think you're gonna want to stay the night, not once you know—"

"Hush," Maddie said, and kissed him.

No ordinary kiss, this. It tasted of every wickedly wonderful thing they'd ever done together in the gloom of the stables or here in this room. It brought back heat, image, and sensation, and had him standing for her helplessly.

It contained all the longing he'd felt since the last time they'd been together and had it rushing upon him.

"Umm," she murmured deep in her throat, and kissed him again, her tongue lavishing the inside of his mouth with attention. "Buffalo's Best."

"Eh?"

"The beer." She laughed, a seductive sound. When Maddie laughed like that, Gilbert knew what was coming. He'd learned that much through pleasure sharp as pain.

But she wouldn't want him, if she *knew*.

Would she? He longed to ask whether she wanted Nilsson this way too, if she'd already had him, but his body screamed at him, insisting he didn't need to know. His flesh wanted what it wanted, what only Maddie could give him, hot and slow.

She pressed her body against his, wound her arms

around his neck, and kissed him yet again, the act a blatant promise of things to come. He could smell her sweat from practice—her Maddie smell—and feel her small breasts through her shirt. His hands came up without his permission and cupped them, thumbs on her nipples.

"Oh God, Gilbert. Oh God, oh God, I need—"

"What? Tell me what." All sanity had left him, departing like an airship across the lake. He whispered into her ear, "I'll do anything."

"Will you?"

"Try me." He should tell her first, tell her what he'd gone and done. But—

"I don't know where to start. Yes, I do. I've been starving for the taste of you." She sank to her knees, had him free of his trousers before he could blink, her fingers working the buttons with preternatural speed. Bliss ensued, the pleasure so intense the room went bright, then dark, then red. He caressed her hair and wondered how he'd existed even one day without her.

That searing experience proved to be the beginning rather than the end of the night's activities. Afterward, they went to bed, where Gilbert licked Maddie up one side and down the other before indulging his own desire, while she came apart on his tongue. Still they craved one another and, seeking satisfaction, they mated throughout the night, until they fell asleep at last, near dawn.

Gilbert woke to find Maddie draped across him, her hair tickling his nose. His head hurt. His whole body hurt, in a good way. But nothing approached the torment gripping his mind.

He loved this woman. He wanted and needed her.

What would she do when she found out he'd switched sides?

She slept deeply, cheek against his chest, breath skittering across his bruises. Would this be the last time he ever held her? Yes, because once she found out he'd gone over to the Freighters, she'd wash her hands of him.

Well, but he could try to explain about the money for a farm, and all the horses that would be booted from the stables once the mechanicals arrived in force. About the better life he wanted for himself, for her and Roddy. But it had all got so tangled up now. Because she was going to turn on him, fiery woman that she was, and he still didn't know if she had feelings for Nilsson.

Damned pretty boy.

And, by God, that reminded him: he was going to have to stop Nilsson's monster shots, in net.

Tonight.

He'd signed on with the Freighters for the money, yes, but mainly out of pique, the belief that Maddie didn't care for him anymore. But didn't last night prove she did care?

No, because as he'd reminded himself over and over again, desire wasn't love.

He caressed her cheek with his finger, traced her bottom lip and her breast. Her eyes fluttered open; she smiled at him.

His world rocked.

"Morning," she said. "How do you feel?"

A good question. He felt like hell. He loved her; he hated himself.

Not waiting for an answer, she asked, "You ready?"

Ready? Did she want to do it all again? His mind reeled. Could he? Hell, yes.

But before he could reply to that, she went on, "Ready for the game, I mean. Tell me we're going to win."

"Ah, that."

"Of course, that. How can you think of anything else? We're up two games to one. We can take it tonight."

Right. He truly would have to be a brick wall. "Maddie, listen—"

She scrambled up, naked as the day she was born. He watched helplessly while she donned her shirt, leaving it unbuttoned, and sat back down on the edge of the bed.

"Let's meet up at the stables at four o'clock and go to the rink together. I admit I'm feeling nervous—nervous but confident. I'm going to need your moral support."

"There's something you need to know."

"What?"

Gilbert pushed himself up in the bed. "I won't be playing for the Boilermakers tonight."

Maddie's mouth fell open. With the morning light in her eyes, at that moment, she looked so pretty he could barely stand it.

"You're skipping the game tonight? Why?"

"Not skipping the game. I'm not playing for the Boilermakers anymore."

Her eyes narrowed. "What? You quit?"

"I quit the Boilermakers. I'm playing for the Freighters, instead."

"Say that again!"

"I'm gonna be in net for the Freighters tonight. Brewster doesn't know. You're the first one I've told."

She sprang to her feet and stared at him with a look he'd never before seen in her eyes. "Traitor." She whispered the word before she roared, "Traitor! And you didn't think to tell me that before I banged you silly all night?"

"I should have. I wanted to. I—"

"God damn it, Gilbert! Why? *Why?*"

He might have cited the money, or the care of the horses. Instead he said, "I didn't think you wanted me anymore. I thought—"

"Is this still about Nilsson? You stupid ass!"

"I've seen the way he looks at you. The way you cozy up together."

She stamped her foot. "Could you be any more of an idiot? You have no idea how wrong you are." She came forward onto the bed and glared into his eyes. "I love you, you bloody fool!"

"I love you, too. More than I can ever say."

"Well! And now look what you've done. You'll just have to switch sides again."

"I don't think I can."

"Of course you can. Just come back to the Boilermakers."

Gilbert shook his head. "They know where my mother is—on native lands in Northern Ontario. She's sick. They say they'll help her if I win." His face creased in a frown. "It was the final argument that turned my mind."

"Oh, Gilbert! What are we going to do?"

"Well, I could be wrong, but I think we'll just have to let the best team win."

Chapter Twenty-Nine

"All I have to do is stand here, right?" Turner, the Boilermakers' backup goalie, looked terrified. And with good reason, Maddie thought. Ron Lemon had sent word earlier that Gilbert had defected to the Freighters, and Brewster had shared the bad news with everyone right before pitching a fit in the changing room.

"I'll kill him," Brewster repeated three or four times, seething. "I'll hand him his head on a plate. How can he play for the God-damned Freighters? He's from Buffalo, isn't he?"

"Raised here, Mr. Brewster," said one of his scouts, "but apparently his mother's from Ontario."

"It's a loophole," said a second henchman regretfully.

"I don't want to hear about any damned loopholes! He's turned his coat and I wouldn't have him back now if he begged."

"But Mr. Brewster…" Coach edged up. "That leaves us with Turner."

"Oh God." Brewster blanched. "I'll have Lemon's guts for this. The mayor of Fort Erie's guts. Gilbert's guts!"

He glanced around at the other team members, all of whom, with the exception of Maddie, looked stunned. "I want you to show no mercy tonight, understand? Rush the net, fire every hard shot you can at him."

Maddie gulped. "But, Mr. Brewster, sir, Gilbert could be killed."

"Good. At least that will get him out of net."

****

Turner looked too petrified to move. Then again, he rarely moved in net anyway. Gilbert, in the Freighters' goal, went through his paces and limbered up, not making eye contact with any of his former team mates, most of whom made a point of skating past him to deliver ugly stares, or with the people in the stands.

Word had got out well before the start of the game that Gilbert had defected to the Freighters. Boilermaker supporters shouted insults at him and threw things until the referees moved to eject the offenders.

No one wanted to miss this game despite—or maybe because of—Gilbert's change of horses.

Could the Boilermakers win without him?

With him in net, could the Freighters lose?

Murphy skated by and glared at Gilbert as he might at a rabid cur. Rogers made a point of ignoring him, and Shandy swooped in and warned him, darkly, he'd better watch out. Culligan, next, called him a bloody turncoat, just as Maddie had, and said he'd take his head off if he got the chance.

Well, what had Gilbert expected?

Nilsson swooped by next, gave Gilbert his glowing smile and wished him luck.

Maddie skated in soon after, scowling. "Be careful. They're planning to take your head off."

"I know. Culligan told me."

"Mr. Brewster's given orders to hit you hard. One of Nilsson's shots could kill you."

"I appreciate the warning."

She scowled harder. "Might be better just to let us win. That way it will all be over."

He eyed her. "I don't think that's gonna happen."

"No?"

"Uh-uh."

"All right, then. Game's on." She edged closer. "I love you."

With that, she skated away at full speed, backward.

My life has become damned strange, Gilbert thought. Then the game started and he had no time to think at all.

He discovered right away that playing in front of the Freighters' goal had few similarities to standing ground for the Boilermakers. The Freighters had always been straightforward shooters, more concerned with putting their opponents in the boards than intimidating their goalie.

The Boilermakers now came at Gilbert with everything they had, skill, strength, and guile in equal measures. He endured twenty-two shots in the first half alone.

And stopped them all.

Maybe because of the night's passion with Maddie, maybe in spite of it, he discovered he was in top form. At the end of the half, his new team mates came and congratulated him.

The Boilermaker fans resumed throwing things, including a wide assortment of tools flung by the union members. Fortunately, they had poor aim.

"You all right?" Maddie skated by.

"Sure. Why?"

"Look out in the second half. Coach has given

everybody orders to take you out—you're playing far too well."

****

"MacGillicuddy! A word, if you don't mind."

"What is it, Nils?"

Nilsson appeared troubled, or as much so as an automaton could. He lowered his voice and leaned toward Maddie's ear.

"Excuse me if I'm wrong, but you are in love with Gilbert, yes?"

Maddie stared, and heat crawled up her body. "What do you know about—"

"Love? I have been well-instructed in all human emotions." He muted his tone to a whisper. "It makes me more convincing."

"You're convincing, all right," Maddie told him, thinking of how jealous Gilbert was.

"So I understand about love. I could tell at once you have affectionate feelings for Gilbert."

"Well, so?" Maddie returned nervously.

"Coach has told me to take him out, the sooner the better. He wants him removed from goal whatever it takes, and the Freighters' backup goalie in."

Maddie looked into the automaton's blue eyes. "You won't do it, will you?"

"I admit, I am conflicted. I like Gilbert and would not wish to injure him badly enough that he was unable to continue play. Even more, I like you and consider you my friend. I would not wish to cause you distress."

"If you do to Gilbert what you did to the Freighters' goalie—that would cause me great distress."

"Because you love him."

"Yes. I love him."

"At the same time, Coach has given me instructions, and I was created to follow instructions."

"Were you, though?" Maddie challenged him. "I thought you were created by the hybrids."

"I was."

"And they're reaching to create more than just," Maddie whispered the word, "*machinery.* They want you to develop and grow, don't they? To possess traits of your own, like compassion. To be a genuine Swedish hockey player."

"I am Swedish hockey player," Nils repeated, almost by rote. He hesitated. "Does a Swedish hockey player have compassion?"

"I'm sure some must. You do, or you wouldn't come to me now, out of concern for Gilbert—and me. You'd just aim your best shot at his head."

"*Ja,* I do not doubt you are right. Very well, since you are my buddy, and I do not wish to cause my buddy distress, I will refrain from pulverizing Gilbert. But you must warn him."

"I already tried. He seems to think he can take care of himself."

"Then I will warn him, in turn. The Boilermakers must score. We must win this game."

"I know. Nils, thank you."

"For what?"

"For—for being my buddy."

He flashed his wide smile and winked. "You are most welcome."

****

"A word of warning, Former Team Mate. I have instructions to take you off the ice during this next period."

“Oh.” Gilbert stared into Nilsson’s ice-blue eyes, not sure what he saw there.

“Just so you know, I do not intend to follow those directions.”

“You don’t?”

“No.”

“Well, uh—thanks very much. I appreciate that.”

“But I will have to make it look good, which means a lot of near-misses. So beware of that. And the others are out to get you, for real.”

“All right.”

“It might help if you’d let in a goal.”

“That’s not going to happen. I’m grateful for the warning and all that, but I’m not letting in any goals if I can help it.”

“You are certain of that, are you?”

“I’m certain. The Freighters are winning this one.”

Nilsson skated away, without another word.

The first killer shot came straight off Rogers’ stick, aimed not for the space behind Gilbert, but at his head. The fact that it hit the post instead might have saved Gilbert’s life. Rogers delivered the shot with a glare and a curse, and Murphy barreled in.

After that it became all pot shots at the goalie, every time the Boilermakers got near Gilbert’s net. By a miracle, none of them got past him, mostly because he stopped them with his body. Nilsson peppered him with shots—to the arms, to the chest, to the shoulders—some of them accompanied by a wink.

Near the end of the half, which felt like an artillery drill, the Freighters scored on Turner. One-nothing and time was running out.

“You fellas have to step it up and score more

goals!" The Freighters' coach, LaPlatte, bawled at them during a time out. "That one's not gonna hold up. Why can't you score on their goalie? The man's a block of wood. He just stands there. Meanwhile, Gilbert is taking a beating. Can't you keep them players off him?"

"When we hit them, we get warnings. You told us not to take dumb penalties, Coach."

"We don't want to give them extra chances to score, no. But keep 'em off Gilbert, understand?"

"Nobody can knock down that big Swede, Coach. And nobody can hit that MacGillicuddy. He just slips out o' the way."

"I don't want to hear excuses. Get out there and keep that lead. We lose tonight, there's gonna be hell to pay. And Gilbert…" LaPlatte leveled his gaze at Gilbert. "You've been grand, just grand. Keep it up."

He would, if he could.

Chapter Thirty-One

"I can't believe it. I can't believe they won," Coach moaned the words as the Boilermakers sat in their changing room, dejected. From the rink, they could still hear the various supporters jeering and stamping with disapproval and exultation, respectively.

"I can, Coach," Rogers lamented, "with Gilbert in goal for them." He swiveled around to glare at Brewster. "Mr. Brewster, couldn't you have kept him from leaving? Offered him more money or something?"

"I never had the chance. I didn't know he meant to leave till it happened."

"Offer him more now."

"Damned if I will. We're gonna win without him. We'll show that turncoat, and Lemon, and the mayor of Fort Erie too."

The Boilermakers looked at each other.

Brewster turned on Nilsson. "And you—I thought I told you to take him out."

"I tried, Mr. Brewster. He is very nimble."

"So he is, damn him."

Behind Brewster's back, Nilsson winked at Maddie.

"We need to win the next game," Brewster declared. "You men have the skills to do it. Those Freighters are heavy-handed clods. You gonna let 'em beat you?"

"No, boss!" they all hollered. Far too much rode on it.

****

"Who is he?" demanded Mr. Stanley, pointing at the large, burly man who stood at the entrance to his stable.

"He's my bodyguard," Gilbert replied sheepishly, continuing to shovel manure.

Mr. Stanley gaped. "Why do you need a bodyguard?"

"Lot of people out to get me, Mr. Stanley. Because of the hockey tournament. It's stirred up quite a bit of bad feeling."

"So you're telling me I have to put up with this?" Stanley gestured at the guard impatiently.

"Just till tomorrow night, sir. Then the tournament will be over, one way or the other. Series is tied up now, two games to two. My boss wants to keep me alive till then."

"I thought I was your boss."

"You are, sir." Gilbert answered uncomfortably. This was why he longed so desperately for independence, a farm where he might be his own master.

"I've been more than patient. I've let you off early for practice—even let that halfwit boy who's cousin to your teammate hang around here."

Gilbert glared at him.

"Speaking of which, you'll have to get Jessop out of here today."

"I'm sorry?"

"The old horse—out. I've been more than generous about that, also."

"But I've been paying for his feed."

"I need the space, Gilbert. I've just received word our second mechanical horse will be delivered tomorrow. So get him out today, right? Or I will."

Stanley hurried off. Gilbert glanced at the bodyguard who stood like a rock, set his shovel aside, and went to Jessop's stall.

The old horse raised his head from the feedbox with a snort and looked at Gilbert with trusting eyes. Gilbert fondled his mane and crooned, "All right, old fellow, we're for it now—you, and me with you. I've got to find somewhere to shift you in the next few hours, before practice."

Damned mechanical horses, he thought. But the truth was, he'd grown to like Piper and didn't mind the prospect of another coming in, except for the effect on Jessop. Less manure, more coal, that was all.

He rubbed the old horse down, giving special attention to the tender places where the harness rode so many years. Then he went out and called to the bodyguard.

"Hey, Alouette, I have an errand to run, just as soon as I find someone to cover for me here. Do you want to come with me?"

"I'm supposed to go everywhere with you. Where are we goin'?"

"To find a stable for a horse."

"This is a stable for a horse."

"Yeah. Another one."

****

Maddie looked up from her sweeping and eyed the two figures standing in front of her. Who would have thought Rita and Roddy would hit it off so well? In the space of a day, they'd bonded and, in fact, become virtually inseparable.

They did make an odd-looking couple, though, the tall, gangly, redheaded lad with the earnest expression and the battered steam unit with the chronically worn finish.

Yet they stood united in purpose. As if to prove it, Roddy threw an arm around Rita's upper torso.

"Say yes, Maddie," he wheedled. "Please."

"I don't think it's a good idea, Roddy," Maddie responded. "The last thing I need is you getting in trouble again."

"How can I get in trouble? It's just a practice. If I say I'm your cousin, they'll let me in."

"You don't understand, Roddy. Emotions are high and feelings are all ramped up. If other supporters show up, anything could happen." She switched her gaze to the unit. "Rita, I thought I asked you to look after him."

"Forgive me, Maddie, but I am looking after him. I will not let him attend this event unaccompanied. And if I may say…" Rita hesitated, which seemed uncharacteristic of her.

"Say what you wish. We're friends."

"I believe Roddy should be allowed to make his own decisions. He is a young man and craves his independence. I understand this because I too crave my independence."

Maddie stared.

"It is a fair and honorable impulse," Rita stated, "taking one's destiny into one's own hands."

Roddy grinned. "We attended a meeting of the Automaton Liberation League this morning," he confided. "It was…inspiring. There was this police officer—"

"Patrick Kelly," Rita supplied.

"Patrick Kelly, that's the fellow. He said if we don't take chances, we'll never know who we can be." Roddy lowered his voice farther. "Just look at the chance you took, Maddie, playing hockey, and how that's turned out."

"Yes, well," Maddie said rather weakly, "I guess it's all right, if they let you in." Better they should come to practice, she thought, than tomorrow night's game, where things might get rough, indeed.

****

"You're late, Gilbert," LaPlatte snapped when Gilbert reached the open ice, where the Freighters drilled. "We need all the practice time we can get. And don't you know things can't start till you're in net?"

"Sorry, Coach. Had to see a man about a horse." He and the bodyguard, Alouette, grinned at each other. During the course of the day, he'd discovered Alouette spoke very little English. Of course, Gilbert spoke fluent French, so they were able to get along.

And today had been something of a bonding experience. They'd met a man…oh, what a man they'd met!

Jamie Kilter ran the Buffalo Anti-Cruelty League and had a shelter for animals down on Niagara Street, most of them formerly abused in one way or another. A big man, and one Gilbert would not want to face in a fight, Kilter had a face half-disfigured by burns. He also had a son and a very pretty—and very pregnant—wife.

He'd agreed to keep Jessop temporarily till Gilbert found some suitable property. Not for long, he warned. Kilter didn't have the room, and the space he did have would be needed for cases off the street.

Gilbert and Alouette had led Jessop there at snail's pace, all the old horse could now manage, and wound up having to fight their way back again, when thugs better known as Boilermaker fans beset them.

At least Jessop was safe.

LaPlatte's eyes narrowed. "There is blood on your face." He unleashed a spate of rapid-fire French at Alouette, adding for Gilbert's benefit, "Have you been scrapping? Isn't the beating you take in net enough?"

"We ran into a bit of trouble," Gilbert admitted, with another grin for his bodyguard. "Met up with a crowd of Boilermaker supporters on our way back here."

"*Oui*," Alouette agreed.

"I think they were members of that union. They had a bunch of tools with them." And they'd been eager to use them for a new purpose. Not happy with Gilbert for turning coat, they'd decided pipe wrenches made fine weapons for taking off a traitor's head. Seemed he might be destined to have his head removed, either on or off the ice.

To make matters worse, he hadn't had so much as a glimpse of Maddie all day. Dared he hope she might be at his room when he got there? Waiting for him. Hungry for him.

"Jill-*bear*, are you paying attention?"

"Sure am, Coach."

LaPlatte launched into a lengthy speech about tomorrow's game, how there could be only one possible outcome. They had to win. He praised Gilbert and berated the rest of the team for their perceived shortcomings.

"This has become a skills game," he declared in his thickly accented English. "Brute force will no longer do. These Boilermakers have raised the level of play. You may try and hurt them—smash them off the boards, *oui*. A healthy dose of cross checking. *Mais*, you cannot take any penalties!"

The team—good fellows all, as Gilbert had quickly learned, but not the swiftest of thinkers—exchanged bewildered glances. Even they recognized this as an impossible mission.

"But Coach," said the brawny center, Billington, "nobody can check that big blond brute—Nilsson. I've thrown some huge hits on him. He just wobbles a little and keeps going."

"Yeah, he's a little spooky," agreed another of the Freighters' forwards, Steward.

"That's because he's Swedish," somebody else contributed.

"Forget Nilsson. You are not going to take him out. Concentrate on the others. Rogers, and that damn MacGillicuddy." LaPlatte glanced at Gilbert. "Jill-*bear*, surely you know their weaknesses and can tell us."

Everyone looked at Gilbert.

"Um," he said. He didn't want Maddie taken out. He certainly didn't want her hurt. He wanted her in his bed, all hot and ready for him. He wanted to get down on his knees and ask her to marry him, do it right and proper. He wanted all this to be over, so much it made him ache.

"Don't think you'll get MacGillicuddy," he said. "He's too quick. Better go after Rogers, instead."

God forgive him.

Chapter Thirty-Two

"What are *they* doing here?" Brewster demanded.

He and most of the team peered out through the doorway that led from the changing room, as supporters flooded into the rink. Blue Boilermaker sweaters and red Freighters garb abounded. People pushed and shoved and swore at each other, and the game hadn't even started yet.

Maddie had come to the doorway hoping for a glimpse of Gilbert. She hadn't seen him since early this morning at the stables, when he'd told her he had found a temporary berth for his old horse and introduced her to his bodyguard.

The presence of the bodyguard had cut into any possibility for what Maddie truly craved. But they'd managed a few scorching moments in the rear of Piper's box when the big Frenchman turned his eyes away. Not half of what Maddie needed but better than nothing.

Especially when Gilbert whispered, "Good luck tonight."

"You too."

Now, Maddie felt…but she had no words to describe how she felt. Terrified, her heart going like a steam-powered hammer. Desperate. Hot and cold by turns. Devastated and hopeful. They needed to win. Could they?

She focused on the group Brewster had indicated. They stood in a knot, big men with a couple of mechanical dogs. The steam-powered dogs had become all the rage—they came in many shapes and sizes. These were big and sleek, hip-high on the strapping men.

"Who are they?" she asked. And why shouldn't they be here? It seemed everybody else was.

She'd never seen the rink so crowded or heard it this noisy, even during the previous games. There wouldn't be enough seats; already people fought over them.

If they all got through this alive, it would be a miracle.

Brewster shot her a look. "Those are the hybrids, MacGillicuddy. Mostly cops, members of the famed Irish Squad. See that big guy on the left, with the tallest dog? That's Pat Kelly. You must have heard of him."

Pat Kelly—hadn't Roddy mentioned him? And he looked familiar. He also looked human, as did his companions. Yes, now she remembered—she'd seen him at the police station.

Nilsson pressed against her back and peered around her head. She could feel the heat of him.

"Perhaps," he suggested, "they are here to see me play."

Brewster snapped, "Why should you say that?"

Nilsson's gaze met Maddie's for an instant, and she knew the truth. These were the automatons who had manufactured him, just like the dogs and the mechanical horses. Being here was their equivalent of proud parents coming to watch a child play.

"Maybe they've got a bet riding," Culligan

suggested. "Do hybrids bet? Christ, but they look real, don't they?"

"I hear," Rogers drawled, "the ones they're turning out now are even more impressive. The next generation of automaton, so to speak."

"*Ja*," Nilsson chimed in. "You would never tell one of those new models from a human."

"Them being cops," Murphy suggested, "maybe they'll keep anyone from killing us. O' course," he reflected, "them being Irishmen, they might help the others kill us. It's all too confusin', ain't it?"

Culligan agreed, "I told my girl if I come home tonight, it'll be a sheer blessed event arranged by all the saints."

"You've got to win first," Brewster bellowed. He glared at Maddie again. "Now get out there. You know what's at stake."

She did.

Her knees trembled beneath her as she took the ice. Freighters supporters immediately started throwing things, mostly bottles from some brew they'd brought with them over the river. Culligan had told them he'd tried it and it tasted like piss.

Barely noticing the rain of deadly missiles, Maddie tried to calm her racing heart and think about the game. Mistakes—there was no room for them. No place for shaky hands or fumbled shots. The Boilermakers had to win.

And that meant she had to beat Gilbert. The man she loved more than her own life.

What would come after the game, win or lose—because there would be an after—she couldn't even begin to guess.

She caught sight of Gilbert then, moving into his goal at the far end of the ice. The members of the Boilermakers' union immediately began throwing tools—a wrench, neatly tossed, barely missed his dark head. Young boys, hired for just that purpose, skated by collecting the tools and the bottles.

With her legs suddenly feeling steadier, Maddie skated up the ice.

The Freighters' defensemen looked at her dubiously as she swooped in. The game hadn't started yet—they couldn't properly check her—but she knew that would happen soon enough. Her body was already one big bruise. She could only imagine how Gilbert's chest must look.

"Hello." She angled to a stop in front of his net, with a spray of frost. "You all right?"

He nodded, his dark eyes grave and steady. "You?"

"A little nervous. I'll settle once it starts. They're planning to come at you again."

"They're planning on going after you, too."

She wanted to tell him then how none of that mattered. All that meant anything was the look in his eyes and the love in her heart. She wanted to spend the rest of her life with this man, the ups and downs, whatever the years brought. She could imagine no finer fate.

Yet the outcome of this game might change everything, including how he felt about her.

Not how she felt about him. Never that.

"Well, good luck," she said lamely, and skated back down the ice.

His voice floated after her. "Luck."

****

Gilbert blinked the sweat out of his eyes and tried to ignore the pain in his shoulder, which had just stopped one of Nilsson's best shots. Every member of the Boilermakers had already made a run at him, and the look in their eyes was enough to make his hair stand on end.

So far he'd managed to keep the puck out of his net, and the Freighters had put two past Turner, who stood like a walleyed post at the far end. The first half was almost over—*almost*.

The rink boiled with emotions like a teakettle set to bubble over, the shouts, screams, threats, and imprecations rising into the sky. Daylight swiftly died in the west; the big lights had been switched on, and the steam plant throbbed like a giant heart. Just like an overheated boiler, the place felt primed to explode.

He had to endure only a few more minutes, then get through thirty more after that, before life either ended or began.

At that thought he saw the play moving up the ice toward him at a tremendous rate. His defensemen moved out, but the Boilermakers—specifically Murphy, with Rogers and Maddie in tow—were much too quick for them. The story of this game so far, Gilbert thought.

The Freighters' rover, Brandt, put a check on Rogers, who had the puck. It squirted away from him and Murphy picked it up. Gilbert had a terrible glimpse of Murphy coming at him, face contorted in a snarl before the impact came, the big center hitting him feet first and falling, shoving Gilbert back into his net with such force the apparatus leaped into the air before landing in a skid.

Gilbert's head hit the ice; the bright lights above

him wavered and blinked. The last thing he heard was the throb of the steam plant, stuttering in his ears.

Where was the puck?

The lights abruptly went out.

"Gilbert? Gilbert!"

Maddie's voice seemed like a thread, a filament of light that tugged at his senses, ahead of a rush of sound that crashed over him just the way Murphy had.

The noise, a physical assault, made him want to cover his ears. But he wasn't sure he could move. Above where he lay on the ice, people shouted and argued, their voices tangled with the cries from the stands.

"It was in!"

"That was goalie interference, you dumb ass!"

And the perennial, if belated question, "Is he alive?" Yes, that was Maddie.

And someone else, "Who cares? Get him out of the way. The Freighters will have to put in their backup."

Well, thought Gilbert, still lying there, that wouldn't be good. Conroy was almost as bad as Turner. In fact, if Conroy had been a decent backup goalie, Gilbert wouldn't be in this predicament.

He blinked at the glaring lights. "I'm all right."

No one heard him. They continued to dispute whether the goal counted and whether a penalty should be called. Twelve figures or more swam above him, along with a bright spot that must be Maddie's face.

He heaved himself to his feet. The Freighters' supporters in the stands roared with approval. The members of the Boilermakers' union tossed wrenches with bad intent.

At least, Gilbert reflected, these were smaller

wrenches—they'd tossed all their heavy ones earlier on.

He looked behind him and saw both the puck and blood on the ice, within the arms of the net. But the net had been dislodged, mainly by Gilbert's head.

Would that kind of goal count?

Murphy thought it should. His shouting match with Brandt exploded and punches were thrown. Both of them crashed into Gilbert and he went down again.

Someone pushed into the netting beside him. Maddie? But no. He found himself gazing into the ice-blue eyes of Nilsson, now full of compassion. The big forward helped Gilbert up with strong hands.

"All right, buddy?"

"Sure. I've got a hard head."

"That is good."

Gilbert reflected on it. "Am I still your buddy?"

Nilsson flashed his wide smile. "For sure."

"What's happening?"

"The refs are calling the goal."

"What!"

"They are also calling a penalty."

"That doesn't make sense."

"I agree, buddy, but I suspect they wish to survive when they leave here tonight."

"Oh." Gilbert hadn't thought about the refs. But they all needed to survive.

Suddenly, LaPlatte was in front of Gilbert, screaming in his face, "You good to play?"

"Sure, Coach."

"All right, then. Wait till they position the net and clear away all the tools."

This, Gilbert reflected, had to be the strangest night of his life—and only half the game done.

Chapter Thirty-Three

"Drop the feckin' puck!" The cry came from high up in the stands and sounded distinctly Irish. Maddie, hovering at center ice, wondered if that was one of the hybrid automatons. Surely they couldn't become so involved they'd shout out, could they?

She didn't know; she no longer knew what day of the week it was or how long this game had been going on. It felt like years, yet here they were, still only part way through the second half.

The score now stood at two-one, Freighters. Billington had scored on Turner again late in the first half, which had turned into a mad free-for-all. Maddie had been checked every time she so much as thought of touching the puck, and smashed into the boards repeatedly. In fact, all the Boilermakers had taken a beating.

All except Nilsson, whom no one succeeded in knocking off his skates. Oh, he'd been hit—he'd even been cross checked and shoved into the boards, but he skated on.

God, but he was strong. Superhumanly so, one might say…

The rest of the Boilermakers showed the effects of the battering. Rogers had blood, still only half dried, all down one side of his face. Murphy, who'd taken a shoulder to the face, had one eye swollen nearly shut.

She, Maddie, hurt from head to toe and suspected only the heat of battle kept her moving. Even Turner, who did little more than move from side to side in the net and let the puck bounce off him, had a bruise on his face the color of a plum.

They had to score real soon, even things up, and then go ahead. Because down at the other end of the ice, Gilbert had been magnificent. There was, simply, no other word for his play.

"Drop the puck!"

It dropped. Rogers won the draw and flipped the puck to Nilsson, who started up the ice. Maddie started too, as if drawn by ropes. Shandy skated part way up, and Culligan stayed back to guard Turner, like the faithful collie dog he somewhat resembled.

Nilsson found his position in front of the Freighters' net and set his shoulders for a shot. Gilbert went into a crouch. But instead of shooting, Nilsson flipped the puck to Maddie. Finding it suddenly on her stick, and the Freighters' defensemen bearing down on her, her mind blanked.

Except for one single thought: God, don't let me get checked again.

She shot the puck wildly, mostly in an effort to get rid of it before the hit came. Nilsson, turning circles in front of the Freighters' net, corralled it and caught Gilbert for once unprepared. Nilsson chipped the puck up high. It cleared Gilbert's shoulder by a scant half inch.

Goal!

The rink erupted with deafening shouts and the pounding of feet, both human and mechanical. The ground rocked as the thumping joined with that of the steam plant. Maddie imagined that, beneath its shore ice, the river rippled.

Tied, two-two.

Was Gilbert all right?

The two thoughts, fully synchronized, flooded her mind even as Nilsson made another of his graceful turns, this time with his stick in the air.

She glanced at the Freighters' net and saw Gilbert's dark eyes burning. All hell would break loose now. They had less than ten minutes left to win or lose the game.

One of them would have to lose. Her stomach flopped over at the thought. As she had before, she wondered what would come after that.

If the Boilermakers lost, would Mr. Brewster, wanting revenge, send poor Rita to the scrap yard? If the Boilermakers won, would Gilbert ever forgive her? He wasn't a prideful man, but could he be with a woman who'd dusted him at the most vulnerable moment of his life?

Play resumed. The Freighters upped the ante, determined to score in turn, playing the kind of hockey that had got them where they were.

Hit. Bash. Pulverize.

Every time anyone looked at the puck, a Freighter took him out. As a consequence, they took some warnings—not as many as they should—and the Boilermakers had plenty of scoring opportunities.

But for the next ten minutes, Gilbert, a determined expression etched into his face, proved bulletproof. He leaped. He reached. He pirouetted in the goal. He sustained a hit to the side of the head that should have taken him out.

Not a puck got past him.

The crowd howled—approval for Gilbert from the Freighters' supporters, cries of protest from those backing the Boilermakers. A rumbling roar seemed to be coming from the automatons. With three minutes left on the clock, Coach called a time out. The Boilermakers gathered beside their bench.

Coach looked like a madman. Heavy face flushed, hair all standing on end, and eyes bulging from his head, he glared at each of them in turn.

"Can't somebody take that bastard out?"

"You mean Gilbert, Coach?"

"Of course I mean God-damn Gilbert. He's the only thing standing between us and a win. Don't you want the glory? The fame? Don't you want all that money in your pockets?"

"It's not about the money now," said Rogers, surprisingly. In Maddie's estimation, it had always been about the money for Rogers. "It's about proving we're the best."

He looked momentarily confused, a baffled look coming over his sweat-streaked face. "Only, *he's* the best. Best damn goalie I've ever seen."

Coach grunted before glaring at Nilsson. "Can't you take him out? Would you rather be shut down?"

Nilsson flinched. The others stared. No one but Maddie understood the threat Coach made—but she did understand it, and wondered at the uneasiness that flooded Nilsson's eyes.

Then, incredibly, Nilsson drew himself up. He leaned toward Coach and said, "That would not be fair. I have earned my place on this team. And there are a hundred supporters in the stands who would not take kindly to me being *ousted*."

Now Coach flinched. "Just take Gilbert out."

"That would not be fair either. Gilbert has also earned his place. Despite the Freighters' method of play, this is a game of skill."

"I don't want to hear your philosophy, you damned pretty boy. Get out there and win this game. Life ain't fair, d'you hear me? Neither is hockey."

"Well, I have to say," Nilsson gave his considered opinion, "it should be."

****

The next three minutes lasted an eternity. How, Gilbert wondered as he flung the damp hair out of his eyes and gripped his stick with fingers gone numb, could time be so flexible? It dragged during an afternoon shoveling manure. It flew on a rush of heat when he had Maddie in his arms.

Upon that thought he saw them coming at him again. The Freighters' defenseman, Steward, stood in front of Gilbert's net, but the Boilermakers approached in a phalanx of three—no, four, for there came Maddie on the side. Nilsson, in the lead, had the puck on his stick.

Neider, the Freighters' other defenseman, delivered a check that barely rocked the big Swede. Nilsson came on, his fair hair streaming.

Why didn't the man sweat?

That odd question flashed through Gilbert's mind before Nilsson made his shot. The puck crashed into Gilbert's knee with a force that made nothing of the thin pad. Pain engulfed him.

Ah—he was crippled. Crippled!

He wanted to fall on the ice, wrap both arms

around his leg and howl. Instead he attempted to corral the puck, which jiggled around between his pads.

It squirted away and Nilsson picked it up again. The Boilermakers began passing the puck.

A separate game within the game, as Gilbert knew it to be. He'd seen it practiced dozens of times when he was still part of the team. They set up in an elongated formation and shot the puck back and forth among themselves. Rogers. Murphy. Nilsson. Maddie. Nilsson again. They wanted to distract him, Gilbert, confuse him, keep him wondering which of them would actually shoot. They wanted to make him blink. Then one of them—probably Nilsson—would shoot the puck in.

Probably Nilsson. But he couldn't be sure. Whatever he did, he couldn't blink.

Rogers got possession of the puck. He was a sneaky devil and could shoot it in at an acute angle if he chose. But Brandt delivered a hit on him and the puck shot away toward center ice, where Billington recovered it and moved away toward the Boilermakers' goal.

Gilbert could breathe again.

No, he couldn't. A minute and a half left.

And here they came once more.

Chapter Thirty-Four

"Shoot the puck!"

The cry now came from everywhere in the stands. Boilermaker supporters were seated in among Freighter supporters—numerous fistfights had broken out and the miscreants had been hauled away by members of the Irish Squad. Others, apparently waiting outside the rink, filed in to take their places.

Maddie observed all this with only half her attention. But she heard everything. The supporters stamped their feet in time with the demand, in time with the clock counting down.

She needed to shoot the puck.

It felt as if her mind and will had become one with those voices. As if their desire to score fueled her own.

If she or one of her teammates didn't score in the next minute, the game would go into overtime. And she didn't think she could survive overtime.

Drenched in sweat, breath rasping in her lungs and legs quaking beneath her, she skated backward up the ice, running interference for Nilsson behind her, who had the puck. She interposed her body between the Swede and Steward, the Freighters' brutal defenseman, took a piece of the hit intended for Nilsson, and fell onto the ice.

For an instant she lay like a turtle on its back, eyes blinded by the glaring lights above.

"Shoot the puck!"

Willpower got her up. The Freighters' rover, Brandt, had gained possession of the small, black disc that had apparently achieved supreme importance, and moved toward Turner with it.

No.

Throughout the game, the Boilermakers had survived by keeping the Freighters' forwards away from Turner, who continued to stand in the net like a steer at the slaughterhouse. Aching or not, exhausted or not, Maddie had to get in Brandt's way.

Culligan got there first and delivered a hit on Brandt that unseated the puck from his stick and allowed it to spurt away.

Employing a burst of speed, Maddie picked it up.

The crowd went wild with elation and disapproval, in equal measures. Maddie started up the ice, so deafened she could hear nothing else. Close behind her came her three forwards. As she neared the Freighters' goal, they broke formation and spread out.

The Freighters' defensemen sailed toward her in what seemed like slow motion, one on either side. Murphy took the nearest out with a check that sent him into the boards. Maddie saw a no doubt momentarily clear path between herself and the goal.

In the goal stood—

The man she loved, black hair drenched with sweat and dark eyes fixed on her in a stare of pure determination.

If she won, he lost. If she lost—

A stick hooked her from behind, catching her just below the knee. She fell and hit the ice with force enough to jar every bone in her body and steal all breath. The puck shot away, and the howls from the crowd increased.

"Penalty shot! Penalty shot!"

Suddenly Nilsson was there, beside Maddie. He helped her up and patted her on the head with a big hand. Her other teammates gathered around. For an instant the lights wavered. They towed her to their bench, where Coach screamed into her face.

"Penalty shot!"

"What?"

Coach's face looked purple, an impossible color. He yelled, "You're going to get a penalty shot, MacGillicuddy. You, up against Gilbert. For the whole thing. You've got to make that goal, understand?"

****

Gilbert's heart—already overworked and the victim of gross abuse on his part—stuttered in his chest when he heard the call. Brandt had hooked Maddie from behind as she took her shot. She'd have a chance to take that shot over, one on one against him. It was a fair call, but—

Christ, how had it come to this? Him against the woman he loved.

He eyed her as she set up at center ice. Almost no time remained on the clock—if she made the shot, this would be the game.

He couldn't let her score. This win meant his future, all he wanted to achieve.

But Maddie was his future, wasn't she?

He looked at her—face streaked with sweat, hair flattened on her head, eyes fixed on his, burning. She started toward him on those fleet feet of hers, the puck dancing back and forth between strokes of her blade, and the trip seemed to take forever, and to happen in the blink of an eye.

He crouched in his net; he set himself, stick at the ready. He felt—

The touch of her hand as she slid it down his body, fingers lingering in a tender caress. The slide of her tongue against his skin as she lavished him with pleasure, coaxing him to surrender his will to her and relish the pure, raw intensity of bursting at the seams. He tasted the tangy sweetness of her and, as she zoomed toward him, gaze locked, saw the light that flared in her eyes just before she gave him everything.

She shot the puck. He could no longer hear the crowd. His ears seemed to shut down and everything fell away, as it did when they came together and she breathed in his ear.

I love you. Love—

His body jerked in reaction, shifted to one side. The puck came up, up, urged by the flick of Maddie's wrist. It climbed and rattled against Gilbert's left shoulder. He twisted.

The puck sailed into the back of the net.

Bedlam ensued. Gilbert's hearing rushed back, and it sounded like the crowd took the rink apart via mere sound. He stood there in his net staring at the woman he loved, seeing her look back at him until her team mates mobbed her, the steam horn blasted, and it was done.

Done.

Objects rained onto the ice. Gilbert, frozen there in his net, had no idea what they were—more tools, probably, and bottles, lots of bottles. A few boots and hats.

Gilbert's team mates—the Freighters—skated to

him and, one by one, bopped him in the head. A friendly gesture, under the circumstances, in answer to a staggering defeat.

And a victory? He might never know.

Chapter Thirty-Five

"It's a stunning victory for this city," Mr. Brewster declared when at last they exited the ice. "A plum in the pie, a feather in the cap for Buffalo. An honor the like of which this great metropolis may never see again!"

Surely he exaggerated, Maddie thought sourly. There would likely be other hockey games, other series, for that matter.

But, she had to admit, at the moment it didn't feel like it. At this instant in time, it felt as if this win began and ended everything.

Her team mates wouldn't stop yapping and hollering with glee. Coach looked like he might well suffer from apoplexy. Safe in the changing room, away from a crowd become outright dangerous in its exuberance, Brewster passed out bottles of Buffalo's Best and slapped them all on the back, continually crowing.

"This will teach the mayor of Fort Erie a thing or two, eh? We dusted those Canadians."

"And here," Rogers hauled Maddie's arm aloft, "is the hero of the hour! What a shot! What a goal!"

Maddie wondered why she didn't feel more elated. Everyone else certainly did. But no, wait—she knew why. She'd left the man she loved standing back there on the ice. And she'd seen the look in his eyes.

Suddenly she couldn't breathe. Why had she shot

so hard? Why hadn't she held back on the shot, or pulled it at the last second so it didn't get the full power of her wrist? Why hadn't she let him win?

If she loved him—and she did—why had she put her all into that blast and sent his hopes tumbling into oblivion?

Would he ever forgive her? Could they get past this and be together again?

There'd been doubt between them even before this happened. Now he had to face the consequences of this loss.

She'd looked back at him as they dragged her off the ice, hoping, hoping…

But he'd already left.

Where would he go tonight? Back to his room, alone? Off with the rest of the Freighters to lick his wounds? He'd fought so hard—well, they all had.

And she'd handed him his defeat.

A split second's decision, followed by reckoning. The story hadn't ended, it had merely begun heading in a new and possibly devastating direction.

But in the Boilermakers' changing room, the celebration went on. Beer flowed like water. People thumped Maddie on the back. Supporters broke in and joined them in their revels. For a while chaos reigned, until the supporters were ejected again.

Not until the newspaper reporters arrived, along with the mayor, did Maddie grasp that all this must have been carefully orchestrated.

And that it would probably go on most the night.

But no, she thought, as someone dribbled beer over her head, she needed to go look for Gilbert. She needed to find out what had happened to her life.

"Are you all right, buddy?" Suddenly Nilsson bent over her, looking concerned.

Could an automaton feel concern? She didn't know, but his perceived sympathy made tears flood her eyes.

"I beat him. Oh, what am I going to do?"

Nilsson parted his lips to answer. She felt sure he did have an answer, but just then the Irish Squad burst in and gathered around them, large, loud, and very Irish. The celebration resumed.

Things got a bit foggy after that. At one point, Maddie became aware that Mr. Brewster had his arm around her and spoke directly into her face.

"Good job, MacGillicuddy, on beating Gilbert—that turncoat!—and on keeping mum. There'll be a big reward in it, hear? Both from me and from the Boilermakers' union. And that other little matter at the laundry? Forget about it."

So she'd succeeded in protecting herself, had she? But was it worth tossing Gilbert under the steamcab? Her beer-soaked brain struggled over it and gave up. It didn't matter, now. Nothing mattered, except that she needed to find him, talk to him, and discover whether they still had a future together.

Roddy arrived then and threw himself into Maddie's arms.

"This is my cousin," he declared to anyone who would listen. "My cousin!"

Someone shook her hand. Looking up in confusion she stared into a pair of very green eyes.

Oh yes, she'd seen them—seen him before. The big automaton, member of the Irish Squad, one Pat Kelly by name.

"I wish to congratulate you, Mr. MacGillicuddy." He winked. "That was quite a shot. As I am sure you appreciate, we members of the Automaton Liberation League had a lot at stake on that game." He observed her keenly for an instant. "Forgive me saying, you do not appear very elated by your victory."

"I'm not. I had to beat Gilbert, see, and he's my—best friend."

"Ah." Kindness flooded the green eyes. "It is a grand thing to have a best friend."

"It's the very best thing." If your best friend also happened to be your lover, Maddie reflected, well, you were blessed. "I'm just not sure our—our friendship—can survive that penalty shot."

Pat Kelly lowered his voice. "Mr. MacGillicuddy, I am a keen observer."

"Are you?"

"Yes, a very keen observer, indeed. I would not say this to just anyone, and I will not breathe a word—ha!—of it. But at that moment when you took your shot, I thought I saw Mr. Gilbert jerk aside."

Maddie stared. "Are you saying—" But oh, yes, the suspicion had already been in her mind, or perhaps in her heart, ever since she'd released the puck from her stick. It had remained through all the shouting, beer glugging, and celebration, only to find confirmation in Pat Kelly's steady gaze.

Had Gilbert let her win?

But…why? It opened him to all kinds of repercussions, criticism and condemnation. People would be angry at him, both for losing and for turning coat beforehand. There were gangs of enraged and intoxicated supporters out there, Boilermaker and

Freighter alike.

"Oh God," she whispered.

"Calling upon a deity may well bring comfort, but in my estimation, there is no certainty that it alters events. Might I, out of gratitude for your support for our man Nilsson, offer my assistance?"

"Eh?"

"Is there anything I can do?"

"Yes." Light filled Maddie's head. "You have a squad of elite policemen at your beck and call, right?"

"I do."

"Could you look out for Gilbert? Make sure he gets home all right? The streets will be dangerous tonight. Find him for me, Officer Kelly. Don't—don't tell him I asked, but please let me know he's safe."

"We can surely do that. Give me his address; we will look there first."

She complied.

"And, Mr. MacGillicuddy—"

"Please call me Maddie."

"Matty, can I give him any message from you?"

Maddie thought about it. A thousand things she wanted Gilbert to know, yet she shook her head helplessly.

"Thank you, Officer Kelly, but no. I suspect whatever I might say, I need to tell him myself."

****

Gilbert's head hurt. In fact, his whole body hurt. Well, that wasn't unusual following a game. The only time he hadn't hurt since all this madness began had been when he held Maddie in his arms. Then all pain, all thought of pain, melted away from him, blasted in the heat of passion.

And something more than passion, to be fair. Had the love he felt grown from the desire, or the desire from the love? Damned if he could tell. Now the tenderness lay beneath the heat like bedrock beneath fertile soil.

Neither would be doing him much good anytime soon.

But where was he?

He lay flat on his back, just as he had on the ice. But this time no lights blazed overhead. It was dark, and in the distance he could hear voices shouting, the sound of footsteps. Someone—several someones—running away.

Something bad had happened to him, something really bad.

He wondered if he could get up. The transition from light to darkness seemed too abrupt. There had to be events in between. He struggled to remember.

Following their loss, his Freighter teammates had been surprisingly decent about it. A lucky shot, they told him. MacGillicuddy had a quick release. Nobody could have done a better job in goal for them.

The Freighters' supporters had not been quite so forgiving. From the moment the team left the rink, surrounded by bodyguards and hustled directly into a steamcab, they'd screamed and attacked the vehicle, rocking it and throwing bottles. From there they went to an office on West Ferry that the Freighters management had been using for their headquarters. There, Lemon made a speech and handed out the pay, all of what he'd been promised, win or lose.

Afterward, the Freighters went away to catch the ferry across the river, complaining how much easier it would be if only somebody would please build a bridge. Gilbert was left on his own. Even his trusty bodyguard, Alouette, went away back to Canada. No longer considered valuable, and once more lugging his own equipment, Gilbert started off through the dark streets toward home.

Only these weren't the streets with which he was familiar. Now the city felt alive, dangerous, and primed to go off, almost as it had last fall when the automatons started that big uprising.

A forlorn feeling seized him, despite his conviction that he'd done the right thing, back there on the ice—the only thing he could have done. It made him feel vulnerable.

It took only a few blocks to persuade him he *was* vulnerable. Of course, he did go armed with a hockey stick, which made a fine weapon. Still…

Loud footsteps clattered, echoing down the dark street. The sound of a drunken laugh came from near at hand. The hair on the back of Gilbert's neck stood up.

He rounded a corner and paused. A crowd of ruffians—or possibly hockey supporters, it was hard to tell the difference—stood in front of him. By their blue sweaters, he could tell they were in fact Boilermaker supporters.

It occurred to him then he should have shed his Freighters sweater before leaving West Ferry Street. Too late now. Before he could blink, they moved, came at him with bottles, wrenches, and fists—all raised.

"It's Gilbert!" somebody hollered. "That damned turncoat!"

He dropped his gear, all but his stick which he lifted high. He set himself, just like in the net.

Yeah, he remembered it now—the blinding impact. A bottle to the side of the head, possibly a wrench to the back. They'd ripped his stick away from him, but not until he hurt a bunch of them in a quick, hard fight. No doubt thinking him dead, they'd left him—here.

An alley?

He groaned and got up, forcing his body to move, dimly aware it took three attempts to climb to his feet. He made his way from the place where he'd been dragged, noting as he left it the pool of blood where he'd been lying.

At the mouth of the alley, he collapsed once again.

Chapter Thirty-Six

"Maddie, there's a policeman at the door, one o' those Irish ones."

Maddie stirred from a sleep that felt like death. She hurt all over, as if she'd taken a thrashing, and the inside of her mouth tasted like stale beer.

Or vomit.

Memory returned to her in pieces—the hockey game, the multiple hits she'd taken. The celebration after. Countless bottles of Buffalo's Best.

So this was how it felt to be a man.

Roddy shook her by the shoulder and spoke again. "Maddie!"

She peeled her eyes open one at a time, by sheer willpower. Sunlight flooded the shabby room. Both Roddy and Rita stood over her, Roddy's expression combining excitement and concern.

"It's that Patrick Kelly fellow. Has he come to arrest one of us?"

God only knew. But wait—Patrick Kelly. An offer to help. *Gilbert*.

She hauled herself up by Roddy's strong arm and crawled from the bed, donned a long shirt over her underwear, and went to the door.

Her heart rose and then sank abruptly. Outside, indeed, stood the hybrid automaton, Patrick Kelly. She did not feel encouraged by his grave expression.

"Mattie, good morning. I wished to inform you that Mr. Gilbert has been found."

"Found?" All the breath fled Maddie's body. "It's not good news, is it?"

"I am afraid not. He was picked up at the mouth of an alley not far from his residence. He has been badly beaten."

"Beaten?"

"Yes."

"By whom?"

"It is impossible at this point to tell."

Maddie's thoughts raced. "Can't he tell you?"

"He hasn't regained consciousness as yet. The physicians are not certain that he will."

The air flickered all around Maddie, went dark and light in quick succession, kind of like when she took a hard hit on the ice.

Kelly stared at her kindly. "He is in hospital right now. I suggest you go to him as soon as you can."

Numbly, Maddie nodded. "Will you wait while I get dressed?" she asked, and shut the door in his face.

She dressed as a woman, in her rough clothes from the laundry, a white blouse and brown stuff skirt.

"Stay here," she told Roddy. "Rita, will you look after him, keep him from going out?"

"But—" Roddy began to object.

"The streets aren't safe. You heard what happened to Gilbert."

Gilbert. Oh God, oh God, oh—

"But—" Roddy repeated.

She turned on her brother fiercely. "Don't make me worry about you too."

When she hauled the door back open, Kelly did not

look surprised to see her clad as a miss instead of a mister. Of course, she thought, he'd already tumbled to the truth about her while watching the games, even if Nilsson hadn't spilled the beans. She realized, with a shock, she need not keep that particular secret any longer. She would go to Gilbert as the woman she was, the one who loved him.

****

"This is my fault," she mourned as she and Kelly rode together in the stuffy steamcab. In the close confines, she could smell the big automaton, a not-unpleasant whiff of hot metal, coal, and serge uniform.

She wondered how it felt to be an automaton. Despite her friendship with Rita, she'd never truly considered the question. But she had no doubt Pat Kelly did *feel*.

"Why do you say that?" Kelly asked.

"I'm the one who put that shot past him. That made him the loser—hated by both sides. Only—" She choked.

"Yes?" Kelly encouraged.

Maddy met the automaton's green gaze. "It's like you said last night, Officer. I'm not sure I did win—I think he did jerk to one side. He might have been trying to block the shot he expected I would make. Or he may have let that puck in."

"I saw what I saw, Maddie. Whether he jerked aside through reflex, or by intention, I truly cannot tell, though I may draw a conclusion. As may you. Why do you suppose he would deliberately let you win?"

"You know why. I know why. Because he l-loves me. And then, and then I went off carousing, let him go out into those streets alone, with all his teammates departed for Canada. I never even gave his safety a thought."

"You did, though, Maddie. You asked me to look out for him, did you not? It is because you asked me to look out for him that he was found so promptly, which may have saved his life."

Maddie began to weep, a stream of tears such as she'd not shed since her parents died one after the other, leaving her alone in a bleak world with Roddy to support.

She wasn't alone, now. She had Roddy and Rita and other friends. But if she lost Gilbert, the devastation might well surpass what she could bear.

"Humans," Kelly mused, "are curious beings, a source of endless fascination. They are capable of great cruelty, and also great sacrifice when the heart is involved. Miss MacGillicuddy, did you know I am married?"

Maddie shook her head.

"To a human woman. My lovely Rose." A note entered the automaton's mechanical voice that made Maddie lift her face and mop her cheeks. "I once suffered a terrible head injury—like, yet unlike, that of your Gilbert. Thinking me lost to her, Rose tried to take her own life. She did not want to remain in the world without me. I understand your fear and distress. But I must say to you, the last thing Gilbert would wish—as I well know—is for you to lose yourself in your unhappiness."

"I need to pull myself together."

"Yes, if only for his sake."

Maddie clasped shaking fingers. "I can. I can do that." She could do anything, for him.

"Brave miss."

"Why has the cab stopped?"

"We have reached the hospital."

She reached out and seized the automaton's hand. "Will you go inside with me?"

"Of course I will."

****

"He's very strong. That's a big plus in his favor." The physician, a tall man who wore a grave expression, spoke with false heartiness that grated on Maddie's nerves. In the present circumstances, it seemed almost obscene.

She barely recognized the man in the hospital bed. She should have known him by his hair, thick and black, but much of that had been shaved to treat the wound—wounds.

His face, a mass of bruises that matched those on his chest, had swollen. One eye—the left—lay buried in a well of tender flesh. So she couldn't really tell him by his eyes, either.

Dark, beautiful eyes regarding her with steady passion as he reached out to kiss her. Long, sweeping eyelashes when he slept. That wild light when she touched him with her tongue, when he touched her.

Ah, his hands—she recognized those, a worker's rough hands, yet so quick and graceful. Strong. One of them lay folded on his chest. She reached out and took it between hers, raised it to her lips, and kissed it.

"Who did this to him?" she asked, but she knew the answer. She had. She'd encouraged him to play hockey—he'd never wanted to. He'd only joined in to be with her. She'd even been the cause of him changing sides when he thought she had feelings for Nilsson.

Stupid idiot. Couldn't he tell she'd never love anyone but him? Just wait till she told him Nilsson was a machine.

If she got the chance to tell him.

It hit her then, in full: he might never wake up, never look at her or speak to her again.

She turned to the physician. "What are his chances?"

The physician eyed his patient and considered the question. He looked reluctant to speak the truth, which made Maddie's heart flutter in her chest like a distressed bird.

"Perhaps a fifty percent chance that he'll come out of this, thirty percent that he'll come out of it unchanged."

"Unchanged?"

"Without permanent damage. In short, that he'll still be the man you know."

Maddie stared at Gilbert in horror. She caressed his hand with hers. His knuckles were all abraded. He'd fought back.

He was a fighter, all right.

"Come on," she whispered. "I'll not give up on you, Huritt Gilbert. Whatever you do, don't give up on me."

****

The hockey game went on and on. It seemed to have no beginning, at least not one Gilbert could remember, and to reach ahead into eternity. There was just the ice, stretching away in front of his net into gray infinity, with clouds of fog rolling along over its surface.

Figures appeared and disappeared amid that fog;

for the most part Gilbert couldn't identify them. He dared not leave his net to get closer, and only occasionally did they approach him.

They seemed to be going about their own part of the game, calling to one another, shouting and even arguing. Not all of them were dressed for hockey. Even he failed to wear his sweater. Looking down at himself, he saw that, instead, he wore the rough clothes in which he went to work at the stable, fit for shoveling manure and rubbing down the horses. Yet he wore a glove and had his stick in his hand—living his regular life, yet playing.

Strange.

Where was Maddie? He couldn't spot her amid the clouds of fog—or was that steam? He thought he caught a glimpse of Nilsson, his fair hair flying.

And here came a man skating toward him determinedly. Gilbert recognized him, and his face split in a wide smile. "Pa?"

"How you doing, son?"

"I've been better. I seem to be stuck here. I don't know how to get out of this net. Awful glad to see you, though."

"And you." His father's blue eyes twinkled at him with well-remembered affection, and warmth flooded Gilbert's body, in response.

"Say, Pa, did you see a girl down at that end of the ice? A tall girl with bright red hair? Or she might be dressed as a man."

Jacques Gilbert winked at his son. "I saw her, *oui*."

"Will you go back and ask her to skate down to this end of the ice?"

"I am not allowed to go back, son. I must move on

to the next life. I will be a little boy, born in less than nine months."

Gilbert's jaw dropped in surprise.

"But when she is ready, this girl, she will come to you, *non*?"

"She isn't down there with a big, blond Swedish fellow, is she?"

"Do not worry about him. He is no competition—he is not even *human*."

"What?"

Jacques smiled and skated past Gilbert, only to disappear into a cloud behind the net.

But, what ho—someone else approached.

She skated a zigzag course and had a puck on her stick. Tall for a woman, like Maddie, only she wasn't Maddie. She paused to spin on the ice and her black braids flew out behind her.

Gilbert knew her even though he hadn't seen her since he was three years old. He watched as she made her way closer to him and paused again, ready to shoot at the net.

"Hello, Huritt."

"Ma?"

She had a broad, lined brow and his eyes. *His eyes*. No, that couldn't be right. He must have *her* eyes.

"What are you doing here?" he asked. "Are you dead? Are we all dead?"

"What would make you think that, Huritt?"

He gestured helplessly at the ice, with his stick.

"I came to tell you I am proud of you. You turned out good. Real good. Your father did a fine job raising you."

"Uh, thanks. I'm glad you think so."

"And I have some advice, if you want it. If you don't, just ignore it. But here it is: it's best to choose with the heart. It is what I did when I chose your father. Sometimes those choices turn out bad, later. But this time it got us *you*. I like the choice you made on the ice back there, with your heart."

"Ma, can you skate back down the ice? Can you find someone there for me? Or are you moving on to somewhere else?"

She smiled, a wide smile, and that looked like his too.

"Sure, I can go back."

"Will you find the tall, red-haired girl and ask her to come down here to me? Tell her I need her. All right?"

"I can do that. But first let me shoot this puck."

She wound up and shot directly at him. The puck smacked him in the forehead, and the pain flared up again.

Chapter Thirty-Seven

"My mother shot me in the head with a puck."

"What did he say?"

"I do not know."

Someone spoke just above the place where Gilbert lay—two someones, voices he didn't at once recognize.

"At least he's talking. That's a good thing, right?" That voice he knew—Maddie's voice. His ma must have sent her after all.

The knowledge that she was right there, so near him, made him want to open his eyes. He drew a deep breath and, with some difficulty, managed to get the right lid open. The left one, however, proved disobedient.

Faces swam into focus like floating moons. Two men, one of whom looked vaguely familiar. And Maddie.

He smiled at her. "You came."

"Of course I came." She looked different, her hair brushed and semi-tamed. She wore a shabby white blouse, and her eyes brimmed with tears.

"Did my ma send you?"

"Is she here?" Maddie glanced around, looking startled. "No. Officer Kelly, here, brought word you were in hospital."

Officer Kelly. The green-eyed fellow was a cop.

Earnestly, Gilbert told Maddie, "My ma hit me

with the puck. She's got one hell of a shot. Like you."

"No, darling, I don't think that's what happened. You got attacked on the street and beat up, don't you remember? You were found lying near an alley, all battered."

Darling? She called him "darling." What did that mean?

"Sir." Officer Kelly stepped forward. The other man, who Gilbert figured must be a quack, if he was in the hospital, stepped away. "What do you remember about the attack? We cannot hope to find the miscreants unless you are able to give us a description."

"I don't remember much." All that filled his head was the awareness of Maddie looking at him the way she was now, and the thought of Maddie touching him, claiming him, making him whole.

She glanced at the copper. "Maybe he'll remember later. Do you think we could have a few minutes alone?"

"To be sure," Kelly replied mildly, and he also left, disappearing much the way the folks had disappeared into the fog, back in Gilbert's dream.

It must have been a dream, mustn't it? He felt slightly disappointed by that.

Maddie sat down next to the bed where Gilbert lay, and squeezed his hand, which seemed to be gripped between both of hers. The tears in her eyes overflowed and trickled down her cheeks.

"Aw," he said, "don't do that."

She laid her head down on his chest and sobbed, a storm as intense as the passion she'd previously showered upon him. His Maddie, he realized, felt things very deeply, even though she didn't always show it. In that way, she was like him.

"Maddie, don't," he begged again. He could smell her hair—it smelled nice, like soap. He buried the fingers of his free hand in it, the way he had when she pleasured him.

"I was so scared I would lose you," she lamented. "And it would have been all my fault."

"How's that?" He tried to shake his head, and thought better of it. "I don't understand how anything could be your fault."

"I beat you on that penalty shot and set off rioting in the city. Do you remember the hockey game?"

He did, now that she mentioned it. The whole thing swam back at him, coming in pieces down the ice of the dream he'd had. "Yeah, I think I do."

She raised a face streaming with tears, all red and blotchy, but still beautiful. She told him, "I've been thinking, ever since the game, I should have pulled that shot. I should have gone wide, missed the net, let you win. How could I have let winning that game come between you and me?"

He searched her eyes tentatively. "Has it?"

"Hasn't it? This is all my fault, Gilbert. You didn't want to join the team. You only did it because of me. You switched sides mostly because of me too, didn't you? 'Cause you thought I had feelings for Nils."

Nils. "Don't you?"

"He's my friend. And we were keeping each other's secrets."

"Eh?"

"He knew I'm a woman. And I found out he's an automaton."

"What?"

"I couldn't tell anyone, not even you. But do you see how ridiculous it was for you to be jealous of him? He and I are just friends. I'm in love with *you*."

Nils Nilsson, an automaton. Well, damn. "You still in love with me?"

"If you can't tell that by now, Huritt Gilbert, there's no hope for you."

Gilbert's heart gave a great leap before taking up a deep, steady rhythm. "It seems I've missed a lot."

A new look invaded Maddie's eyes. "I knew I loved you—well, a girl doesn't do the things I did with you unless she loves a man. But it wasn't till I thought I was going to lose you that I realized just how much. I looked smack-dab at what my future might be like without you, and I don't think I could endure it."

"Oh, don't start crying again, Maddie. You won't have to endure it."

"But your poor head—"

"Made of rock, isn't it?"

"The doctor said every time you get hit in the head with the puck, it damages you a little more. Then this attack on top of it…"

"Kiss me," he requested, and her eyes widened.

"What?"

"Kiss me, Maddie."

She did, softly and sweetly. Strength flowed into him, and he felt her tears on his face.

"Please don't cry," he begged when the kiss ended.

"I can't seem to help it." Her fingers clenched his so hard, it hurt. "Tell me one thing."

"What?"

"That we'll find a way to be together. I don't care where, or what we do. Go back to our old jobs. Get new ones. Live on the money I won. It's an awful lot of money."

"Is it? I made some money too—for turning coat."

"I'll share mine with you fifty-fifty, fair and square, if you'll marry me."

"That sounds like a very decent offer. But I'll need to get back on my feet first."

"Of course."

"And I'll have to take care of a few things. There's Jessop—he's with a fellow called Jamie Kilter down at the Buffalo Animal Sanctuary, but I can't leave him there forever."

Maddie's smile became brilliant. "There's nothing wrong with your head, is there?"

Apparently not. His thoughts zinged like lightning bolts. "And Mr. Stanley said he was bringing in the second mechanical horse. That means old Justice will get the boot too. I'll need to find accommodations for him."

"I can help with that. I have friends who can maybe get Justice out of there."

"Yes. Friends like Nils." Gilbert considered it. "So if he's an automaton—"

"One of those new hybrid ones, built by the other automatons."

"—and you're a woman, it means the whole hockey tournament was illegal."

"I guess so."

"And nobody knows?"

"Nobody outside Mr. Brewster, and all he cares about is his pride. I'm not sure what I care about, besides you." She touched his face tenderly. "Gilbert, tell me one thing."

"Yeah?"

"When I took that penalty shot—you remember that?"

"Sure."

"Did I really beat you? Or—or did you let me have that goal?"

Gilbert closed his eyes for an instant and thought about how much he loved this woman. He thought about what love meant, and what a man did for those he loved.

He opened his eyes and looked at her again. What did she want him to say? It no longer mattered, did it? Except to her.

"All I can tell you, Maddie MacGillicuddy, is—it was a hockey shot in a thousand, and only you could have got that puck past me." Now, and forever. "Only you."

Chapter Thirty-Eight

"Are you sure you're well enough to leave the hospital?" Maddie fretted, and danced nervously from one foot to the other. Used to looking after Roddy and, to a lesser extent, Rita and the others at the laundry, she nevertheless found Gilbert—a large and severely hampered male—a far different proposition.

What if he wasn't ready? What if he collapsed on her and took a fall? What if he reopened the wound on his head? What if she did the wrong thing, and let him down?

She tried to put the brakes on those thoughts, and sucked in a big breath. When had she started feeling responsible for everyone? Roddy, the other players on the team, especially Nils… She decided it had started when her parents died.

It needed to stop now.

Roddy was a big boy who, as Rita and others had assured her, needed a chance to stand on his own feet and make his own mistakes. Nils, a fully functioning automaton, also had his way to make in the world.

Gilbert—well, Gilbert was over six feet of rough-and-tumble former hockey player. She wanted to be his lover, not his mother or his nursemaid.

She smiled at Nils, who had turned up at the hospital to help her collect Gilbert and had a cab waiting outside.

"I have to be ready," Gilbert answered reasonably. "They're kicking me out of here, aren't they?"

The swelling around his left eye had finally gone down. His face looked like a patchwork of bruises in various colors, as did the rest of him. He wore a bandage on his head, set at a rakish angle. Maddie still mourned the loss of most his hair.

She began chattering nervously. "We're going back to your room for now. I hope that's all right. There hasn't been time to arrange anything else. Roddy and Rita are staying at my place."

"Rita?"

"My friend from the laundry, the automaton."

Gilbert's brows twitched. Nils grinned.

"I will be happy to help you locate other quarters," Nils said. "And to stand up for you at your wedding. I am told weddings are very special events."

"Ah, well," Gilbert said, and shot a look at Maddie. "That's very handsome of you, Nilsson. I don't doubt you'd make one heck of a best man."

Maddie flushed. Leave it to Nils to introduce a subject that had been tormenting her. Gilbert hadn't actually responded to her proposal of marriage the other day. Of course, his head had been bounced about like a puck in the net. She didn't know if that accounted for why, or if he didn't actually want to marry her.

"And I understand," Nils continued, while escorting them down the hospital corridor and out the door into the cold, clear day, "you are interested in purchasing a farm."

Gilbert stared at him. "How do you know that?"

"Yesterday, I went to help out at the stables where you work. I arrived in the midst of a situation. Some of my colleagues were, in fact, delivering a new mechanical horse there, and an elderly horse named Justice was being evicted."

Gilbert paled beneath his garish bruises. "Justice! I'm too late?"

"Not at all," Nils assured him. "Since I'd been apprised of what might happen to Justice earlier, by Maddie, I called upon my fellows to use their wagon to help him. We took him to the Buffalo Animal Shelter and got to talking, there, with a man named Kilter—as folks do."

"As folks do," Gilbert repeated, sounding stunned.

"Mr. Kilter mentioned you'd confided to him your desire for a farm."

"Yeah, he's keeping my other horse for me."

"Indeed."

"But Nilsson, it's not that easy, buying a place. Property's expensive."

They paused on the curb, bathed in the sunlight of a bright winter's day. Traffic—foot, steamcab, and horse-drawn cab—streamed by on the street. The air smelled like river water, mixed with coal smoke.

Nils turned very blue eyes on Gilbert. "I hope, Buddy, you will let me help with that."

"Help? With the farm, you mean? But you're a hockey player."

"Swedish hockey player," Nils confirmed. "I was constructed using the corpse of a Swedish man killed in a brawl. If you look at the back of my neck, you can see the mark where the knife entered his body, in a killing stroke."

"Uh," Gilbert said. "That must be uncomfortable for you."

"Not at all. I like knowing from whence I came. It is like you, Maddie, knowing your ancestors came from Scotland or you, Gilbert, knowing your mother was Algonquin. All of us being constructed as part of this new generation will know. We will have identities. But anyway, I would like to make you a wedding gift of the money I won in the hockey tournament."

"Nils!" Maddie gasped. "That's awfully generous of you. But won't those who built you expect to receive your winnings?"

"No. I have been informed the winnings are mine, to do with as I wish. I have few needs of my own and would like to invest in the two of you."

He flashed his wide smile at Gilbert. "Do you know how to farm?"

Gilbert laughed, and pressed one hand to his chest. "No, I don't, but I do know horses, and my plans are more for a refuge than an actual farm, though I imagine I'll learn how to grow their feed and all the rest of it. I don't suppose that bodes well for your investment."

"I am not worried. I have every faith in each of you, and even more in the two of you together."

"Thank you, Nils," Maddie said, and embraced the automaton.

"Yeah, thanks." Gilbert extended his hand. "But I'll need to sort through some things before I'm ready to take you up on your offer."

Nils clasped his hand heartily. "Meanwhile, we remain buddies?" he asked.

"Buddies, for sure."

Nils' grin widened impossibly. "Here is your cab, waiting. I thought you might enjoy riding in this one."

Maddie turned in surprise. The cab standing at the

curb was large and dusty, the horse big, silver, and shiny.

"Piper!" Gilbert exclaimed.

The mechanical horse lowered its head to Gilbert's shoulder and blew steam.

"He remembers you, Gilbert," Maddie said with delight.

"Of course." Nils agreed. "Our kind never forget our friends."

****

"Maddie, we need to talk."

Maddie's stomach sank in response to Gilbert's words. Oh no. She'd been afraid it was all going just a bit too well—his miraculous recovery from the beating, his seeming ability to put the repercussions of the hockey game behind him. She'd hoped it was over.

It wasn't, though—not really.

She turned and looked at him where he lay propped up in his bed. There really wasn't any other comfortable place to put him, here in his shabby room.

He deserved better. Now that she, Maddie, had some money, she'd make sure he got it. But she needed to rein in her runaway thoughts. She'd already decided she couldn't make his decisions for him.

Yet he looked so helpless lying there, all broken. No, wait; she saw nothing helpless in his dark gaze.

"You've got some messages, here," she said, stalling for time. The envelopes had been lying just inside the door when they arrived from the hospital, probably having been shoved under.

"I'll look at them in a minute. Come and sit down, Maddie."

Here it comes, Maddie thought. He's been

thinking, remembering the hockey game and the way she'd bested him. Or had she truly bested him?

She perched on the side of the bed facing him, legs tucked underneath.

Gilbert reached out and took her hand. "The last few days have been pretty confusing. Waking up in the hospital like that, not remembering everything straight off. I think I remember it all now, though."

Oh damn. She'd half hoped it would be like Mr. Trinedore at the laundry.

Gilbert hesitated, seeming to struggle for a moment, and emotions stirred in his eyes. Gorgeous eyes, those, in which a woman could get lost for a lifetime. But would they have that together?

"A lot's happened," she acknowledged.

"You can say that again. But out of all that's happened, I think I'm pretty sure of one thing."

He wanted rid of her. He wanted to start the farm on his own, go back to a simple life like the one he'd had at the stables with his horses, before she'd come along and complicated everything.

"I figure—I figure I'd better ask you properly. Do it right, if I've ever done anything right. Maddie MacGillicuddy, will you marry me?"

For an instant, Maddie's world ground to a halt. Like an overused automaton at the laundry, it stuttered and died. She saw only Gilbert's dark eyes and the light there, that which burned for her alone.

"Yes." So breathless had she gone, even she couldn't hear the word. She spoke it more bravely, "Oh yes. I can't imagine anything else."

"Neither can I. From the minute I met you, I couldn't. I want a life with you and Roddy, and Rita, the horses and—whoever else comes along. But there are some things I'll need to take care of first."

"Like what?"

"I'll need to get Jessop and Justice away out of Jamie Kilter's sanctuary. That was just temporary, and I don't want to take advantage. I'll need to find a stable—"

"I'm pretty sure Nils is working on that. He really is a great guy, Gilbert."

"I know."

"And even if—even if he had been human, he couldn't hold a candle to you, in my heart."

"I know that too, now. Maddie, I might have to go away for a while."

"What?" Her fingers clenched on his. "Why?"

"I need to go up to Ontario and look for my ma. Part of why I played for Lemon was…I believed he had some kind of hold on her. I think she might need help."

"Oh."

"I'm not even sure she's still alive. If she is alive, she might not know Pa's dead."

"Right, then. You need to go find her."

"If I can."

"If you can. It's the honorable thing to do."

"Honorable?" His face wrinkled in a grimace. "Most people in this city think I'm a turncoat and don't have any honor. You sure you want to tie yourself to that?"

"I'm sure."

"Eventually, if I can scrape up the money, I do want a farm, just like Nilsson said—somewhere outside the city. Maybe in Eden. Have you ever heard a prettier name?"

"I have the money. I already told you that. You're not going to get all male-prideful over that, are you? What's mine should be yours also, understand?"

"What's ours is ours."

"Yes." She linked her fingers with his. "I could go with you. To Ontario, to look for your ma, I mean."

"Maddie—"

He was going to say no. He didn't want her with him after all.

His dark eyes met hers, full on. "This is something I think I need to do on my own."

People went away from her. This was a thing she had learned. All too often they didn't come back. It was a hard lesson.

"I'll come back," he said just as if he heard the thoughts in her mind.

She leaned forward to kiss him. "Just make sure you do."

Chapter Thirty-Nine

"Hey, Gilbert, you never read your messages."

Gilbert had no desire to move. The light in the room had faded. On the bed, where Maddie and Gilbert lay together with their fingers entwined, peace reigned. He still hurt too much to stir, and anyway, completeness had found him once again.

"Can't be anything important," he murmured. "Not as important as you."

"As us," she amended. "You know, when you go to find your mother—if you want to bring her back to live with us, she'd be welcome."

"Thank you, Maddie."

"We're going to be building a life, and it occurs to me there'll be room for all kinds of people in it, including mechanicals."

"And animals."

"And animals," she confirmed.

Gilbert narrowed his eyes. "It occurs to me more and more cab horses are going to be replaced. They'll need somewhere to retire. A refuge like Jamie Kilter's is fine for one or two, but he doesn't have room for many. Trouble is, if I start a refuge, how am I going to support them?"

"Like you've said, on a farm, we can learn to grow feed, along with other crops to sell. My grandparents farmed, in Scotland."

"But we'll need a steady income right from the start."

"How about starting a hockey school?" she asked tentatively.

"A what?"

"Hockey fever has seized the city. It's all anyone's talking about. Folks want a permanent team. I was thinking of getting in on the one Drane Rogers is organizing."

"Oh?"

"Me and Nils both talked about it, actually. But on the farm, we'd have room to build a rink. We could take youngsters for a week at a time, instruct them. Roddy could help; he's a real good skater, and I think he'd be good at it."

"Do you think people are gonna want to come take lessons from a turncoat?"

"When he's as good a goalie as you, yes. They'll get over it, Gilbert. Think about it, will you?"

"Sure I will."

She kissed him, slid off the bed, and lit the steam lamp. Next she brought the two white envelopes and dropped them in his lap. "Here, read."

The first missive proved to be a letter informing him an account had been set up in his name at the First Bank of Buffalo by one Nils Nilsson.

"Well, what do you think of that?" He passed it to Maddie with a feeling of deep gratitude. Things were coming together, all his dreams within his reach, for the first time in his life.

He opened the second envelope while Maddie perused the first letter. Opened it and froze.

Because the second letter proved to be an offer, an

incredibly handsome one.

"Maddie?" he said.

"Hmm? This is really kind of Nils, isn't it? He's a man of his word, and those are hard to find."

"Maddie, will you read this?" he asked, and handed her the second sheet.

He watched as she read, and the color drained from her face. "Oh! But—"

"It's from a team in Montreal, a legitimate hockey team."

"I see that."

"They want me to go there and take a job as goalie. They had a scout here at our games. And look at the money they're offering me!"

She lowered the sheet and turned her beautiful, hazel eyes on him. "It's an amazing offer, Gilbert. And—and well-deserved. They'll be lucky to get you."

"I don't know about that."

"I do." She touched his hand, and brushed his face with her fingers. "Gilbert, offers like this don't come along every day."

"You're right, they don't. But Maddie, Montreal?"

"Yes."

"It's so far."

"I'd come with you, Gilbert, if you wanted me."

"Of course I'd want you there. But—" Gilbert thought about it, really thought. The surrender of all the dreams he was building here in this city that, for all its darkness and light, sins and blessings, felt like home.

He took the letter from her, folded it carefully and put it back into the envelope.

"No," he said.

"Gilbert, they want an answer by return post."

"And I'll send them one." He turned to her, caught her face between his hands and gazed into her eyes. "It was never the hockey I liked so much. It was being near you," he confessed. "I don't want a life that's me playing hockey and you following after me. I want a life that's ours. I want to build it together, see?"

"Here, in Buffalo?"

"Here in Buffalo."

He kissed her, a vow and a promise of passion to come. "I figure," he whispered then, "you've got your eye on the goal."

"Oh, I do," she assured him. "And just between you and me, Huritt Gilbert, I fully intend to score."

A word about the author...

Multi-award-winning author Laura Strickland delights in time traveling to the past and searching out settings for her books, be they Historical Romance, Steampunk, or something in between.

Her first Scottish Historical hero, *Devil Black*, battled his way onto the publishing scene in 2013, and the author never looked back. Nor has she tapped the limits of her imagination.

Venturing beyond Historical and Contemporary Romance, she created a new world with her ground-breaking Buffalo Steampunk Adventure series set in her native city in Western New York.

Married and the parent of a grown daughter, Laura has also been privileged to mother a number of very special rescue dogs and is intensely interested in animal welfare. These days while she's writing, you can always find her latest rescue, Lacy, nearby.

Her love of dogs, and her lifelong interest in Celtic history, magic and music, are all reflected in her writing. Laura's mantra is Lore, Legend, Love, and she wouldn't have it any other way.

Thank you for purchasing
this publication of The Wild Rose Press, Inc.

For questions or more information
contact us at
info@thewildrosepress.com.

The Wild Rose Press, Inc.
www.thewildrosepress.com

www.ingramcontent.com/pod-product-compliance
Lightning Source LLC
Chambersburg PA
CBHW051525260626
47170CB00003B/792

* 9 7 8 1 5 0 9 2 3 0 4 7 1 *